Logging Back into Life

RJ Hutchins

Alison,
Thanks for your
support! I hope
you laugh at least
once— You have a
great laugh.

RJ

Sue
Thank you for motivating me to start.
I hope you enjoy how it ends!

Mark
Thank you for continuing to support my dream and offering
encouraging words to keep going. You helped remind me that
my grandma was always with me.

Shel
Thank you for reading and offering feedback and
continual support.

Brendan
Thank you for your creative work on the cover.

Megs, Kitty and Shaley
Thank you for always being excited about my dream.

For Clara.

One

Edward slumped in his chair, looking around at his desk. He wasn't quite sure what to make of his new job. A lot had happened in the whirlwind of the last few weeks. He wasn't expecting to be between places, a state away, and starting a new job.

"Edward Simmons, let me introduce you to Maggie Jenkins."

Edward looked up at his new boss, Steve, a gaunt, pale man, with thinning, sandy red hair. He was only a few years older than Edward, despite being two levels higher at the agency. Edward thought he looked old for 36. He worried this was what he had to look forward to - premature aging due to the stress of advertising. He knew this world all too well. That's why he had left the first time.

"Hi, welcome to the agency," Maggie quietly interjected.

Edward was still trying to take it all in, his thoughts causing a delay in response. "Hi, Maggie, it's nice to see you again."

He noticed how tired she looked. He didn't remember the dull, pale circles under her eyes last time. Edward did, however, remember her beautiful smile and bright blue eyes. They reminded him of Kate's.

"Oh, that's right, you met during interviews. I forgot. Well, I'll leave you two to get started." With that, Steve was gone.

"Edward, can you give me 30 minutes? I need to answer a few client emails before we get started." Maggie was professional and curt, albeit aloof.

"Sure."

Edward turned back to his desk. There sat a desktop

computer and a stack of files from past projects. *A desktop computer? What year is this?* he thought to himself.

He sat there for a moment, considering. He could look through the past project files, but it didn't appeal to him. He was no stranger to advertising, already having worked at another agency as a client manager. He never pictured he'd have to go back to the agency world, though, but he needed a job quickly. Reviewing old project files didn't seem to be the best way to learn. *Was this the formal training program?* he wondered. *Co-workers' time when they were available and reviewing old files?* He couldn't help but question if he had made the right decision. It was a recurring thought that had haunted him for days.

The silent agency felt like a mausoleum. Advertising was supposed to be fun, lively. At least it used to be at his old agency. Edward put his face in his hands for a moment and pondered his decision to move back home.

Home. The thought seemed foreign. Edward didn't even know where home was anymore. He hadn't lived in Michigan for nearly seven years now. After a brief job in Atlanta, where he realized the heat of the deep south didn't suit him, he had settled in Chicago. Chicago. That felt like home, at least it did until recently.

He had been developing a solid career as a senior marketing manager. He had also been well on his way to getting married to a beautiful, happy redheaded girl with an infectious smile and big blue eyes. Their senses of humor had clicked from the very first time they were introduced at a friend's party. They soon were one-upping each other with one-liners and had the room in belly-laughs. At the end of the evening, he didn't ask for her number. He didn't have to. She volunteered it. "I hope I hear from you soon."

And she did. One date turned into two, and two eventually turned into a form of cohabitation alternating between their apartments. He loved her in a way he didn't know possible. Yes, she was beautiful, but more than that, her spirit seemed to fill Edward with a sense of happiness he had never really known. Edward had never even considered marriage until Kate. After her, he tried dating, but no one was quite like her. His heart still hadn't healed.

"Hi, Edward, great to see you again! We're all really excited you're finally here!"

Edward was jolted out of his thoughts by Jan, his new creative director. Edward stared at her for a brief moment taking in her bright pink glasses, slightly shaved head, and height. She was a towering woman with a slight grin. He wondered how well they'd work together. Edward was a bit embarrassed he was caught daydreaming on his first day.

"Why don't we grab lunch today, and we can talk about the upcoming projects on deck. I'm so happy you're here. We're drowning!"

That statement caught Edward by surprise. Drowning? It's how he felt a lot lately trying to make sense of everything going on in his life. He wondered how they could be drowning. It's so quiet he wasn't sure if anyone really worked there.

Edward turned back to his desk after Jan left. Project 65733 – Family Circle Print Ad. He opened up the file to see a creative brief and budget. The file looked pretty standard. It wasn't long before his thoughts shifted back to the last few weeks.

He wasn't sad to be leaving Chicago, or so he thought. He needed a change. The ghosts of Kate were everywhere. If he were honest with himself, he still loved her. He probably always would. She ignited a part of him he didn't know existed. She had also shattered his heart.

Just when he had started to pick up the pieces and try to date again, he got the call.

"Hey mom, what's up?"

"Your grandma has been in an accident," she said

softly, her voice shaking.

"Is she ok?"

"She's stabilized. She's in ICU. She's on the ventilator."

The news hit him like a punch in the stomach. Edward and his grandma had always been very close. Edward knew his grandma, Elsie, was tough for 83, but at that age, how tough can you really be?

"Should I come home now? Wait for news? The holidays?"

"I can't answer that for you. I don't know what's going to happen. I know you're busy. I will support your decision. You know she'd understand."

Edward left to see her the next day.

Edward's attention soon shifted to the owner of the agency, Michael, yelling obscenities in his office down the hall. Edward had been given the unfortunate first cube at the end of the hallway leading to Michael's office. He heard every soul-crushing put-down Michael yelled at his under-appreciated employees.

"Pull your head out of your ass. Don't come in here this confident of shitty work."

Edward again asked himself if he had made the right decision… *What's done is done I guess,* he thought. *I'll just do my best to avoid him.*

The rest of the day was sort of a blur. Lunch with Jan was ok, if not a tad awkward. She seemed defensive, almost testing Edward. He then spent some time catching up with Maggie on procedures. All very formal interactions. He didn't really envision her as someone with whom he'd become friends. He couldn't wait to go home.

"Have a good night," said one of many random co-workers he didn't really care to meet on her way out. Five o'clock. Day one in the record books.

Edward hadn't found a place to live yet. The job search was faster than anticipated. Within six weeks, he was

4

permanently back in Michigan. He was thankful he was able to find work easily in metro-Detroit considering the economy, but it also meant he was crashing on his parents' couch until he could find a place. Thirty-one, back at his parents, and still single - this wasn't the plan.

That night, as Edward tried to sleep, with his mind racing about his first day and needing to find a place, he thought back to his decision to leave Chicago. He made the decision on that first five-hour drive from Chicago.

What if she doesn't make it? What if I don't make it in time to say goodbye? A sense of guilt fell over him for not being home more over the last seven years. Elsie was more than Edward's grandma, she was his biggest supporter and best friend. His name Edward was even selected as a nod to the E in Elsie. He couldn't remember a time she wasn't a big part of his life, from reading Highlights magazines together to attending his little league games.

I should've called more, he thought to himself. *It was only five hours, why didn't I make an effort to get home more?*

Naturally, he thought of Kate. He didn't blame her. She loved his family. But in your 20's, Chicago with your girlfriend is more exciting than the suburbs of Detroit with your family. And with two careers, it was hard for them both to get away. He didn't like to be away from Kate if he didn't have to, so in the last few years, trips home were relegated to the traditional holidays.

"A lot of good that got me... Bit..." The half-spoken word lingered in the car. He still couldn't bring himself to process his anger toward Kate. That was part of the problem. Everywhere he looked in Chicago, he was reminded of how good it was with her. Dressing up to go to the theater. Runs along the lake. Neighborhood bar crawls. The endless laughter. Then it was over.

I don't know. Maybe this is God's sign, he thought with

just under an hour to go in his drive. *If Chicago is Kate, maybe it's time for a fresh start. Maybe I need to focus on my family for a while and being there for Eltz like she's always been for me.*

Edward didn't consider himself a rash man. He had always been very deliberate with his career choices. In fact, Kate often described him as pragmatic. But after several months of being in a fog after Kate, and a job that lately hadn't really challenged him anyway, he decided that if Elsie stabilized he would move back to be closer to her.

"God. If you'll let her make it, I'm in. There's not much left for me in Chicago anyway. I've torn up my 20's. I've had a good time. Please."

After another 30 minutes, Edward pulled into the hospital's parking lot. Between him continually running his hands through his dark black hair during the drive and spurts of tears, he needed to compose himself. After a deep sigh, he headed toward the ICU.

"Hi mom, how is she doing?" Edward whispered as he hugged her tightly. He waved to his dad, brother and uncle sitting nearby.

"Well, she has stabilized. She's been doing breathing treatments to strengthen her lungs. She has fluid on them, so she's not out of the woods yet. It's really a miracle she survived. I mean, at 83, who survives a rollover accident? Only my mother... tough old bird."

They laughed. It felt good to be there with his family. For the first time in a long time, despite the weight of the situation, he felt almost whole again. In that moment, he made up his mind.

"I'm moving home. As soon as I can find a job, I'm back. This is where I need to be."

His mother didn't respond. She didn't know if it was the moment or fear talking, but inside, she was elated. Edward noticed the slight smile on her face.

It was the last image in his mind that night as he finally drifted off to sleep.

<u>Two</u>

Over the next few months, Edward fell into his new normal. He had traded a lake-view apartment in Chicago for a ground floor one-bedroom with a view of the parking lot. He was struggling with the transition. Had the new job been exciting or fun, or if he had friends left in the area, or *something* maybe it wouldn't have been as bad. He didn't let his mind go to the place of if he had *someone*. He was thankful for the ability to visit Elsie, especially now that she was recovering in the assisted living facility.

Hey, at least I'm not on my parents' couch anymore, he thought as he got ready for work. He laughed to himself at how different his life was from just six months ago when he was thinking about how he was going to propose. Dragging himself out of bed still wasn't easy, but it was getting easier, even if just slightly.

"Edward."

It was Maggie's usual curt greeting as he walked past her in the morning. He still couldn't figure her out. They were both account directors, yes, but he got a sense of competition he didn't quite understand. He was the new guy, and at his current ambition level, he wasn't looking to climb the ladder anytime soon. So, if there were a promotion to be had, she could have it. He didn't really feel she was sabotaging him; she also wasn't volunteering to go the extra mile to make sure he was successful.

"Morning, Mags, how was your night?"

"First. Maggie. And it was fine. Thank you."

As usual, she didn't give anything up personally. Edward smiled as he sat down at his desk. He sort of liked pushing her buttons. He just didn't get what her deal was. His first client call didn't start for another 15 minutes, so he googled "Maggie Jenkins LinkedIn." He clicked on the first result. She had gone to a mid-tier state school and had her Bachelor's degree in marketing.

Hmmm... maybe that's it, he thought. *Maybe she's a bit self-conscious or threatened.* Edward had gone to Michigan for undergrad and to Northwestern's part-time MBA program while he was in Chicago. He had blue chip credentials, plus his time working on the client side, which is coveted in the agency world.

"Are you ready?" Maggie asked three minutes prior to their meeting.

Edward quickly closed his browser window hoping she hadn't seen what was on his screen. Edward and Maggie split responsibilities managing one of the agency's most lucrative businesses, both reporting to Steve. This morning, they were having a kick off meeting for strategic planning for the upcoming fiscal year.

"Let's do this!" Edward beamed.

Maggie turned around and rolled her eyes as they walked toward Jan's office. Despite the somber nature of the agency, Edward tried to infuse some energy where he could, and when his spirit allowed. The bright red, blue and yellow walls couldn't mask how lifeless the agency really was.

"Hey dipshit, why don't you learn what the fuck it means to be creative!"

He could hear another rant from Michael against some poor soul as he walked away from his desk. He sighed.

"Hey Jan! Ready to wow these guys?" Edward chirped behind Maggie as they walked into Jan's office.

Maggie again rolled her eyes, which Jan noticed and grinned. Jan also noticed how tired Maggie looked lately. Edward was too new to remember Maggie at her best, but lately, she had a little less energy. The bags under her eyes had started to show. Jan knew Maggie was extremely private, so she didn't pry.

It did have her a bit worried, however. The account was

about to double in spend, which is why Edward was hired. Steve was not a "doer." He fancied himself some high-powered exec that couldn't be bothered with the actual execution. Jan wondered what Steve actually did, except kiss Michael's ass. Jan realized her partners in leading this expansion were a new account director and one that looked like she could fall over from exhaustion at any minute. Jan had allowed the account team to cut corners for a while when the business was smaller. A half-filled creative brief. A job order that didn't include the specs. She could, because she knew the client better than anyone, having won the original business with Steve. She knew she couldn't continue like that, though, as she also needed to build her creative team.

"Mags and I are pumped to get this kicked off," Edward continued.

"Maggie. Please. At this point, it's purposeful."

Edward knew his light-hearted ribbing wasn't being received as he intended.

"Ok, Maggie. No problem. But let's get pumped to get this going. I really am looking forward to rocking this with you."

The meeting was pretty uneventful. The clients, each individual brand directors, went through their respective objectives and budgets. Edward would take the more male-targeted performance health brands, while Maggie would focus on the "mom" brands. After the call concluded, Edward was quick to leave for lunch.

Maggie lingered for a minute. "Jan, I think that guy's sort of a douche."

Jan laughed. "Yeah, but that douche is now your partner, and we need him if we're going to get all of this done. We both know Steve isn't going to do any real work."

Maggie couldn't argue with the logic. She sighed. "I honestly don't know how we're going to get it all done, with or without Edward." She knew she meant she didn't know how *she* would be able to get it all done.

"Listen, we've worked together a long time. We've been through this before. Day by day."

Again, Maggie couldn't argue with Jan's logic. Day by day. It was how she had been operating for a while now.

"But seriously, a bit douchey, no?"

Jan raised one eyebrow, not knowing if Maggie was threatened by or attracted to Edward. Maggie could almost read her thoughts.

"Not even a little… you old pain in the ass."

Edward came back from a quick lunch and noticed Maggie was still in Jan's office. Jan, like the rest of the agency, had been professional since he started, but not necessarily welcoming. Everyone around him seemed to be friends with each other - like an old boys' club he wasn't allowed to enter. He wondered what he had missed.

"Whatever, I can't worry about it," he whispered to himself.

Edward logged back in. He heard Maggie walk back to her desk just as her phone was ringing.

"Hey, Steve. Yeah, I can meet tomorrow. 10:30? Works for me."

"Ass," she whispered not thinking anyone could hear her.

Edward's eyebrows jumped in surprise. Maybe he and Maggie had something in common after all. He wasn't a particular fan of Steve's himself, but since everyone seemed to gush whenever Steve was around, he figured he better just keep it to himself. This was the first time he had gotten any indication from Maggie, though, that she wasn't a fan either.

"Maybe she's just having one of those days. Maybe it's me!" he laughed out loud.

Maggie wondered what he was laughing about now. She rolled her eyes again. She opened her calendar to send an invite to Steve for tomorrow at 10:30 am.

"He couldn't be bothered to leave his office to walk over here to talk to me?" she fumed to herself. "I've been keeping this account afloat for months, and he can't even talk to me face to face? Cool it, Mags, it's a waste of energy..."

She laughed at the irony that she referred to herself as Mags but would be damned if the new guy could be so informal. Now it was Edward's turn to wonder what she was laughing about.

"Edward."

It was the same formal, curt address on her way out for the night. It was 6:45 pm, and Maggie had to jet.

"Hi, Brian. How was your day?"

She sat quickly and caressed his hand, slowly rubbing the light hair on the edge of his hand.

"Treatment this morning was rough. I didn't feel like eating, but they made me."

"You have to keep up your strength. You promised me you would eat."

Brian tilted his head with no change of expression. They both seemed to know what the other was thinking. Whether he ate or didn't eat, it really didn't much matter. It may buy him some extra time, but the prognosis remained the same. Three to six months.

"Come on. The cafeteria jello appeared in Gourmet magazine recently, didn't it?"

Maggie's corny sense of humor broke the tension. Brian smiled. She didn't feel like she had been very funny lately, especially at work. She was happy she could at least make him smile. She continued rubbing his hand as Jeopardy started. 7:30 pm. It was the same nightly ritual they had had for weeks.

After Jeopardy, the TV droned on as the two talked about nothing in particular. At 9:30 pm, Maggie whispered to Brian as he started drifting off, "I have to go.

I'll be back tomorrow. Please eat what they give you." She leaned over and kissed him on the forehead.

She had stopped saying, "I love you," months ago. Their relationship had been dying slowly when he was diagnosed with cancer. For weeks prior to his diagnosis, she considered breaking it off. She knew she had stayed as long as she had out of convenience. She was focused on her job, and he was busy developing new apps until all hours of the night. It was just easier to cohabitate and have the occasional quickie.

She was surprised then to see him one night at 7 pm. "Mags, we need to chat."

This is it, she thought. *He's divorcing me. Me!* She was annoyed that he had the balls she didn't.

"Listen, I don't know how to say this. I guess I should just say it."

"You don't have to. I know what you're going to say," Maggie stopped him.

"No, no, I don't quite think you do. Mags, I have cancer."

She furrowed her brow out of confusion, not really reacting. After a few seconds, she finally broke the silence.

"But you're perfectly healthy. What do you mean, you have cancer?"

"I haven't been feeling well lately. I didn't want to bother you. I know you're stressed at work. I wasn't sure it was anything really anyway. So, I made an appointment a few weeks back when you were traveling to see your client."

"A few weeks back! When were you going to tell me? Am I even the first to know? Or did you tell some chick you're banging? I thought you were fucking leaving me!"

Maggie was spewing some hurtful accusations out of fear, frustration, exhaustion. She didn't really believe Brian was cheating.

"What the fuck are you talking about?" Brian snapped back. Then he saw the tears in Maggie's eyes, and he knew she had just put up her defenses, which is her m.o. to protect herself. He just wrapped his arms around her. They hugged as tears streamed into his shirt.

"Maggie, I'm going to start treatment soon, so I knew I had to tell you. I know you have a lot on your plate at work, so I've been trying to spare you anything else to deal with - at least until the new guy can help take some of the load."

After a few minutes, Maggie composed herself. "Ok, so what's the prognosis? What kind of treatment? And did they give you a sense of how long you'll need to be off work?"

Maggie rapid-fired a series of questions so quickly, Brian didn't have time to answer one before the next shot at him. He knew this was Maggie transitioning back into take-charge mode, and she was already planning out in her head how they'd get through this.

"Maggie, it's not that simple."

"What do you mean?"

"The prognosis isn't good. It's pancreatic cancer. Stage 4. It has metastasized."

The color drained from Maggie's face.

"I've decided to fight. The doctors said I have a very low likelihood of survival. They've given me six months realistically, but, they also said because I'm relatively young I have a better chance, albeit small. I'm not going to throw in the towel. I know it's not fair to just drop all this on you, but I wanted to be sure. Weigh my options."

At no point in the conversation had Brian said, "I love you," nor was it offered in return. But Maggie recognized he was trying in his own way to protect her despite being given a virtual death-sentence. She also realized she couldn't leave him now. For better. For worse. And Brian was on her insurance, which made her job even that much more critical.

"When do you start your treatment?"

"Next Monday."

They had sex that night like they hadn't in years. It was the closest they had come to expressing love for each other. A single tear rolled down Maggie's cheek as she was drifting off to sleep.

"I don't know how I'll get this all done..."

Three

Maggie's meeting reminder popped up at 10:15 am - *Meet with Steve. Ugh*, she thought to herself. *Like I don't have enough on my plate right now than to meet with him. I wonder what the hell he wants.*

"Hey Maggie, I was going to stop by Jan's office in a few minutes to go over the projects that are due in the next two weeks. Do you have time?" Edward asked over the cube wall.

"I can't. Meeting with Steve in a few minutes."

Edward couldn't help but wonder what the meeting was about. He had barely talked to the guy outside of their bi-weekly one-on-ones.

At 10:29 am, Maggie walked over to Steve's office.

"Good morning, Maggie. Come in. I decided to do performance reviews for the Crandon team a bit early this year. I know in the coming weeks it's going to really pick up, so I wanted to be judicious with your time. Let's review your performance."

Maggie was a bit annoyed, although she tried to hide it as best she could. Performance review? Steve hadn't even asked her for a list of her accomplishments as he normally does. Did he even seek out peer reviews? This felt like another Steve power play where he, the almighty omniscient one, would bestow upon the world his views. Maggie was surprised she could fit in the same office with his ego.

"Maggie, your work is solid. You're our go-to. We know we can rely on you to build the needed client relationships. I couldn't be happier to have you as part of my leadership team."

Maggie listened intently without making any change in facial expressions. She was still trying to mask her utter annoyance at this guy's audacity.

"I've talked to Michael, and we agree that based on your leadership and efforts, we're going to give you a 5% raise this year. I would've liked to earmark more for you, truly, but until the new account revenue comes in, I need to make sure to reward the rest of this awesome team."

Maggie let that hang in the air without responding. During her last mid-year check-in six months ago, she and Steve had discussed a promotion to senior director on the business. That was until they hired Edward.

After what felt like an awkward eternity, Maggie started, "and Steve, where do I stand with promotion to senior director?"

"Well, Maggie, I know we talked about that. I still think that is the next step for you, but now is not the time. I think once we get this next piece of the business up-and-running, and Michael feels confident, it's going to be a no-brainer, slam-dunk."

She hated his sports analogies, but she hated his inconsistency more.

"Steve, this was the same conversation we had six months ago - that in six months, it would be a 'slam-dunk.' You know I've been carrying this thing for months, not only because I'm committed to this team, but based on our agreement that it would lead to my promotion."

"Maggie, I understand your concerns. You know you are a valued leader of this team, but with all the upheaval, an expanding team, and with Edward starting, I need to wait a little longer. Again, I'm hoping that you recognize the 5% is higher than anyone else on the team, and I'll do my best to make up for it during your promotion."

Maggie knew it wasn't worth her time to fight this. It wasn't going to change. She was filled with rage. She didn't know whether to blame Steve, Edward, or both. She didn't believe for a second that Michael was even consulted on the decision. He let Steve decide on personnel matters. She thanked Steve for his time and returned to her desk, where she quickly grabbed her purse and left for lunch - at 11:01 am.

She didn't want to cry. She certainly had no intentions of crying at work, but as she pulled out of the parking lot, tears streamed down her face. She wanted nothing more than to quit on the spot - to grab Steve by the proverbial balls and tell him to "figure it out" without her, but she knew she couldn't. Now more than ever, she and Brian needed the money for impending medical bills, and more importantly, her insurance.

She pulled into the Chili's about 5 miles away from the office - not that she particularly loved Chili's, but because she knew it was just far enough away that the likelihood of seeing any co-workers over the lunch hour was slim to none. She asked for the farthest booth from the entrance. Upon sitting down, she asked for a double rum and diet. As she ate and sipped her drink, she looked out the window with no real, coherent thoughts. It was the first time in months she finally exhaled. She wasn't worried about the next project deadline, Brian's diagnosis, trying to get it all done. She just stared aimlessly.

After her second double and diet, she looked at her phone. 12:55 pm. Maggie couldn't believe she had been gone almost 2 hours. She hadn't done that... well, ever. Maggie didn't really care. She wasn't overly concerned about time today - most of her afternoon was free from client meetings because they were having an all-agency town hall.

When she finally did walk back into the office at 1:15 pm, Edward heard her sit down. She slammed her file cabinet shut after putting her purse inside. He thought better than to go over the projects he just reviewed with Jan.

At 2:15 pm, a reminder popped up on Edward's calendar for the town hall. He wasn't quite sure what that even was. He stood up and looked over the cube wall to ask Maggie. He noticed her puffy eyes and remnants of her make up.

"Yes?"

"Oh, hey" he whispered. "I just wondered what this town hall meeting is. Is it mandatory?"

"It's just some smoke and mirrors BS where we go over the agency's latest wins."

Edward hadn't ever heard Maggie be so negative. Curt yes. Negative no.

"Ok, thanks. Listen, let me know if I can be of any help to you. I'm happy to jump in. And before 2:30, you may want to freshen up a bit before we all convene."

Maggie didn't know whether to be pissed that he pointed out that she looked like shit, which she knew she did, or cry more that this guy who she blamed and calls a douche just offered to help her. She hurried off to the bathroom to put some cold water on her face. As she looked in the mirror, free of any remaining makeup, with eyes still swollen, she mouthed to her reflection, "Pull it together."

At 2:30 pm, Michael excitedly kicked off the meeting in the agency's atrium, a large open space meant for collaboration that no one ever really used, ironically because if Michael saw you sitting there, he thought you were socializing, and not working. Everyone knew to be seated and ready to go, as to avoid the public shaming he would provide.

The start to the meeting was pretty standard. Company financials. New business. Good creative. Michael then turned it over to the individual team leads to introduce their new team members. The meeting droned on for its usual 45 minutes or so. Maggie hadn't really been paying attention. She stared forward with a blank look. Then instead of ending the meeting, Michael hurried back to the mic.

"Before we end today, I want to make a special announcement. As you know, the Crandon team has worked tirelessly over the last several months and just won a very large piece of new business, which has allowed us to expand that team even further. I couldn't be happier with their work and commitment to the agency. That's why today, I'm pleased to announce that Steve Raymond has been promoted to senior vice president of client service. Let's congratulate him!"

Maggie literally felt sick to her stomach. *That fucking weasel,* she thought to herself. *It had nothing to do with 'waves' or 'needing to have things settle.' He couldn't have senior VP and senior director promotions on the same cycle. He totally fucked me over when I've done all the work.* She couldn't believe it. From 3 pm to 5 pm, she just watched the clock and played on her cell phone. She read no emails. She didn't answer the phone. She waged her own form of silent protest, and for the first time since she was an account coordinator, she left right at 5 pm.

Edward heard her push her chair in and leave, but unlike other days, she didn't address him as she left. Maggie may not have been his best friend, but she was always professionally polite. He couldn't help but wonder what was up.

"Hey, Jan, have a sec?"

"Sure, but just a few minutes. I have a team brainstorming yet tonight."

"What's up with Maggie? She wasn't herself today."

"Listen, Edward. I can't get into this with you. You're too new, and I'm not going to jade you. We need you, and we need you positive. You've really helped to bring some much-needed energy to this team, and I can't thank you enough. But when it comes to Maggie, we go way back. We've been through a lot together, and today's announcement was utter bullsh…" Jan stopped mid-word. The look on her face indicated she had already said too much. It was all Edward needed to hear.

"I get it now."

He felt vindicated that his suspicions of that guy were right. Steve was, in fact, the snake in the grass he suspected.

Four

A few months had passed since Edward's grandma had her accident. Recovery had progressed, but not quickly, considering she was in her early 80's. Edward felt bad he hadn't seen her as much as he had intended when deciding to move back. As life sometimes can, it had gotten away from him. He fell into his routine, and with new projects mounting weekly, and Maggie hit or miss, work became a bigger focus than he ever planned.

"Hey, Mom. What's up?" Edward answered as he picked up his cell phone late one Wednesday night.

"Hi, honey. I wanted to check in. We haven't heard much from you lately."

Edward knew this approach. It was half concern and half guilt. After more than 30 years, he still wasn't immune to the Guilt Queen's reign of terror.

"I know, Mom. It's just work has been crazy. I feel like my co-worker is starting to check out, and as the new guy, I can't really say anything. It's taking more of my time than I anticipated."

"I thought this was 'just a job.' Isn't that why you took this one? So you could be more invested in the family?"

"Hey, I'm invested!"

"Edward, when was the last time you saw your grandmother?"

Checkmate. Like a punch to the stomach that knocks the wind straight out of you, the Queen had landed her final blow.

"You're right, Mom. I'll plan to go see Eltz this weekend."

"I don't want you to go if you're too busy. You know she understands."

He sighed heavily. For a Queen, she certainly

transitions to martyr quickly. She was as agile as a gymnast in emotional maneuvering, and as effective as a ninja.

"Mom, I want to go see her."

After a slight pause, "So, what else is new, honey?"

Clearly having achieved her aim in calling, she was now free to move on to digging into his life to see if there was any*one* new. After chatting for a bit, Edward hung up and laughed.

Someday, I'm going to get better at handling her, he thought to himself.

Saturday morning, Edward woke up at 6:30 am as he would on any given work day. His internal alarm clock was as annoying as ever, especially considering he was free to sleep in. Knowing Elsie would be up, Edward decided to get a jump on the day and hopped in the shower.

"Large hot coffee, 2 creams, 1 sugar." Edward ordered his usual as he pulled through Dunkin' Donuts.

"Wait. Wait. Also, could I also have a medium black coffee with a Splenda and cream on the side?" Today, he would have coffee with his Eltz.

"Good morning, Eltz!" Edward beamed as he walked into Elsie's room. He had heard her TV on as he walked down the hall, so he knew she was up.

"Well, Eddie!" Her face glowed from her wide smile. She was as happy to see him as he her.

"How are you feeling?"

"I'm ok. I want to go home."

Elsie's face turned from the wide grin to solemn, but only momentarily. As if to course correct, Edward could see his grandma switch back to being family matriarch. Her role as mother and grandmother wouldn't allow for the grandchildren to worry. That wasn't the natural order of things. She could worry and care for them, not the reverse.

"Gram, I hear you're doing great. Making progress. Hopefully you can go home soon. Have you had any visitors lately?"

Edward had gotten used to asking about visitors when he talked to her - asking what was new seemed rhetorical considering she hadn't been able to get out of bed for weeks.

"No, not really."

Edward just smiled. In talking to his mom, he knew the family had conducted a virtual parade through the assisted living facility taking turns visiting. He knew his oldest cousin Daphne had just driven over an hour to see her mid-week.

Instead of calling it out explicitly, he asked, "Gram, how's Daphne? I hear she stopped this week."

"Oh, she's good." She wrinkled her nose as she spoke, as if to say, nothing new there.

Edward laughed out loud. "Oh, Gram."

"What!"

She may not be able to get out of bed, but she certainly hadn't lost any of her spark today.

"And what about you? What's new with you, Eddie?"

Eddie. She was the only one that still called him that. It was his childhood nickname that he railed against in his teen years. And yet, the only one that paid no mind, and for whom, he didn't seem to mind either, was his Eltz.

"Well, Gram, I'm working a lot these days. That's really all that's going on. We continue to get more projects, which is great, but my team is slammed. There never seems to be enough time to get ahead, and my colleague has just recently been sort of checked out. I'm not sure what's going on with her. I think it's because she hates me."

"Oh, Eddie. Who could hate you?"

"Her!"

"Don't assume. You don't know what's going on in her

life. Remember what it was like for you after Kate?"

Two solid punches landed. Edward knew where his mother got it from. All hail the Queen Mother. Although this wasn't necessarily guilt, she still knew how to impart life wisdom that left him feeling close-minded and winded. All he could do was nod.

Saint Elsie... As Edward looked at her frail form, it still couldn't mask how strong she was. He still saw the stubborn, strong, proud German woman that he revered. And even at her weakest, she was still guiding him. He thought back to a few Thanksgivings ago, when she showed up with her almost blind friend, Betty. Betty was over 90 and lived alone. Her remaining family lived a few hours away. So, Elsie, over 80 herself, often would pick her up to get her out of the house, including taking her to her doctor appointments.

Out of concern, Edward tried to reason with her, at least what he thought was reasoning.

"Gram, you're over 80 yourself. Are you sure you should be taking Betty? That's a lot of stress."

"Edward..." (when she started with his full-name, his ears perked up. This was serious.)

"This is my church. I couldn't call myself a good Christian if I can't help my friend."

And with that, nothing more needed to be said. Edward knew she wouldn't be changing her mind. It was in these moments when he was reminded she was the best person he knew.

"Eddie, why did you get so quiet?"

He smiled at her as he snapped out of his daze. "Just thinking, Gram. You're probably right about Maggie. I should not assume."

"Good boy."

"Hey, I need to use the restroom quickly. This coffee has run through me. Do you need anything while I'm up?"

"Some water would be nice, thank you."

When Edward returned, Elsie had fallen back asleep. He didn't want to wake her, but he also wasn't ready to leave. He looked at her peacefully sleeping, noticing that she was a good 40 pounds lighter than the stout woman that he spent so much time with growing up. He was happy to be able to have this time with her, not knowing how much was left.

He picked up the remote control about to turn on the TV, but just as quickly he set it back down. He realized he hadn't had this level of solitude in weeks. He turned the recliner in her room and put up his feet. He stared at her for a bit as she shallowly breathed. Tears welled in his eyes when he realized these moments were fleeting; he wouldn't always be able to talk to her. What made him the saddest was after all these years, he still needed her.

She was his biggest fan, his consummate cheerleader. Edward was the baby of the family, and for as long as he could remember, there was a special bond there. Everyone in the family knew it. Without it having to be said, Edward was the favorite. Elsie and her Eddie were inseparable.

Edward and his brother would spend countless hours with their grandparents growing up - the benefit of parents that had kids in their early 20s. His brother had a close bond with Edward's grandpa, Wally, and Edward with Elsie. If she was going to town, he was right alongside her. If they were playing cards, he was her partner. If his brother and cousin were picking on him, she was the first to defend him. Every game. Every school event. She was a part of it.

Now here he sat in his early 30's crying because she was still teaching him, and he wasn't ready to let her go. Amidst a still broken heart, a life in upheaval, a shit-storm of a job, and despite her being frailer than he had ever seen, he needed her more than she needed him. It terrified him - the thought of his life without her. He didn't think he could handle much more. After several months of just trying to get through, he finally broke down and sobbed. He had to get up and leave. He couldn't let Eltz see him like this. She didn't need to worry. As he got into his car, he committed to visit Elsie at least once per week, regardless of how busy life got.

— —

Edward tried to keep his commitment to visit Elsie, but there wasn't much time for anything else. Maggie had become a virtual ghost around the office, so he had been acting as the sole account director. He still wasn't sure what was going on in her life, and he struggled to remember to give her the benefit of the doubt. No one called it an official leave of absence. During an early morning meeting with Jan, Edward, out of frustration, let out an ill-timed joke calling it a 'leave of presence.'

Jan quickly got up and shut the door. He could see on her face that he pissed her off.

"Listen. I get that there is some bad blood or hostility or some shit between you and Maggie. That's between you. I wasn't going to say anything to respect Maggie's privacy, but I can't afford to have any negativity bringing this team down. Her husband's dying of cancer. She's his primary caregiver in his final weeks. I get that it's shitty timing. The absolute worst, in fact, but it is what it is. Maggie and I go way back, and I will do my part to support her. I'm asking the same of you. You got a problem? Keep it to yourself. And don't bring my team down. There's too much to do without you adding to the shit pile. Got it?"

Jan saw a genuine look of remorse on Edward's face. He felt like shit. Elsie's words echoed in his ears, "You don't know what's going on in her life."

"Jan, thank you. Truly, thank you for letting me know. I'm an asshole."

"You're human. But for now, we need you to be *super*

human, so knock it off already!"

They laughed. As Edward got up to leave, he hugged her. She was taken aback, but sensed there was more going on in his life than he had shared as well. As he left her office, she whispered to herself, "Jesus... this is the fucking Days of our Lives."

Edward got back to his desk and thought about sending Maggie an email saying he would cover work - that he understood her priorities needed to be elsewhere. He wanted to express genuine sympathy. Yet he knew he couldn't - he wasn't supposed to know. It all made sense now. Why she kept her walls up. He also realized it meant she wouldn't be back anytime in the near future. He sighed heavily at the prospect of several more months at this pace.

When I'm working, at least I don't think about Kate, he thought to himself.

The day drudged on, and at about 3 o'clock, he heard Maggie at her desk.

"What are you doing here?" he asked concernedly peering over the cube wall.

Maggie had never heard this soft tone from Edward before. She wondered what was up, but she only had a few minutes so she didn't give it too much thought.

"I needed to stop in to fill out some paperwork. I also wanted to check in with you on how everything is going with Crandon." Reality was, she just needed to get out of the house during the hospice nurse's visit.

"It's fine. Don't worry about it. Jan and I have it covered."

She wondered why he was being so nice.

"Ok. Well I'll be back soon. So, you don't have to worry. I *will* be back soon."

Maggie hit print and shut down her computer. After turning in some mandatory forms to HR about her leave, she left without talking to anyone else. She wasn't strong enough to discuss Brian's condition with anyone today, especially Jan. She knew she would break down. Maggie pulled into her driveway 20 minutes later. The hospice nurse was preparing to leave.

"He's resting quietly. He's in a little bit of pain, as is to be expected."

"Is there anything I can do to help?"

It was the same question Maggie asked every afternoon before the nurse left. She increasingly felt helpless to the situation, a frustrating rage slowly building inside her with no real outlet. Maggie's Type A personality was being crushed under the weight of futility.

"No, Maggie. You're doing everything you can for him. You're meticulous in his care. I can't commend you enough."

It didn't seem like enough. Nothing seemed like enough. Maggie walked into the guest bedroom to check on Brian. Since he had been released to come home several weeks ago, Brian insisted he not disrupt Maggie's life any more than it already was. He would set up his hospice bed in the guest room. As he slept, Maggie picked up his hand. As she had for months before, she ran her fingers over the light hair on its edge.

"Hey, Mags. Where'd you go? Did you get done everything you needed to?" Brian groggily whispered barely opening his eyes.

"Hey B. I just had to go into the office for a few minutes to fill out some paperwork. Thanks for letting me get that taken care of."

"Mags, come on. No thanks necessary. I should be thanking you. You don't need to be here 24/7 - you know I appreciate everything you do for me. Too much really. I wish I could repay you, but it would take me two lifetimes, and unfortunately, we know I'm on borrowed time. Mags, I know I don't say this enough. Hell, I don't know when I last said it, but I love you. I guess I realized when you were gone, that if I wasn't awake when you got back, you may not know how I felt. We have had our ups and downs, but I've always loved you."

A single tear rolled down Maggie's cheek as she clutched his hand, unable yet to respond. As she looked at him, she saw his strong chin, perfect nose, and five o'clock shadow. He was considerably thinner from his treatments from when they met, but he was still handsome. She noticed all the things that attracted her to him when they first met. Maggie's lips quivered as she responded.

"Brian. After all these years, I love you too. And I have a constant pit in my stomach knowing that we only have a little bit of time left."

"I know, Mags, and I'm sorry."

"B, you didn't ask for this. No one deserves cancer."

"I'm sorry that I didn't appreciate you more on our bad days. I'm sorry that I can't have that time back. And I'm sorry that I'm leaving you alone to deal with everything, and there's nothing I can do."

Maggie couldn't respond this time. She stood and stroked his hair before leaning down to kiss him. She walked out of the room.

She went into the bathroom and turned on the bathtub to dull out the sounds of her crying. As she sat on the edge of the bathtub, she wept into her hands.

"You asshole," she whispered. "You make me fall for you. Marry me. Then ignore me. I was perfectly fine to leave you, and then you had to go and get cancer. To make it even worse, after months of taking care of you, and actually talking again, I've fallen back in love with you. Why did you have to make me fall back in love with you? Only to leave me…"

Maggie's chest heaved heavily as she cried. "I don't want you to leave me."

— —

Edward hadn't seen Maggie for a few weeks after she stopped into the office. Every morning after seeing her empty desk, he thought about emailing her, but what would he say? They weren't close. They weren't even friends. Yet he still felt a genuine concern for her, that was also tinged with guilt. He considered asking Jan, but he knew better than to broach the subject. For the time being, it wasn't his business, and if or when she comes back, he committed to himself to try harder to work with her.

The initial upheaval of new work had started to balance out, which allowed the team to better manage the workload. Edward was starting to leave work at a reasonable hour, between 6 pm and 7 pm. It was the first time since he moved back to Michigan several months ago, that he felt he was able to decompress in the evenings. He even started finding time to return to the gym. As he left work that night, Edward thought to himself that it was too nice for the gym. He was going to go for a run when he got home. It would be nice to be outside and get some fresh air.

About 10 minutes into his drive, Edward's cell phone rang. It was Jan. He thought it odd, as she rarely calls.

"Hey Jan. What's up? Did I forget something that was due today? I'm not far from the office. I can turn around if I need to."

"Hi Edward. No, nothing like that. You didn't forget anything. I wanted to let you know that Maggie's husband passed away yesterday. We all just found out after you left, and I didn't want you to come in tomorrow and not know what was going on."

"Ok, Jan. Thank you for letting me know," was all he could muster before hanging up.

Edward turned off the radio and drove in silence. He asked himself why this was bothering him so much. Yes, it was sad that she lost her husband, but he barely knew her. And he didn't know her husband at all. He considered his last year. He acknowledged that a lot had changed. His mind drifted to Kate. His heart was still broken, and perhaps he could empathize with what Maggie must be going through. He thought about Elsie and almost losing her, knowing that she would never quite be the same active grandma that he had always known. When he got home he quickly changed into his running clothes. He jogged in silence for almost an hour, trying not to think about anything except escaping.

His return to physical activity had started to show in his physique. He was trimming down with a flat stomach and tightening pecs. As he wrapped his towel around his waist after his shower, Edward looked at himself in the mirror.

"Not bad for a middle-aged guy. Maybe it is time to try dating again," he chuckled to himself.

Edward didn't know what to expect when he showed up at work in the morning. A good portion of the team had worked with Maggie for years, and he was sure there would be a somber overtone to the day. He went in to Jan's office right away.

"Hi, Jan. Thank you again for calling me last night. Sorry I ended the call so abruptly. I was just taken aback by the news. That's not what I was expecting."

"Yeah, never fun to be the bearer of bad news. I really feel for her. It's going to be a long road back. I don't know if she even realizes, but she's been gone for the better part of 3 months. Her whole world was taking care of him. She will probably be a little lost for a while."

"Absolutely. We'll do our best to help her."

Jan's eyebrows raised in surprise at Edward's statement. Since she called him out, he had become a true team leader, shouldering a heavy load and infusing much-needed positivity into the team. But he never again spoke of Maggie. His sudden support of her seemed interesting.

"Agreed. It's all we can do."

"Lord knows Steve won't do it!"

They both laughed in unison, a much-needed relief to the somber start of the day.

"So, Jan, what are the funeral arrangements? Will the agency do anything?"

"Honestly, I'm not sure. We can talk to the team in our morning staff meeting about what we may want to do for the funeral, flowers or something." The team decided to contribute for a bouquet of white lilies.

Edward got an instant message from Jan later that morning stating the calling hours would be the next two days followed by the funeral tomorrow late morning. The next morning, Edward headed to the calling hours before going to the office. He felt compelled to finally show some level of support. When he got toward the front of the receiving row, he saw Maggie in a simple black pant suit, with a pink blouse, and matching swollen eyes. He waited patiently with his head held awkwardly down. He wanted to show support, but he wondered if she would welcome it.

Edward jumped a bit when a woman he didn't recognize tapped him on his shoulder. She was well-dressed in a white sweater dress and black pants and heels. Her thick, brown hair framed her round face, and her warm smile was the genuine kind that instantly put you at ease.

"Hi. Thank you for coming. Excuse me for stopping you, but I've known Maggie and Brian for years. I don't think we've met, though. I wanted to introduce myself and again thank you for coming to show your support. I'm Renee, Mags' best friend."

Edward tried not to laugh upon hearing her friend also referred to her as Mags - it was neither the time nor place.

"Hello. I'm Edward. I work with Maggie on the Crandon team."

"Oh. Hello," was all Renee returned with a raised eyebrow. She smiled again, this time a tad less warmly, before walking away.

Edward started to question whether he should have even come. Again, he wasn't sure why he felt he needed to show his support. It just felt like the right thing to do. He looked down at his feet contemplating leaving, as to not upset Maggie. Perhaps she'd wonder even more than Renee why he was here. Maggie saw him waiting, before he realized. He looked up and made eye contact with her. It was too late now. When he got to the front of the line, she hugged him, much to his surprise.

"Hi, Edward. Thank you for coming. Thank you for everything the last few months. Jan told me how much you've helped keep the account afloat. I can't tell you how much of a relief it was to just step away and take care of…" she paused. "Well, to take care of what was most important. And Edward, thank you also for the thoughtful flowers."

"The team wanted to send you something to show our support."

"No, the flowers *you* sent. That was an incredibly kind gesture."

Edward scanned the room and saw the small arrangement of gerbera daisies he had picked. He wanted to send something more colorful than the team had picked to try to provide a morsel of cheer. The card simply read, "Maggie. I'm very sorry. Edward."

Maggie hadn't seen Edward in several weeks. Jan had kept her up-to-date, but in generalities. She knew work wasn't Maggie's priority. Maggie still wasn't sure they'd end up friends, but she did feel that perhaps she misjudged him. He didn't have to acknowledge her loss. If he did, he could've just participated in the group flowers. Yet, he took the time to send personal flowers and come to the calling hours to show his condolences. Amidst the life lessons Maggie had learned the hard way recently, giving someone another chance was near the top of the list.

"Maggie, of course. Again, I'm very sorry. Take all the time you need before you come back. We have it covered."

"Thank you. Truly."

Edward gave a quick nod of respect to the casket. Despite the obvious physical toll of cancer, he could see how young Brian was. He appeared handsome. Edward looked at a few pictures in the funeral home. In many pictures, Brian and Maggie were laughing or goofing around. He had never seen that side of Maggie. Since starting, she had always been guarded, aloof. He now understood why. Maybe he misread her too. He thought again to Elsie's sage wisdom, "Don't assume. You don't know what's going on in her life."

Five

Crandon annual planning had taken longer than Edward anticipated. His 7 pm nights quickly shifted to 9 and 10 pm departures, as he was balancing the grind of daily work and annual planning for both his and Maggie's businesses.

8:58 pm. He glanced at his computer's clock considering whether he should continue plowing through or call it a night. He looked to his right at the calendar. He quickly realized it had been four-weeks since he had visited Elsie.

"Damn it, Edward. You promised yourself this wasn't going to happen. You gotta keep your priorities, buddy." He vowed to himself he would leave work by 6 pm tomorrow and go to see her.

"Elsie, how are you?" he beamed as he walked into her room with a large bouquet of white daisies, her favorite.

"Oh, I see you brought a peace offering."

She may not be as physically nimble, but today she certainly was as mentally sharp.

"You got me there, Eltz. How are you?"

She shrugged her shoulders slightly, as to say not much is new.

Edward proceeded with his usual first question. "Any visitors lately?"

"Your mother was here earlier. I don't know what I'd do without her. She is helping me so much until I can go home and manage my bills and such again."

Elsie spoke as if she'd be going home and managing her own affairs again. Edward knew better. She wasn't going to be able to live alone again. This was her new norm, but he wasn't going to be the one to discuss that.

Edward could never anticipate what kind of

conversation he was going to have when he visited. Somedays it felt like it was a carbon copy of the previous visit. Then there were days when she could still impart a life lesson. Today would be the latter.

"Eddie, how have you been?"

"Gram, if I'm being honest, there are days I'm barely hanging in there. I go day to day, and I know it's a terrible excuse, but that's why I haven't been to see you lately."

At first, she furrowed her brow, as if to say that's not an excuse. After letting him know in her own way that she didn't love that he'd been absent lately, she started, "Eddie, I don't believe there's anything you can't do."

"Ha! Gram, thanks for the vote of confidence, but I'm not so sure lately."

"Let me tell you. When Richard left me, I had to figure out how I was going to feed four kids, balance a household, and work three jobs. There were days when I didn't know how the bills would get paid. My brothers would bring me sugar and flour just to make sure I could feed my kids."

Edward sat in stunned silence. He had never heard his grandma be so candid before. She rarely talked about the time before she married the only man he knew as his grandpa. For his whole life, they were financially comfortable. Add to that, Elsie very rarely left "grandma" mode to talk so openly. He had no idea she had struggled so much.

"But I did it. Looking back, I don't know how. Thanks to the Grace of God for my brothers. There were some dark days, where I'd pray pretty heavily to the Lord, and beg Him to help my children. Then one day, as I was waiting tables at the local pub, I met your grandpa. That was the turning point. And had I not had job #3, I wouldn't have met him. I think things worked out pretty well, don't you?" she said with a wry smile.

Edward nodded his head in agreement. His grandpa

was a wonderful man. He had married a divorced woman with 4 kids and raised them as his own, on a factory worker's salary. Edward never knew how his grandparents met, but he certainly didn't envision that it was at the local watering hole. With the benefit of hindsight, things worked out well indeed.

"Thanks, Eltz. I needed to hear that. I got this. I do."

"Eddie, I'm happy to hear that because if there's one thing I've learned, it's we have to work to pay the bills, but life is more than just work. You need to find love. Why don't you date, Eddie? I want to be at your wedding. Nothing would make me happier. I'm not getting any younger!"

He laughed awkwardly, not sure what to say. The Queen Mother of Guilt again surfaced, and he wondered if she and his mom talked often on this subject.

"Young man, I asked you a question. I'm waiting."

Oh Lord, she wanted to actually have this conversation. He wasn't quite prepared. Still unsure exactly what to say, he knew she wouldn't accept "work" or "busy" as an answer.

"Well, if I'm being honest, Gram, I'm not sure I'm over Kate yet. Well, maybe I'm getting there. I don't think about her quite as often as I used to. I have only looked at her Facebook page once in the last month. Who has the time?"

He was now nervously rambling. He wasn't even sure if she knew what Facebook was! He paused hoping that answer would suffice, and they could return to more mundane topics.

"Eddie, Kate was a lovely girl. We all loved her too, but you can't mortgage your future on your past. You have to move on. But before you do, I have a question for you. What happened there? We never really knew."

Edward's eyes got large as saucers. He really wasn't prepared to relive that day. However, perhaps he should -

maybe it was time. If he felt he could talk to anyone about it, it was Elsie.

"Gram, where do I begin? I loved her. Like really, really loved her. I was ready to marry Kate. In fact, I had started ring shopping. I even had asked her dad for permission. I was planning how I would propose. There weren't really any signs that she felt differently."

"Oh, Eddie. I didn't know."

"It is what it is now."

"So?"

"Well, it was a random Tuesday after work. I'll never forget that day. It was a great spring day in Chicago. I was hoping we could go grab dinner and sit outside. Having been cooped up all winter, you want to get out. I got home and asked if she wanted to go to dinner. I didn't really wait for her response - just assumed she'd be game. I went into our room to change into something more casual. I asked her how her day was and continued talking between the rooms, like we did most days."

"I could tell from her responses that something was off. I wondered if something had happened at work, or if someone in her family had died."

"Kate, is something wrong? You don't seem yourself."

"Edward, we need to talk."

"Yeah, of course. What is it?"

"I don't really know where to start. A few months ago, I got contacted by an international conglomerate about running one of their teams in London."

"I was a bit confused as to where this was going. Kate had never mentioned anything about applying for or considering a new job."

"Did you apply for it? How come you haven't mentioned it?"

"That's just it. No, I didn't apply for it. One of their recruiters found my profile on LinkedIn. Even then I didn't give it much thought because I didn't think I was quite qualified for the level of job they wanted to discuss with me. It's kind of like a once in a lifetime opportunity. I couldn't turn it down. I start next month."

"What? When were you going to discuss this with me?"

"Again, I just didn't think it would happen, so I figured why rock the boat. You seem so happy."

"Well, aren't you happy? I would've said *you* were happy too!"

"I am happy, and I do love you. I just know me, and if I turned this down, I would always wonder 'what if.' It's *my* moment, and I have to take it."

"Ok."

"I stopped and let silence fill the air. I still wasn't quite sure then what this meant for us. Since she just dropped this on me, I wasn't going to let her off the hook and ask more questions. I waited for her to continue. After what seemed like eternity, Kate grabbed my hand."

"Edward, I've been doing a lot of thinking. This job is going to take up most of my time. I'm going to be in a new city, working a ton. I just don't think it's fair for me to ask you to move with me and not have any time for us."

"So, I don't get a say in this? What was I? The backup plan? How can you so cavalierly walk away from us?"

"No! You were never the backup plan! I never saw this coming."

"Right. But if being with me doesn't fit into your life, no matter the circumstance, I'm just the backup plan - what's convenient for you now. What the fuck, Kate? I was going to ask you to marry me! And you what? Flush it down the *loo*. Is that how you'll say it now that you'll be in fucking London? Well cheeri-the fuck-o."

"Kate started to cry, and I started to yell."

"Oh no. You don't get to cry. This is your choice. You're actively choosing to move away, and seemingly telling me that I'm not part of the move. So, don't cry to me."

"I ripped my hand away from hers so I could get up and pace. Just two hours before I was happily thinking about ways to propose, and then my world had been crushed."

"I'm sorry, Edward. I don't know how else to explain this to you. This is a once-in-a-lifetime opportunity, and while I do love you, I don't want you to begrudge me for taking you away from your career and your life here."

"You are my life! Don't you get that? If you're in London, that's where my life is. Why wouldn't you talk to me about this? How can you say you love me, but it not be enough to try to discuss this as a couple?"

"Because it's not a decision I was going to make as a couple. I made this decision for me, as selfish as that sounds. I needed to decide on my own, without your input. I couldn't let this pass."

"Ok, I get that. I get that it's a great opportunity, but what I don't understand is why you didn't think I'd be happy for you or go with you. Why is it one or the other - your job or me? It doesn't have to be that way. I'll move to London, if that's what it takes to stay with you."

"Kate sighed. She knew she was breaking my heart. She tried to hold back the tears. It was to no avail. Tears rolled down her cheeks."

"I know this isn't what you want to hear, and I don't know how to quite explain it myself. I don't have a good reason. Just in my heart of hearts, after considering this for a while, I just see me going alone.

This is something I have to do. In my head if I stay with you, I'm going to be a mom with 2.5 kids and a minivan. And that doesn't equate to where I'll be in my life in London. I can't explain it other than that. I need to forge a new path."

"That makes no fucking sense! We've both talked about wanting kids. This isn't a life-sentence I've bestowed upon you. If you don't want kids, then why didn't you say so? How did I become all that is wrong in your life?"

"I didn't say that! You're an amazing man. In my heart, I just feel like I have to go this one alone. And perhaps I'm walking away from the best thing that will ever happen to me, but I don't know I can give this 100% if I'm trying to also be dedicated to you."

"So now I'd be a distraction from this newfound devotion to career? But I wasn't hindering your career here. So, again, backup plan. Good for the time being. Great to know, Kate. I only wish you had told me I was the backup plan sooner, so I didn't get my heart completely crushed. Of all the people in the world, I never pictured you'd be the one to hurt me."

"She got up without another word, grabbed her purse and walked out. I guess she figured it was no use trying to explain it further. I was dumbfounded. I couldn't believe she could drop this news and then just walk out. I was pissed, so I continued yelling at the door behind her."

"You're a bitch! Did you ever really love me at all? Did your dad know when I asked for his permission thinking 'that poor sap?'"

"And that's it, Gram," Edward finished. "I was angry for the first few days and needed time to cool off. By the time I was ready to see her again and talk, she was gone. I didn't know it was happening that fast. I haven't seen her since."

"Well first young man, watch all that foul language!"

He laughed slightly before asking, "Gram, that's what you got out of my story?"

"You didn't let me finish! I'm really sorry, Eddie."

"The hardest part, Gram, is she didn't choose someone else. There was no warning. There was no reason. For whatever reason, I just wasn't enough. How do you learn to love or trust again after that?"

"You should never feel that way. The heart is complex. She made a choice for her. If she didn't want to be with you, then you have to let her go."

"Easier said than done, Eltz. I loved her, in a way that was pretty consuming."

"Just because you move on doesn't mean you didn't love her. It means you're willing enough to find someone who is capable of loving you as well."

"Yeah, but you have to first learn to trust or be open again to getting hurt. I don't know if I can go through that again, if I'm being honest."

"What choice do you have? Life is not to control, but to live. For that, you must let go."

He sighed. He sighed as if to exhale the burden of the last year and a half. He sighed as if to wonder how this feeble old woman was still impacting him in a way he didn't think still possible. Most of all he sighed not knowing if he was really capable of moving on. But he knew she was right.

He smiled at her. "Gram, you're right. You're always right. I love you."

<u>Six</u>

Elsie's voice echoed in Edward's head for weeks. "Life is not to control, but to live. For that, you must let go." It was easy to put off getting back in the dating scene while Maggie was out. He was forced to focus on work. However, he received an email from Steve to the Crandon team that Maggie would be returning in two weeks. If he were honest with himself, he didn't know how he felt about her returning. Since the start of her leave, he had been able to fully lead the team, despite the initial difficulty and long hours. And after the funeral, he let go of the concern for her. In fact, he hadn't really thought much about her lately. He now worried that things would return to their tumultuous beginning.

"Hey, Jan. Got a minute?"

"Sure, Edward. What's up?"

"Did you see Steve's email this morning? Maggie's set to come back."

"I did! Isn't it great? I can't wait to see her again. You must be happy to get some help yourself. You can finally share some of the burden."

"That's just it. You'd think I'd be excited to get some of this off my plate, right? I'm a bit worried, though, about the dynamic when she gets back. It's been a few months now since she's been part of the team."

"She's an old pro. She'll slip right back in, and before you know it, it'll be like she never left."

"I hope so. I'm sure you're right. Have you talked to her?"

"I haven't actually. After the funeral, she went MIA. I gave her some space initially and then reached out via text message, but I didn't hear back from her. I didn't think too much of it. I figured she just needed time and didn't want to think about work quite yet."

Edward nodded his head in agreement. He looked at Jan and realized how far they had come in such a short time in their own working relationship. They now gelled so well - Edward with his knack for finding a consumer insight, and Jan's ability to run with that insight and turn it into interesting creative. As she spoke, he worried Maggie would throw a wrench into that as well, but he didn't dare say that. He knew Jan was fiercely protective of Maggie.

"Well Jan, I guess we'll see in two weeks how she feels about coming back, won't we?"

"It's going to be great! Hey, I can't talk much longer. I have a creative team huddle."

"Ok, no prob." Edward half-heartedly waved as he walked out of her office and back toward his desk.

"Don't worry!" Jan beamed in return.

Why is this bothering me so much? he thought as he sat back at his desk. He knew the answer. Work was a good distraction. He still wasn't concerned about climbing the corporate ladder, though. He barely spoke to Steve, so it wasn't as if he were playing the office politics game. He admitted to himself that it meant he would have more time on his hands.

He opened the top drawer of his desk and took out a small post-it note on which he had written Elsie's advice, "Life is not to control, but to live. For that, you must let go."

"So be it, Gram," he whispered to himself. With that brief moment of courage, he took 30 minutes to start his first online dating profile. He read the first question: "How would you describe yourself?" He laughed to himself, "Over this already?" He laughed even harder at the next question: "How would your friends describe you?" "Needs to get laid... badly."

He didn't want to spend much time at work focusing on crafting the perfect profile, if there were such a thing. He just needed to get off go. He hurriedly filled out as many answers as he could. Finally, he needed to add a few pictures.

"Ugh, I really hate this."

He pulled out his phone and looked to see if there were any pics that he felt were not too embarrassing. He found a recent one at a baseball game with his friend, and then he came across a selfie he had taken with Elsie on a recent visit.

Hmm, I'm not sure how'd she feel about being on my dating profile, but these women should know she's the most important woman in my life right from the get go, he thought as he uploaded the picture.

After uploading, he logged off and took a look at his calendar to see his schedule for the rest of the day. He also thought he should probably start thinking about a transition plan for when Maggie came back.

The day went by quickly as always between the rush of meetings, client calls, and creative reviews. He hadn't given much thought again to Maggie or his new dating profile. Needless to say, he was quite surprised that evening then when he already had 3 messages and 2 winks in his email from women that saw his new profile.

"Oh, I'm really not ready for this! But there's no time like the present."

He clicked on the link in the first email. His online account opened in a second window. The first woman was attractive, but not really Edward's type. He decided to read what she had to say anyway.

Hello, sexy! Great profile. I haven't seen you on here before. We should meet for a drink!

He was taken aback by her forwardness as a woman. Usually it's the guy that makes the move. He wondered to himself if he was too old-fashioned, or if this is just how dating is in the cyber age.

Should I respond? Am I obligated to respond? he

thought. He was so confused. He didn't know online dating protocol, and he didn't really want to google, "online dating etiquette." He decided he'd just ignore her message and take the easy way out. He didn't feel great about it, but he also didn't want to digitally say, "you're not my type."

He opened the second message. It was from a young 23-year-old blonde with pretty blue eyes and a round, cherub face. She had long hair with curls at the end that sat on the front of her chest in her picture.

Hello. It was a pleasure to read your profile. I'm Jessica. I especially liked that you had a picture with your grandma. I'm really close with mine as well. I hope we can chat sometime.

She's a bit young for you buddy, he thought. He appreciated that she called out how important family is to her, though. And if he were honest, he couldn't deny that she was pretty. He opted to respond.

Hello, Jessica. Thanks for reaching out. Yeah, I'm super close with my family, especially my grandma. It's been a difficult few months with her health, but I'm glad to have this time with her. What do you do in your free time?

No sooner had he hit send then an instant message chat box popped up from Jessica.

Jessica: *Hi!*

Edward: *Hey - that was fast!*

Jessica: *No time like the present. Since you were on, I figured I'd speed up the conversation.*

Again, Edward was befuddled by the speed of talking to complete strangers in the online dating environment.

Edward: *Ok, no problem. How was your day?*

Jessica: *It was ok. I had to work, and then I grabbed some drinks with my friends.*

Edward: *Sounds fun. I just worked, hit the gym, and now checking out this online dating thing. It's all new to me.*

Jessica: *I didn't think I had seen your profile before! Welcome to the joys of online dating. It's all downhill from here.*

He laughed at her last comment. He liked her spunk, and since she had said she grabbed drinks with friends, he figured he'd be forward too.

Edward: *Well happy to be here I guess. Care to grab a drink sometime with me?*

Jessica: *Sure. That would be great. When are you free?*

Edward: *Most nights after work. You tell me when you're free. We can make it work.*

Jessica: *Thursday, 7 pm. You tell me where.*

Edward: *Done. Let me get back to you on the location.*

Jessica: *Sounds great. I have to run but look forward to meeting you soon.*

Edward logged off without reading the other message or looking at the 2 winks. He shook his head in amazement. "Do I really have a date? What the fuck? I guess I'm doing this. I'm back in the game."

Elsie will be happy, he thought to himself, and then he thought better of telling his family he was back in the dating scene just yet. He wasn't ready for the onslaught of questions that would cause.

He had to figure out where they would meet for a drink. *Should I pick a place where they also served food in the event we want to stay for dinner? Is that too presumptuous? If it is going badly, would food obligate me to stay?* He was out of practice and feeling like a teenager again.

Pull yourself together man! You've been on dates before. The hard part is over. I'll worry about this tomorrow. I'm going to bed. With that, he put off having to deal with it further for the night.

"Hey Jan, where's a good place around the office to grab a drink after work?"

Jan looked up to see Edward leaning on her office doorway. She was a bit surprised, as Edward had never asked her much about anything social outside the office.

"Well what are you looking for? A bar? A restaurant? Drinks and appetizers? There's tons to choose from within a few miles of here."

"Probably drinks and appetizers I guess."

Jan's face got a huge grin on her face, and Edward knew he was busted.

"You have a date! With whom? Details! How'd you meet? When is it?"

Why do women get so crazy about these things he wondered? He sheepishly crashed in the chair opposite her desk.

"Jan," he paused embarrassed, "I started online dating. Shoot me now."

She howled in laughter. She wasn't quite sure why she found this so funny, but she knew it just was. Here was this smart, attractive, ambitious guy, and he was in the sea of barracudas.

"Gee thanks, Jan. You can stop laughing now."

"Well, it's just that you're so private. I didn't know if you were already dating. Asexual. Gay."

"Again, thanks, Jan. If you haven't noticed, we've been a little busy around here for the last several months! Who had the time?"

"You do now, kid! Maggie's almost back. She's going to love this!" Jan's voice kept getting giddier as the conversation went on.

"No. No, no, no. This isn't going to be watercooler fodder. Promise me!"

"Ugh. You're no fun. Fine…" Jan's nose curled up in frustration. "But you have to at least keep *me* posted on how it's going."

"You're killing me. As if this isn't hard enough already for me. Now I have to report back?"

"Yes. Oh yes. And to answer your question, I'd go to Ken Smith's Steakhouse. It's about .3 of a mile from here, and they have a great bar and appetizers."

"You're evil, and thank you." Edward smiled wryly as he walked out. He recognized Jan was his work best friend.

— —

Thursday morning came faster than he anticipated. Edward awoke nervous. He was surprised to find a pit in his stomach shortly after his alarm went off.

Why are you making such a big deal of this? You're not a virgin. This isn't your prom. And it won't be televised. Just relax, he thought.

He spent an extra 10 minutes that morning trying to figure out what to wear. "This is lunacy. Get your shit together, Edward." He picked out a black button up and dark jeans. He decided to go with the classics - only after he tongue-lashed himself for being such a girl about it.

He walked into the breakroom at work 20 minutes later than he normally does in the morning. Much to his chagrin, Jan was the first person he saw as she got her coffee.

"Looking good, buster. You got a date or something?"

He shot her a sly grin. "I hate you."

"Nah, because you know without me, your work life would be even shittier than it already is."

"True story! Now pour me some coffee, please."

The day unfolded like any other Thursday, except that Edward really couldn't concentrate on work. He kept looking at the clock and checking his emails hoping Jessica would cancel. At 6:45 pm, his stomach sank as he logged off to head toward his first first-date in over 7 years.

When he walked into the restaurant, Jessica was already there. He noticed she was a bit heavier than in her pictures, but her eyes shined just as brightly. He wondered if all people only post the most flattering of pictures online. She smiled widely when she saw him. It was a great smile.

"Hi, Edward. It's a pleasure to meet you!"

He stuck out his hand to shake hers, but she went straight for the hug. She let it linger longer than he would've expected upon meeting someone new.

"It's a pleasure to meet you too. Thanks for meeting tonight. Shall we grab a seat at the bar?"

"Sounds great."

He pulled out the bar stool for her and had to assist her up, as she was only about 5'3". She kissed him on the cheek to thank him. Again, he was taken aback by it.

"So how was your day, Jessica?" Edward started.

"It was great! I was looking forward to meeting you all day!"

Edward wished he had felt the same, but in lieu of really explaining how he felt, he went with the more polite response.

"Same here."

"What kind of work do you do, Jessica?"

"Oh, I'm an interior designer. Well I hope to be soon. I'm finishing up my degree now. I can't wait to get my first job designing. I want to focus on new higher end homes."

First job? he thought to himself. *What the hell? Welcome to Sesame Street.* He didn't let his facial expression change. He had been out of the game, but he wasn't novice enough for that.

He tried to get a word in edgewise, but she just kept talking. He didn't really mind - it made it easier for him. He'd just listen and take it all in. This went on for the next 20 minutes or so, with Edward uttering a few "oh ok's" and "cool's."

"So, Edward, I went back and re-read your profile

today. Again, I just love how close you are to your family. Now, how would we split the holidays with my family?"

Edward sat in stunned silence. *Did I just hear her correctly? Was she serious?* Edward thought. *Please tell me she was just joking. Thirty minutes in and we're talking about how we'll split up the holidays?*

"Edward?"

He shook his head briefly as to snap out of a daze. "Uh, what do you mean?"

"Well, family is really important to us both. I figured we should really discuss how we'd split up the holidays to make sure we're on the same page. My family does Christmas big! Maybe Christmas with my family and Thanksgiving with yours? Should we rotate? Hmm... although I can't imagine not spending Christmas with my family." She had returned to her speed talking, but this time it appeared as if she were talking to herself.

"I guess I hadn't thought about it." That was the most honest answer he could've given without telling her he thought she was waving her crazy flag.

"Oh, that's ok. We'll figure it out. I can't wait to meet your Grandma. She looks so cute in your picture. I'm sure she'll love me. Grandma's love me."

It was apparent Jessica was looking for her Bachelor of M-R-S degree to accompany the interior design one. Edward let her continue talking for 20 more minutes and a glass of wine. That made the date one full hour, and he felt he had met his obligation. He just didn't feel they had the same level of maturity...or crazy.

"Jessica, it's been great meeting you! Thank you for grabbing a drink with me tonight. I have an early morning tomorrow, so I'm going to have to call it a night. Can you get home or should I call you a cab?"

"Oh...ok. Well it's been great meeting you too, Edward! Thank you for the glass of wine. I hope we can find time again soon."

Edward didn't answer either way, but he smiled politely instead. "Let me walk you to your car, Jess."

"Sure."

He hugged her quickly before opening her car door. The look on her face expressed her disappointment in not getting a good night kiss. But the last thing he wanted was to send mixed signals, so he promptly walked away after bidding her a good night. Edward put his head down on the steering wheel after getting in his car.

"What the hell was that? Is this what I have to look forward to with online dating?"

The next morning Jan almost did an Olympic race walk to Edward's desk when she saw him. She might have run had she not had a hot cup of coffee in her hands.

"Tell me!"

"Really? Not even a good morning?"

"Edward. There is *no time* for niceties! Tell me how the date went."

"Well. Hmm. How do I put this? Thirty minutes in she wanted to know how we were going to split the holidays."

Jan did a literal spit-take and then proceeded to laugh with a loud cackle.

"Jan, I hate you."

"Oh, Edward. That was awesome. When is your next date? Thanksgiving?"

"Have I told you how much I hate you?" he said wryly. "Yeah, there isn't going to be a next date, much to her chagrin, I'm sure."

"Edward, pull up your dating profile. Let's find you your next date."

"Are you serious right now?"

"Absolutely! You're back in the game. I'm not letting you sit on the bench again."

Edward logged into his profile to see 3 more winks and 1 new message to accompany the previous unread message and 2 winks.

"Am I obligated to answer these in the order they came in, Jan?"

"Edward, this isn't client service! It's dating. You respond to the ones you're interested in. God, you've been out of the game too long. Oh! She's cute. Click on her profile."

Edward clicked on the profile of a pretty brunette with shoulder length hair and dark brown eyes. He had to admit, Jan was right. She was cute.

"What do you think?" Jan excitedly asked him.

"Hold on. Let me read her profile."

She was a 31-year-old accountant that liked to travel and read. Edward could work with that. He clicked on the link to respond to her message.

"Let's try this again."

Seven

Renee poured Maggie a cup of coffee. She had been staying with Maggie off and on since Brian passed just to break up the quiet solitude.

"How are you feeling about going back to work?"

"I think I'm ready. I don't know. I can't just sit in the house forever. I have mixed emotions. I miss my team. If I'm being honest, I don't necessarily miss the work, and I certainly don't miss Steve!"

"What about that guy that showed up to Brian's funeral? I know you weren't too keen on him."

"You know what. I wasn't. And truth be told, I'm not sure what to expect when I go back from him. Oh, by the way, his name is Edward. But he really surprised me when Brian died. He personally sent me flowers. He reassured me that he would take care of things at work. Do I think we'll be best friends? Probably not. But I think we can have an amicable working relationship."

"Well you already have a best friend anyway," Renee grinned sarcastically.

"You know what I mean."

"Well that's good to hear. I was sort of short with him when I found out who he was. He probably thought I was such a bitch."

"Renee! Why would you do that?"

"Instinct? Reflex? I don't know - you know I got my girl's back."

"I do. And I don't know that I could've gotten through the last several months without you. This was harder than I could've ever imagined."

"Well, he was your husband."

"I know. But you also know we weren't exactly Romeo and Juliet, Ross and Rachel. I just wasn't expecting to fall back in love with him. I thought we were heading for a divorce, not cancer."

"Mags. So, what now?" Renee tilted her head and softly touched Maggie's hand, wondering if that question was too soon.

"What do you mean?"

"Never mind."

"No, come on. Let's have a real fucking discussion. I can't be handled with kid gloves anymore. Everyone is treating me like I'm porcelain. You do remember how tough I am, right?"

"Fine. Dating? Love? Sex! You're too young to just let your vag dry up!"

Maggie burst out laughing. "Girl, I needed that. I need this. I'm going to be fine. To be honest, I haven't really thought about dating again. I feel like I've been on autopilot for so long with Brian that I don't even remember when *we* dated. Where do I even begin? And when? What is too soon vs. an appropriate time of mourning?"

"That's up to you! And fuck anyone that thinks or tells you otherwise. As you said, you weren't Romeo and Juliet. So, while I know you loved him, you've spent too many years in neutral. It's time to find some real happiness, Mags, and I'm not talking submitting ads to print. Jesus, that job is not your life."

"I know. You're right. It just means breaking out of my comfort zone."

"No. It means getting out of those yoga pants and doing something with your hair."

"You really are a bitch."

"I never denied it, but a bitch you love."

Maggie rolled her eyes as she shook her head in agreement.

"Well I'm going to have to get out of these yoga pants tomorrow. It's my first day back. I'm sort of nervous."

"Maggie, you've been there over a decade. You could run the joint. What's to be nervous about?"

"Ugh, speaking of. Do you know I left a message for Steve to talk about my return, and he responded via email? After working for that guy for this many years and helping him grow this business, he couldn't even pick up the fucking phone to call me back. He responded and copied HR to coordinate. I couldn't believe it."

"Why don't you just leave? Find a new job? How long have I been saying this?"

"Because I like my team. My clients. And right now especially, I don't want to have more upheaval in my life."

"Mags, it's always something. We've been having this same discussion about that hell hole for how long now?"

"Fine. New topic. What about you, Ms. Chambers? How's your dating life?"

"Smooth. Deflect. Ok, well dating is fun as always. The endless parade of tom cats, lotharios, and douchebags makes life interesting."

"And you want me to get back out there why?"

"Because at some point you're going to want to feel the warmth of a man on top of you again, so the sooner you acknowledge that fact, the sooner we can find you a date."

"Jesus, Renee."

"Tell me I'm wrong."

Maggie sighed heavily. "You're not. You very rarely are. It's annoying, but it won't be today."

"Fine. Let's go shopping today. We'll find you something new to wear for tomorrow. You can go back and start a new phase looking great."

"Ok, I can handle that."

— —

When the alarm rang at 6:30 am, Maggie hit snooze 3 times. This wasn't the Maggie that used to be the first one at the office by 7:15 am, putting the coffee on for the rest of the team. She wasn't sure what to expect. She felt bad she hadn't responded to Jan, but she just didn't want to think about work. She also wondered how the dynamic with Edward would be. He's been leading the team now for over 3 months. That can be an eternity in advertising.

"Well, Mags, there's no time like the present. Let's do this."

On the fourth buzz, the alarm was off, and Maggie's feet hit the ground. As she showered, she thought about her conversation with Renee. Good-God Renee. She was outspoken, but she told it like it was. Maggie appreciated her candor.

Could I really go on a date? The thought isn't that exciting. Maybe I'm not ready. Well, to Renee's other point, there's no rush. I'm on my own timetable now. I just need to put one foot in front of the other. And right now, that one foot better hurry up, or I'm going to be late!

She drove to work virtually on autopilot. She had driven this route thousands of time. Nothing was particularly unique about this morning, but everything felt different. She had a knot in her stomach, that only tightened as she got closer to the office. The outfit that looked so good in the dressing room mirror, she now questioned. And what would she say to Steve? It was becoming harder to hide her disdain for him. She pulled into the parking lot, turned off her car, and sat in silence for 5 minutes.

She looked at herself in the rear-view mirror. "You're being ridiculous. Stop stalling. Act like you own the place, and get your ass in there!"

She walked toward her desk. There were the normal quiet rumblings of the morning: typing, sipping of coffee, some hushed whispers. Her traffic coordinator, Angela, was the first person to see her.

"Hello, Maggie. Welcome back. We've been looking forward to seeing you today. Let me know if you need anything as you get settled."

Maggie sat down and sighed. She was thankful the most junior employee at the agency was the first person she saw. Trial-run. She was so warm and welcoming. *Perhaps I made a bigger deal out of this than I needed to. This is my team.*

"Hello, Maggie."

Maggie looked up to see Edward standing over her cube wall. He noticed she was at least 10 pounds thinner than when he saw her at the funeral. The stress and grief must've really taken it out of her.

"Welcome back. I'll let you get settled. I'm sure you have a bunch of emails to dig through. I didn't put time on your calendar today so you can have the day to get acclimated, but let me know when you're ready to talk about the transition plan."

"Transition plan?"

"Oh yeah. Steve talked to me about what brands and clients he'd like each of us to own going forward."

Maggie could only nod. Of course, Steve hadn't talked to her about it first to get her input. The almighty, omniscient one in his infinite wisdom will bestow his decree upon the land.

"Ok thanks," was all she could muster. Edward noticed she had rolled her eyes. That wasn't something the Maggie of old would've ever let someone see her do so cavalierly.

She had only been there 10 minutes, and she was already annoyed. She knew where she needed to go next. After getting a cup of coffee, she headed to Jan's office.

"Lady, where have you been all my life!" Maggie boasted as she walked in.

Jan got up to give her a giant bear hug. "Me? You went radio silent on me, chica."

"I know. I'm so sorry. I just wasn't ready to talk or think about work, so I tuned that part of my life out. I'm sorry again."

"No need. I figured as much. Who can blame you? Like you'd want to think about this place…"

Maggie stepped in and shut the office door. "So, let's get real. What have I missed?"

"Honestly, not much. We went through phase 2 of the expansion. We picked up 3 new brands, all acting as their own pieces of business. Edward's done a great job to manage it all, delegate and lead the teams. I've been impressed."

Maggie looked down. She should be happy to hear that - that she wasn't walking into a tornado. But she also wanted to feel like she was needed, that the account couldn't go on without her.

"Steve's been, well, Steve. He's gotten up at the last 2-3 town hall meetings and taken credit for the expansion, when it's really been Edward and me. That guy, as you know, is a jackass, but what can we say?"

Maggie just nodded. Normally, she would've jumped on the "I loathe Steve" bandwagon, but she was hearing something else in Jan's voice as she talked. She sensed that Jan and Edward had grown close, much closer than when Maggie left. Again, Maggie should be happy - it would make for a better team environment. Yet all she felt were pangs of jealousy. She had worked with Jan since almost day 1.

"How about you, kiddo? How are you doing?"

"I wish I knew, Jan. I'm going day to day. I wasn't really excited about coming back, and you know I used to live for work. It just now seems like there should be more to life than work, sleep, repeat. Losing Brian made me realize that."

"What does that mean exactly? Are you thinking about leaving?"

"Oh no. I was telling my friend Renee yesterday that I'm not looking for more upheaval in my life right now. I need to get back to my routine. I know I'm good at what I do. I think it's important that I'm back, as hard as it was this morning."

"Have you seen Edward?"

"Yeah, he said hello this morning. That was about it. He said the transition plan has been established already. I'm glad Steve sought *my* input," Maggie snapped sarcastically.

Jan smirked. She knew where Maggie was going.

"I have to tell you - I've been impressed with Edward. I think you're going to like working with him. I know you got off to a rocky start, but I think his heart is in the right place. And he's funny. You should hear his dating stories."

Jan bit her lip quickly, as if she had just revealed government secrets.

"Noooo... he talks about that with you?"

"Maggie, I shouldn't have said anything. I'm such a yenta. Forget it."

"Ok. I will...for now. I have too many emails to go through, but this isn't the end of this conversation."

As Maggie opened Jan's office door and stepped out, Steve was walking by.

"Maggie! Welcome back! I'm so happy to see you. You're looking great. Let's catch up later this afternoon. Put time on my calendar."

She couldn't believe it. First, he couldn't be bothered to actually call her back, and now he can't even set up the meeting invite. The first thing he tells her to do is send him a meeting request.

Whatever, Maggie. Let it go. This isn't the way we're going to start our day.

1,123. The bold number of unread emails popped up as she opened her inbox. She knew it would take her the majority of the day to go through them, but she was happy for the quiet distraction. She could ease back into it at her own pace. She turned on her Lady Gaga Pandora station and opened the first unread email.

After an hour or so, she bored of digging through emails. She wasn't particularly thirsty, but she got up to go to the kitchen for water as a welcome distraction. Michael was heading back to his office when she saw him.

"Hello, Maggie. I'm so sorry for your loss again. We're very happy to have you back."

He never ceased to amaze her. For someone who treated people with such contempt and condescension, he could also at times be very caring. She wondered if he had some sort of chemical imbalance.

"Thank you. Honestly, I'm so grateful to everyone for their warmth, patience and support as I dealt with everything. It's good for me to focus on work again."

"Well, happy to have you back. Steve has really built up this business. We need all hands on deck."

Maggie had the presence of mind not to roll her eyes until after she walked away. She couldn't figure out how for such a cunning businessman, he couldn't see Steve for the weasel that he was. That reminded her that she hadn't put time on Steve's calendar yet. She looked at his calendar when she was back at her desk. He had one open half hour window this afternoon.

Maggie did her best to try to stay productive until then, but her heart wasn't in it. Perhaps she came back too soon. *It's your first day. Be nice to yourself,* she thought. Five minutes before her meeting, the knot in her stomach returned. *You can do this, Mags. Stop being stupid. You've handled him for how long?* She exhaled. *It's now or never.*

"Hi, Steve."

"Come in, Maggie. How's your first day back?"

"Just going through a lot of emails right now. Edward mentioned he'd give me time to re-acclimate before we met."

"Great. Yes, I've talked to him already about a

transition plan. I wanted to talk to you about it as well. Since we picked up three more brands, I want to divide and conquer between you. I've asked Edward to lead the charge on the 3 largest, and I've decided you'll lead the remaining 5. I did this so he can maintain momentum on those, and you can have a soft transition back into the pressure cooker."

Maggie didn't know whether to be thankful or infuriated. She understood his point about giving her leeway to come back at a slower pace, but she also couldn't help but feel this was Steve's way of minimizing the risk to the overall account. She couldn't blame him necessarily. This was business, but that pissed her off too. She just sat and half-heartedly listened to his plan for the next few months. She was still too wrapped up in her own processing. She also wondered if this was because Edward was a man, or even worse, was he better than she was? Both thoughts fueled her inner anger.

"Do you have any questions?"

The question caught her off guard as she snapped back to full attention.

"No, I'm just excited to be back. Thanks again."

"No problem, Maggie. And remember, I'm always here if you need anything."

She wanted to laugh in his face. *Need anything? How about the promotion you promised me twice over? Or any credit with Michael for where the account is today?* But of course, she just smiled politely before she left.

When she got back to her desk, she looked at her phone. Renee had sent her a text.

Renee*: How's it going?*

Maggie: *Ugh.*

Renee: *That good, hey?*

Maggie: *It's fine. I just need time to get back into the swing of things I think.*

Renee: *Or a distraction!*

Maggie: *Like what?*

Renee: *I think I may have a date for you?*

Maggie: *I told you I wasn't sure I was ready.*

Renee: *I know, but I can't control that I found someone that could be cool for you to meet.*

Maggie: *What's his story?*

Renee: *Don't know him well. He's a friend of a co-worker. 30. Saw his pic. He's not bad. He's single and wanting to get back to dating himself. I thought of you. Nothing to lose.*

Maggie: *Why do you do this to me?*

Renee: *B/c I love you! So, is that a yes?*

Maggie: *Fine. But if this sucks, you owe me.*

Renee: *Deal. Maybe you'll get to suck! Then you owe me!*

Maggie: *?!*

Renee: *I know, right? You love it. Talk to you later. I'll try to set it up for this Friday.*

And just like that, Maggie had a new source of worry. Maybe Renee was right after all. Maybe she did need a distraction. She certainly wasn't overly concerned about work anymore.

Eight

If Edward thought he was busy when he first joined the agency, online dating proved to complicate things. It was like a part-time job itself! Logging in, answering messages, reviewing profiles, going on dates. Edward wouldn't have necessarily minded if he felt like he were meeting any women in which he was interested. He couldn't figure out how women who seemed promising on paper could be such bombs in person.

He had a third date after work with the accountant. He still wasn't quite sure why. She was quite possibly the most boring person he had ever met. Was he giving her the benefit of the doubt? Was he just passing the time? Or most likely, was it those dark brown eyes and that gorgeous smile? He looked at his watch - 3:05 pm. He had about 4 hours before he needed to leave to pick her up. He opened up CNN to look at the news of the day. He took out a notecard and wrote down 5 topic ideas for conversation so he wouldn't forget. He put his head in his hands. *Are you kidding me? Are we really doing this? You are so bored with her that you're writing down things to talk about and yet you're still going? You must be hard up, dude,* he angrily chided himself.

Date one was a casual dinner. Edward was excited to meet Emily. She was an accounting manager at a large professional services firm, had her CPA, and owned her own home. Compared to the 23-year-old seeking her MRS degree, Emily seemed much more established. He re-read her profile prior to dinner to make sure he remembered her likes and interests. She loved to travel. Boom. Great topic of conversation. That should be enough to get the conversation flowing.

When he arrived at the restaurant, Emily was already

waiting in the lobby. She was sitting neatly with legs together and hands folded in her lap. She looked every bit the part of a professional - with black button up blouse hugging her body, albeit not too tightly, with stylish jeans and black high heels. She was beautiful in a Jennifer Aniston manner - subtly sexy. When he walked in, she recognized him instantly and stood up to give him a hug. She smiled widely, and Edward was taken with her gorgeous smile.

"Hi, Emily. I hope you haven't been waiting too long."

"Not at all. Looking forward to dinner."

"Me too. Shall we?"

Edward smiled to himself as he walked behind her toward their table. He was hopeful this was finally going to be a good date.

"So, Emily, how was your day?"

"It was good, thank you…."

After she finished speaking, there was an awkward pause as Edward waited for her to ask a question in return. When she didn't, he asked, "so tell me about yourself?"

"As you know I'm an accounting manager. I lead a team of 8 people on a project in the consumer products industry."

Again, Edward waited for her to ask the same question in return as typical conversations go, but nothing. *Was she nervous?* he wondered to himself.

He couldn't wait any longer or this would be a pretty quiet dinner.

"I work in advertising. Like you, my client is in consumer products too."

"Ok."

Ok? That's it? She wasn't giving him much to go on. He was hoping a drink may relax her. Edward flagged the waiter over.

"Hello. Welcome to Horizons. Glad you could join us tonight for dinner. I'm Anton, and I'll be your waiter tonight. Apologies for the delay. We're pretty busy tonight. What would you like to drink?"

"I'll take a Sauvignon Blanc," Emily requested first.

"And I'll have a Malbec please."

Edward was relieved she ordered a glass of wine. Perhaps now they could have an actual two-way conversation.

"So, Emily, I read you like to travel."

"Yeah." (pause)

"What's your favorite vacation you've taken?"

"Probably my first trip to London." (pause)

Edward couldn't believe she wouldn't elaborate on any of her answers. He was starting to feel like he was interviewing her. Unfortunately, he was proving to be no Oprah Winfrey.

"So, why London? I enjoyed my first trip there as well, but the weather was abysmal. And it was super expensive."

He wanted to add, "and my bitch of an ex moved there, along with my heart and soul," but he stopped short.

"Because it was my first trip abroad, and I just hadn't ever experienced anything like that before." (pause)

"Ok, here is your Sauvignon Blanc and your Malbec. Are you ready to order?"

Edward had been so focused on trying to keep the conversation afloat that he hadn't even looked at the menu, but in lieu of waiting any longer and trying to fight for new topics, he encouraged Emily to order.

"I'll take the grilled chicken, with steamed asparagus and baked potato, no butter."

That order is sort of boring, he thought to himself, *but it explains that great ass.*

"And I'll have the sirloin with a blue cheese crust, medium, and a side salad with balsamic."

Edward noticed her wine was half empty, so after the waiter left, he waited to see if she would initiate the conversation. With at least some wine in her, perhaps she would loosen up, but she just smiled as she swirled her glass.

The dinner pretty much went the same way, with Edward asking questions and Emily answering with 1-2 words and giving awkward, "Yeah" responses to statements Edward made. He couldn't believe that a date that seemed so promising could be such a bore, with her personality seemingly matching her order. When the check came, she quickly took the bill.

"I'm going to pay for my own."

Edward knew what that meant. This would be a one and done. He appreciated that she was willing to cover her own if she felt like it wasn't a match, although he would've happily paid for her dinner. At least that explains why she wasn't very talkative. He wondered if she weren't attracted to him in person.

"Thank you for joining me for dinner, Emily. It was nice to meet you. Shall we go?"

She smiled politely and nodded. At least they would both be out of their apparent misery soon. As Edward walked her toward her car, she abruptly turned and kissed him on the cheek.

"Thank you for a lovely dinner. I hope we can do it again soon."

He was dumbstruck. Was she on the same date he had just been on? He didn't know how to answer. He stammered in shock as he just mumbled, "Uh sure... Sounds good."

"Great. I'll be in touch to coordinate."

Edward wondered if he'd hear from her again. Since she said she'd be in touch, he didn't feel obligated to reach out. Nor did he know if he even wanted to. Two days later, he got an email with the subject, *Movie?*

Hi Edward! Thank you again for the fun dinner. You're even more handsome in person. I wanted to see if you wanted to go see the classic James Bond movie this Friday. I'm a surprisingly big Bond fan. Let me know! Thanks! Emily

Bond? She had officially become an enigma. First, he had no indication she was remotely interested, and then she says he's even cuter in person. Now, she's a Bond fan. How can someone so beautiful, intelligent with interests like Bond be so damn boring? Something must be missing. He decided to take her up on her offer. Maybe he would finally see her personality, if she had been able to find one.

Sounds good, Emily. I'll meet you at the theater at 8:00. I checked show times. There's an 8:20. Edward

At least with a movie, he wouldn't have to hold up the entire conversation. That would be Sean Connery's job. Even if she proved to be just as boring, at least he'd see an entertaining flick. He arrived right at 8:00 pm. He didn't want to arrive early and worry about the awkwardness. He still wasn't sure why he agreed to a second date, but at least he could tell Elsie he was trying! This would make for a great story.

He walked into the theater, and as before, Emily had already arrived. She was just as stunning. She somehow managed to make casual look chic. She was wearing khakis, with a white button up blouse, with the top three buttons opened and a denim jacket. She had on a E pendant necklace that hung perfectly in the open V of her blouse and at the crest of her breasts. She had her hair pulled up in a ponytail and smelled amazing. Boring or not, Edward wanted to kiss her. He settled for a hug that he purposefully let linger. She didn't seem to mind.

"I appreciate you offering to cover your dinner the other night, Em, but the movie is on me tonight. I insist."

"Ok. Sounds good."

"Would you like any snacks or something to drink?"

"No, I'm good. Thank you. I ate dinner earlier."

"Ok, then lead the way. I'll let you pick our seats since you were nice enough to invite me to the movies."

She smiled that smile that made Edward want to pull her into him, and quite frankly, was one of her few saving graces at this point. She led Edward toward the top of the theater and sat in the middle of the row. That was also his preferred spot. As they sat down, she wrapped her arm around his and began to rub his hand. At least she was giving some indication she was interested. Perhaps he had been too quick to judge. About halfway through the movie, she leaned into him, and he put his arm around her. He again noticed how good she smelled. He couldn't deny how attracted to her he was. After the movie, he walked her to her car and took her hand.

"I had a really nice time tonight. Thank you for coordinating."

"I did too, Edward. Perhaps we can agree to a third?"

He was batting .500, so he figured why not. His second at bat was much better than the first, so he'd give it a third.

"I'd like that. May I give you a call?"

"Yeah, let me give you my number."

He pulled out his phone and entered her number. He still couldn't believe this was the same woman he could barely hold a conversation with, but he wasn't going to question it. She started to back up from him, but still held his hand. When she smiled at him, he couldn't resist. He finally pulled her into him. He leaned down and gave her a soft kiss on the lips. This time, it was her turn to linger. He opened her car door for her.

"I'll call you soon, Em. Have a great night."

"Sounds great. I'll talk to you soon."

As he walked back to his car, Edward considered that perhaps the first date was just nerves, and he had been wrong. On his drive home, he couldn't stop thinking about her eyes, that smile and how she smelled. It wasn't the

70

same instant spark of compatibility he had with Kate, but rather sheer physical attraction. He figured he'd text her tomorrow and call on the second day. He didn't want to seem too eager.

Edward texted first thing the next morning.

Edward: *Hey Em, thank you again for last night. You looked great. Looking forward to seeing you again. I'll call you soon.*

Emily responded almost immediately.

Emily: *Sounds good. Thank you.*

He had hoped for a little bit more enthusiasm, but he knew her days were crazy. He chalked it up to her job and tried not to overthink it. As the day went on, he hoped she would respond further with some level of flirting. He couldn't believe he was actually anxious to talk to her again. On his drive home, he decided he wasn't going to wait until tomorrow to call her. Unfortunately, it went straight to voicemail.

"Hey Em, it's Edward. I thought I'd try to reach you tonight so we can decide on when we're both free next. Give me a call. Bye."

He expected her to return his call that evening, but he didn't hear from her. He woke up the next morning wondering if she had changed her mind. That's when he knew he really was back in the dating scene as he started to re-evaluate every text and conversation. He didn't like to consider himself a neurotic guy, but he felt uneasy about the amount of time he was thinking about this. He had to get to work, so he put his obsessing on pause.

He looked at his phone when he got out of the shower to check the time. He had a new voicemail.

"Hey, Edward. It's Emily. Sorry I didn't get back to you last night. I was at my client's until 9 pm. I will try to call you after work."

He instantly felt a mix of relief and enthusiasm to see her again. He wanted to touch her, smell her. Beyond what she had in her profile, he still didn't know much about her. He was hoping date 3 would crack that code. He considered what they should do. He really needed something where they could talk, but he didn't want to just offer up dinner again.

Maybe I should invite her here and cook dinner? Is it too soon for that? he thought. He decided to err on the side of caution and forego that idea. He didn't want to scare her, although he would love to be alone with her. He realized he hadn't had sex in months, and it would be hard to resist her. *Got it...ice skating. Even if she's terrible I can hold her hand or hold her up. Either way, I win.*

For most of the day, he had a shit-eating grin on his face waiting to talk to her after work. You'd have to be blind or oblivious not to notice. Even though things had been running pretty smoothly since Maggie had been back, his incessant smiling annoyed her, so she did her best to avoid him. Following the afternoon's status meeting, Jan couldn't resist calling him into her office.

"What's going on with you, Edward? You've been smiling non-stop all day. What gives?"

"Do you remember the accountant whose profile we looked at online awhile back? I'm hoping to talk to her tonight to coordinate our third date."

"Huh? I thought you told me she was boring after your first date. I can't keep up with you."

"Well, to be fair, she was. I'm a bit shocked myself, but we had a great second date. And she's just so damn hot."

"Ah, there it is. She could be a bumbling bimbo, but let her be hot, and guys are right there for date 3. Guys are pigs."

"Hey now. Give me some credit. It's not like that. We had a nice time watching a movie, and we agreed to a third date."

"Ok, Sir Chivalry. Keep me posted then. Any other dates in the hopper?"

"Nah. It's too much work to try to keep up with this. I'm kinda hoping this will take off."

Jan smiled and nodded. Edward took his goofy grin back to his desk and focused on plowing through the rest of his work so he could leave on time. At 6:45 pm, his phone rang. It was Emily! His heart started beating faster as a gut reaction. As to not seem too eager, he let it ring three times before answering.

"Hey, Em, how was your day?"

"Hi, Edward. It was good. I'm tired. Driving home now." (pause)

He waited to give her a chance to continue, but like their first conversation, it wasn't coming.

"Have you considered what you'd like to do for our third date? I'm pretty excited to see you again. I have an idea, but I thought I'd give you the first choice."

"Oh. Well, I hadn't thought about it honestly. I'm looking forward to it too, though."

"What would you think about going ice skating? There's an indoor rink pretty close to my house, and I feel like it would be a fun activity and give us a chance to talk more."

"Oh... Ok." (pause)

"We don't have to if you don't want to. It was just a suggestion."

"I just haven't skated in a while."

"Me either, but I think it'll be fun. What do you say?"

"Ok."

"Great! So, what else is new? How's your week going?" Edward thought to himself that he'd ask an open-ended question and give her a chance to decide what she wanted to talk about.

"It's good thank you. Just working." (pause)

Jesus, woman, give me something to work with here! He was growing more impatient with her inability to hold a conversation or apparent disinterest in learning anything about *him*.

"Sounds like you work a lot. Besides that, what do you do in your free time?"

"Unfortunately, especially during tax season, I don't have a lot of free time. Right now, we're not in tax season, but we're preparing for it. When I have a chance, I grab dinner with friends." (pause)

Still no questions in return, no picking up the conversation. At least he could tell by the sound of her voice, she was tired. So again, he gave her the benefit of the doubt.

"You sound tired. Why don't I let you go? Let's plan for Friday at 7:00. Shall I pick you up?"

"That would be nice, but let's make it 8:00. I won't have enough time to get home and ready by 7:00 after work."

"Deal. Have a good night. I'll see you then."

Edward sat and considered the date on Friday. It would be the third date, and he'd certainly like to bring her home. But what if it goes like date 1? He felt torn about his obligation to her, if any. He decided to just let it happen organically and see how it goes. He wasn't good at that. Hence why he now found himself pre-planning topics for the date just a few hours before it.

Since Emily wouldn't be ready until 8 pm, Edward had time to go home first and freshen up. He tried not to think too much about how the date might end, but he kept picturing her neck and her breasts from the other night. He got hard in the shower. He started to consider whether he should jack off as preventative measures or stay armed and ready for the main event. *Dude, you're really overthinking this now! What the hell has happened to you? Chill out. It's a date, not your wedding day. And if it doesn't go well, hey you tried.* With that, he decided just to hurry up and get ready.

He arrived at her house early. He wondered if he should

wait a few minutes or just ring the doorbell. Since she had been early to the first two dates, he didn't think it would be an issue to be early. When he rang the doorbell, Emily answered in jeans and a tank top.

"Hi, Edward. I'm running a bit behind. I got out of work late. I just need to put on my sweater and put my hair up."

He couldn't help but look down at her body. He hesitated but couldn't resist leaning down to kiss her hello. She grabbed both his arms to steady herself as they shared a deep kiss.

"No problem," he said with a laugh after finishing the kiss. She just smiled.

The car ride to the rink was pretty quiet, as Edward wanted to let her steer the conversation. She did not. When they got to the rink, Edward excitedly bounced out of the car like a kid, but he could sense she was much more apprehensive.

"Hey, come on. It's going to be fun. I promise you I won't let you fall."

"Ok."

There it was again. Edward grew tired of "yeah's" and "ok's." He was starting to realize that no matter how sexy she was, she was probably just plain dull, but he was too excited not to at least have some fun tonight.

"Size 12 please. Hey, Em, what size skates do you need?"

"9 please."

"You heard the lady. And a pair of 9's."

"Em, are you ready?"

"As ready as I'll ever be, I guess."

Edward stepped out on the ice first. He wanted to take off and just skate like he did when he was younger - as fast as he could, forgetting about everything but going even faster. Instead, he turned and smiled at Emily stretching out his hand to steady her.

"I'm nervous, Edward. I haven't skated in probably 20 years. Please don't let me fall."

"Don't worry about it. It's just for fun. The Russian judge isn't here tonight. They're always the hardest, so if you fall on your double axel, no biggie."

She looked at him quizzically. Even his jokes went over her head. He made a fast dash and got behind her and started pushing her.

"Hey, slow down. I wasn't ready."

"You'd never have been ready. Get that cute butt in gear."

He stopped pushing and took her hand. She seemed to find a bit of balance, although she was virtually just walking on the skates.

"Emily, have you skated before?"

"Yes."

"Ok then. You know how to do this. Trust me. I got you. Just stay centered over your middle and lean just a little forward. Let's go."

With that they started skating a bit faster. Edward again skated behind her this time wrapping his arms around her waist and kissing her neck. He made sure she was upright and led her over to the side wall before darting off. He skated around the rink 2-3 times just to finally get the feel of the ice he was craving.

"Having fun, Edward?" She seemed annoyed that he skated off.

"I am. I just needed to wear off some of the rust. Like this."

He pulled her fast away from the boards, and they started cruising down the side of the ice. He was happy with his choice of date activity. He expected wanting to just skate next to her to talk a bit more, but after the car ride, he decided it may be futile. Instead, he would just have fun.

"Edward, my feet are getting a bit sore," Emily said

just a little over an hour in.

"Yeah that can happen when you haven't skated in a while. Do you want to go?"

"Do you mind?"

"Not at all? Are you cold? Do you want to go for a coffee or a hot chocolate somewhere?"

"Why don't we go back to my house, and I can make us some cocoa," Emily suggested, surprising Edward. When they got back to Emily's place, she showed him into the living room.

"Make yourself at home while I make the cocoa."

Edward sat on the couch and looked around. When he picked her up, he hadn't gotten much further than the foyer. He now got a greater sense of the house - it was meticulously clean with many pictures of family and friends mixed with very homey decorations. Again, he wondered to himself how someone whose life looked so full and inviting could be so boring.

"I hope you don't mind. I added a few marshmallows too."

"What would cocoa be without marshmallows! Thanks, Em. I hope you had fun tonight."

"I don't know that I'll head right back to the ice in the near future, but it was ok."

She sat right next to him on the couch. She placed her hand on his thigh when she sat down. Edward was again surprised by her forward nature considering she wouldn't take the lead on any conversation.

"Em, I have to ask. Are you shy? Reserved? We haven't really spoken much since meeting."

"Really? I hadn't noticed. I've enjoyed our conversations."

There was the definitive proof he was looking for. This wasn't going to work out. Should he finish his cocoa and go? His body was telling him to fuck her and walk away, but he had never really been that guy, not even in college.

"I'm just a bit more pensive. I don't feel there is always something to add. When I have something to say, I will, though. I like that you can carry the conversation."

Carry the conversation? He had been giving them piggyback rides up a mountain! He considered picking one of the topics he had written down earlier in the day, but what was the point? He'd be talking to himself anyway. At this point, he was ready to check out and cut his losses. That's when she made the first move. She started gently rubbing his thigh in longer strokes as she sipped her cocoa.

Edward sat there indecisively trying to figure out what to do. He couldn't wait much longer as his erection was quickly getting harder. Finally, he thought to himself, *hey I tried. She clearly wants this.*

He took the cocoa out of her hands and laid her down on the couch. She smiled with no resistance. He was on top of her quickly kissing her neck as he moved his left hand up under her sweater.

"Let's go to my room, Eddie," she said trying to be playful.

"Edward, please. Only my gram calls me Eddie, and I can't think about her right now," he said laughing.

Emily was every bit as gorgeous naked as he expected. And for someone whose personality was so vanilla, she was anything but in bed. Or perhaps it had just been too long for him. They had sex for close to two hours when she finished her third orgasm.

"Oh man, Edward. That was great. I needed that. I was hoping the date would end this way."

"I sort of picked up on that when you were stroking my leg."

"Yeah, well it's been awhile since I've met a guy like you. One that I want to spend time with."

Edward's stomach sank. He didn't know what to say. He didn't want to mislead her, but he knew he wouldn't see her again. He questioned if he had made the right decision, but her three orgasms and his two were good consolation prizes.

"It has been awhile for me too." He stopped there without elaborating further.

"Well, I should go. It's getting late, and I need to get up in the morning to go see my grandma."

"Oh, I thought perhaps you might want to stay over."

"Thank you for the offer, but I need to get up early to go see her. I bring her coffee on a few Saturday mornings a month, but thank you."

"Ok," she said disappointingly.

Edward was relieved to know it was the last "ok" he'd have to hold up in conversation. He quickly got dressed and started toward the door.

"Edward, I really enjoyed tonight. I hope we can do it again soon."

"Yeah…" was all he said as he kissed her on the forehead before closing the door behind him. He couldn't bear to make eye contact. Despite the pit in his stomach, he laughed to himself on the way to the car at delivering as riveting a goodbye as she had given in many of her conversations.

Nine

Subject: Time to connect on Monday morning? (EOM)

The email from Steve was waiting for Edward when he got to work. Jan and Maggie were copied as well. Since the body of the email contained no information, Edward wondered what this was about. He hated Monday morning meetings, as he preferred to organize his week as he enjoyed his first cup of coffee. Steve had also put time on their calendars for 9:30 am. Edward was surprised Steve even knew how to add a meeting.

He begrudgingly headed toward the kitchen to get his coffee. It was 9 am already, and now he was going to have to shift a few things around.

"Good morning, ladies!" Edward beamed when he walked into the conference room. If the coffee hadn't yet started working, his natural penchant for the morning had. Jan and Maggie both grumbled their responses. Their faces indicated they were just as unexcited about the meeting as Edward.

"Any idea what this is about?" Jan said softly as if she didn't have enough energy to kick off the week this way.

"No, and I didn't have any dust up emails over the weekend that would render this a 'client emergency.' Did you, Edward?" Maggie added.

He shook his head no.

At 9:37 am, Steve still hadn't showed up.

"Nice of him to make it a priority to arrive on time considering there was no notice, and yet we all made it." Maggie sighed as she rolled her eyes.

Edward glanced at Jan and winked knowingly at Maggie's decreasing filter. Since Maggie had returned to work, her demeanor and patience had changed. She was still professional, but she was less polished. You could catch her rolling her eyes, mumbling under her breath, getting exasperated. These were things the old Maggie would never have done. Conversely, it also humanized her, and the team no longer kept her at arm's length.

Finally, at 9:42 am, Steve sauntered in as if he were exactly on time, with no apologies for his tardiness.

"Team. I've got news."

Maggie wondered to herself if he got another promotion because of her work, but she knew better than to say that aloud.

"We've been invited to Crandon's strategic planning session. They've decided to bring together all their agency partners to kick off planning all at once and have a full-day thinking session."

Maggie, Jan and Edward glanced back and forth at each other wondering why the urgency of another client meeting. They've made multiple trips this quarter to visit Crandon without Steve's involvement.

"The meeting is next Monday, and I'd like us to spend this week brainstorming new ideas to have in our back pockets heading into the day. I think it'll be important for us to solidify our stance as thought leaders. I want to get a jump on the week. There won't be a billable code, but I'd like us to dedicate, at a bare minimum, 2 half days this week. Maggie, could you put time on our calendars?"

Maggie bit her tongue, but her face turned crimson. He knew how to add this meeting to the calendar, to which he couldn't be bothered to arrive on time, and yet, he asked Maggie to find time as if she were his secretary. She quickly got up to leave the room.

"Oh, Maggie, I'm not quite done," Steve chimed as she headed out the door.

"I'll catch up with Jan or Edward later. I have some things I need to take care."

She had never been so brazen with Steve before. However, her tolerance for him had grown slim, and with

Brian no longer needing the medical coverage and her having received his life insurance, she didn't feel as beholden to the job.

"Ok, wow. She must have had a bad weekend," Steve said frustratingly, completely oblivious to his role in upsetting her.

"Anyway, the meeting is first thing next Monday. So, we're going to need to head out Sunday. I had already planned to be out of town with my family, so I'll be traveling in separately. Would you three coordinate your drive? I have to run to my next meeting, but I'll answer any questions when we meet later. Thanks guys. It's going to be a great session."

Jan and Edward lingered in the conference room after Steve had left.

"It's 9:50. He made a big to-do over an 8-minute meeting? He's growing more ridiculous. I wonder if he even knows what's going on with each of the business units?" Jan asked bewildered. "I mean, this could've just as easily been discussed in our weekly status meeting later today, as I'm going to need to pull in some of the team for brainstorms anyway. He's just so clueless."

"How about Maggie?" Edward asked, raising his eyebrows surprisingly as he looked at Jan. "She's got some moxie. I'll give her credit. She's no wilting flower."

"Yeah, but Edward, it's a fine line. She still needs to be careful. As valuable as she is to our team, you proved that you can manage this business without her when she was out. Steve won't tolerate the attitude forever."

"I have to wonder if she cares, Jan."

"Perhaps. But that's not the Maggie I've known. The Maggie I've known was professional to the nth degree. She would never have let her frustration show like she did today."

"Maybe she's not that Maggie anymore. Death can change you. Besides, I don't want to manage this business alone. That was hell, and a time suck. I took this job to have more time with my family - not to work all the time. I could've stayed in Chicago for that. I need her here. It'll be good to have a little road trip as a team. We can have some laughs. Grab a drink. Build some camaraderie. Maybe that'll help her feel a little better about the situation."

"Let's hope. We'll make the best of it."

"Best of it? Come on, Jan. We can have some fun with this. At least Steve won't be riding with us! Can you imagine how awkward that would've been?"

"Thank God. Even if he made up his family event to drive alone, I don't care. We're better off driving separately."

"Do you think he would purposely avoid riding with us?"

"Oh, who knows. You know how he likes to keep his distance to maintain an air of superiority and separation. It doesn't matter. We're better off with this arrangement. I need to head to my next meeting. I'll talk to you in a bit."

Edward walked back toward his desk. He saw Maggie peeking over the cube wall, virtually waiting for him to come back to his desk.

"So? Did I miss anything?"

"We all need to be there Sunday night for a Monday morning start. Steve said you could ride with him."

"Uh no..." Maggie replied with a look of incredulousness on her face.

Edward started laughing at the look on her face.

"You're an ass, Edward. What's the real plan?"

Edward appreciated that Maggie was at least willing to joke with him now, even if it was in small doses. She still didn't reveal any details of her personal life, nor did she invite him to lunches, but she now spoke to him as a colleague and not an annoyance.

"I don't know yet. Jan had another meeting, so I

assumed we would figure that out later. It's about a 2-hour drive, so we really could leave anytime Sunday. I thought it might be nice if we arrived in the early evening, so we could at least grab dinner and a drink."

Maggie's first thought was that she didn't really want to have to spend any more time with co-workers than she had to. She recognized her attitude of late had deteriorated, and her self pep talks weren't much help in improving her mood. However, she did think it would be nice to catch up with Jan in a more social setting. She still felt guilty for not returning any messages to Jan when she was out. Jan had always been an ally and a friend. The x-factor, however, was Edward. She hadn't spent any time with him outside of work besides the few minutes at Brian's funeral. They worked on different Crandon business units, so they hadn't traveled together on their client visits.

"I guess I'm ok with that if Jan is. Perhaps we leave around 4:30 on Sunday, check in to the hotel around 6:30, for a 7 pm dinner. Would that work for you?"

"That works for me. We can run it by Jan. I didn't have any plans this weekend besides taking Eltz our Saturday morning coffee."

Edward's comment piqued Maggie's interest. Was Edward dating someone? *He must be having better luck dating than I am*, she thought to herself.

"So, this Eltz. Anyone special?" Maggie asked, surprising herself that she would venture near his personal life.

"Yes. The *most* special," Edward answered softly and sincerely.

"Oh? So how long have you been dating?"

The question caught Edward off-guard. He didn't realize Maggie didn't know he was referring to his grandmother. He must not have mentioned her by name before. He decided to have a little game of cat and mouse.

"She's been in my life for a while. I adore her."

"How did you meet?"

"My mother introduced us."

"Your mother? Talk about a momma's boy."

"Indeed. I couldn't have asked for better really."

"So, then are you thinking about marriage?"

Edward couldn't toy with her anymore. "No! She's my grandmother! My mom's mom, so she did, in fact, introduce us."

"Again, Edward, you're an ass," Maggie said, this time with a hint of a smile. She had to admit that was clever.

"So then are you dating?"

The question again surprised Edward. Why was she all of a sudden interested? She had barely made any personal conversation since he started, and now Maggie was interacting as if they were friends. He decided not to question it.

"I'll be honest. I've been online dating for the last few weeks. It's been pretty dreadful. I have some stories. Perhaps, I'll tell you about it over a drink Sunday."

"Ugh, *you* have dating stories? *I* have dating stories."

Edward didn't realize Maggie had gone back to dating since Brian's death. It seemed pretty soon, but then who was he to judge? He just knew that after Kate ripped out his heart, he had no interest in dating for months. And yet after a death, here she was back dating. He didn't ask any questions, for risk of upsetting her.

"Let's connect with Jan this afternoon after status, and we can finalize our plans."

"Sounds good, Edward. And listen, I'm sorry you had to witness my lack of professionalism this morning. I don't know what came over me. I will work on that. It's not good for our team to see that from me."

"Hey, I get it. No need for apologies, but I do agree. A happy, cohesive team is better for everyone overall. Michael and Steve add enough tension and stress around here, without us adding to it."

"Very true. Well it wasn't my finest hour."

Edward just smiled and sat down at his desk to curtail the awkward conversation. He looked at his email first, and despite her reaction to Steve's request, Maggie had already created all the meeting invites and sent them out for the brainstorms. She was a hard worker and really cared about this client. That was the irony. Maggie did the work caring about her team and the clients, while Steve took the credit because he cared about the accolades. Edward wanted to say he didn't care. That he wasn't invested in this job, just as he told himself he wouldn't be when he moved back, but the truth was, it was beyond him not to care.

Edward headed to the first brainstorm that afternoon excited to take a step back and think differently about the business. He had been running so fast over the last couple months keeping up with the demand of current projects and leading the team, that he hadn't really thought about what else the Crandon businesses could, or should, be doing. He walked in, and Jan and her team had already assembled. She had brought with her 2 associate creative directors and a copywriter.

"Hey team. Thanks for assembling on short-notice. I'm glad you could come and help lend your creative juices to the brainstorm," Edward said as he smiled at everyone. He took his role as a team leader seriously and wanted the team to feel his appreciation. "I know there are a lot of projects going on right now, so to ask you to give your time to help with this is a big ask. And we thank you."

"Hey everyone. Glad you got my invites, and you could make it!" Maggie said as she walked in shortly behind Edward. "Steve didn't give us much notice, so I apologize for filling up your calendar without any warning. Let Edward and me know if there are any projects that may need to be pushed because of this. We can negotiate what can be delayed."

Jan smiled at them both and nodded her head in approval. They both handled this firestorm with grace, considering Jan had received quite a bit of pushback from her team about being locked in a room and not working for a good chunk of the week on a moment's notice. For them to acknowledge the situation and show appreciation and flexibility was the best they could've led with.

The meeting was supposed to start at 1 pm following lunch - not ideal for brainstorms as people fought their impending food comas. But considering schedules and timing, Maggie didn't have many options. Everyone had arrived by 1:05 pm, except Steve.

"Should we get started team?" Jan asked at 1:10 pm for the sake of time and productivity. "I know we all have a lot of other things we need to be doing."

Maggie couldn't believe Steve was late again, when he said he'd prioritize this. She looked out the window to see Steve arriving back from lunch with another of his office crony-buds. She was infuriated. Again, her face turned crimson instantly. Edward noticed the look on her face and then looked down to the parking lot. He knew immediately why she was upset. She didn't say anything as she turned back toward the whiteboard where Jan was standing to lead the session.

"Team, when thinking about the Crandon business, what do you think the biggest challenges they face are?" Jan asked to start the conversation.

One of the associate creative directors answered first, and as Jan was jotting notes, Steve walked in at quarter after.

"Hey team. Glad you got started. I'm ready to jump in," Steve said as he quickly took his seat, after which he took out his phone to check his emails.

Again, this irritated Maggie. He couldn't be bothered to show up on time, and he couldn't be bothered to give his full attention.

"Steve, based on your discussions in learning about next Monday's sessions, what are your thoughts on Jan's question?" Maggie asked him point blank with a raised eyebrow as she looked him square in the eye.

Steve knew she was putting him on the spot, which he didn't appreciate. The room knew it too. There was an awkward tension in the room.

"Jan, where did we start?" Steve asked knowing he couldn't avoid the question.

"Sure, Steve. I thought we could start by talking biggest challenges Crandon faces to help develop buckets we want to think against."

Steve gave his thoughts on the state of the business, and Edward had to admit that it was a well-thought out answer. He may not like the guy or how he leads the team, but he was smart. Because Maggie put Steve on the spot, Steve stayed engaged for the rest of the meeting. It was a surprisingly productive session, and Edward had to give Steve credit that dedicating forced thinking time was needed.

"Ok team, thanks for your time. Those 2 hours went pretty quickly, and I'm happy with where we have started," Jan stated before summarizing the opportunities she wanted the team to think against in the next session.

"Hey Maggie, could I talk to you for a minute?" Steve asked as everyone was collecting their notes.

Maggie stayed behind as everyone shuffled out of the conference room.

"Hey listen, you've not been yourself lately. You've been short with me. And today, I didn't appreciate being put on the spot after having just joined the meeting. I know you've been going through a lot personally, but I still expect a level of respect."

Maggie exhaled as to not scream. She paused before answering to compose her thoughts. Respect? She wanted to tell him that you need to earn respect. She exhaled again.

"Steve, I have gone through a lot. Indeed. More than anyone should ever have to. And for almost a year, I was caring for Brian while working tirelessly here to grow this business. I've waited for a promotion you had said was coming never arrive. And today, for you to be late to both meetings that *you* had asked for without credence to our time and all the work this team is trying to deliver, was unacceptable to me. So, I'm sorry if you feel disrespected. I will look to better provide this feedback to you in a more constructive manner going forward."

Maggie smiled and went back to her desk without waiting for him to respond. She knew she had crossed a line she had never crossed with Steve before, so she didn't know what to expect going forward. However, she also felt empowered. She no longer just bottled up her frustrations. She would leave today no longer feeling like the office door mat.

Edward heard Maggie sit back at her desk, but he wasn't sure he wanted to broach the subject just yet. Perhaps they could delve into how that conversation went on their trip, but considering she had just recently started to warm to him, he thought better to just leave it alone for now.

The week proceeded in a similar fashion. The sessions were productive, and the team was feeling confident about the ideas they would have in their back pockets heading into Monday. However, Steve and Maggie barely spoke, or even looked at each other. Jan and Edward did their best to try to minimize the tension. Maggie must have had some impact, though, as Steve arrived on time for every session after that first one.

By Friday afternoon, the team was spent. Most people had worked until 8 pm or later all week. One of the benefits of working at an agency was the relaxed atmosphere, so Edward had planned ahead. He went out at lunch and bought 2 bottles of wine and a 12-pack of beer. At 4 pm, he sent an email with the subject, "Team toast in Jan's office in 5 minutes."

"Edward, you're something else," Jan smirked as he carried the libations into her office.

"Thank you for continuing to treat my team so well. They've mentioned how much it has helped having your energy on the team."

"*Our team*, Jan!"

"Fair enough…" She just smiled with a sincere sense of gratitude that he had joined this craziness.

While the team enjoyed the impromptu happy hour, it was short-lived. Everyone wanted to wrap up any deliverables that needed to be released and leave for the weekend. Edward asked Maggie to stay in Jan's office after everyone else had gone back to their desks. He got up and shut the door.

"I saved the best for last!" He pulled out a bottle of champagne from the box he carried in. "I figured we could have our own toast for co-leading this team as awesomely as we do."

Maggie was touched that he included her. She didn't know why - she certainly was a co-leader, but considering the tension she had added lately and the fact that Edward and Jan had done much of the heavy lifting over the last several months while she was out, he could've just toasted with Jan. She wouldn't have blamed him.

"If we're toasting to co-leaders, shouldn't we have Steve join us?" Jan asked sarcastically.

They all started laughing. For the first time since Edward had started, it felt like they were all on the same page, playing for the same team. He smiled at Maggie, but she looked away, still embarrassed by her behavior this week. He didn't understand her response. All he could do was shrug.

"Ok guys, what's the game plan for Sunday?" Jan asked.

"We were thinking about leaving around 4:30, checking in around 6:30 and grabbing dinner at 7:00. Does that work for you?"

"That works for me, Edward. That ok with you, Maggie?"

"Yep. We discussed it this morning. I think that's a solid plan too."

Jan was a bit surprised that Maggie was agreeing to not only carpool, but dinner together as well. Despite the tension and stress of the week, she was happy to see Maggie and Edward start to work better together. She wondered how long this would last. Jan had worked with Steve long enough to know he didn't take kindly to having his authority questioned. She was worried for Maggie, regardless of how long she had been at the agency.

"Well then I'll see you back here at 4:30 Sunday."

— —

It felt like they were all back there in a blink of an eye. The weekend had flown by for each, as they tried to get caught up on life after working long hours during the week.

"Edward, how was your coffee with Elsa yesterday?" Maggie asked as they got into Jan's SUV to start the trek.

Edward started to laugh. "Eltz. As in Elsie. She's not going to freeze any Nordic kingdoms any time soon! And she doesn't want to build a snowman. But thank you for remembering and asking. I appreciate it. She's doing ok, you know, all things considered. She wants to go home, but she can't. She has her good days and her bad days. She was pretty tired yesterday, so our conversation was limited. Some weeks I'll go, and our conversations are so enriching I want to freeze time. And others, it feels like the same conversation over and over. I guess it's to be expected considering her age and the trauma she's been through, but it really isn't easy for us. I talk to my mom, and she sees her 3-4 times per week. She sees more of the bad days. I know it's hard on her too."

"I get it. Brian had a similar pattern. I'd get to the hospital some nights, and he was wide awake as if the cancer weren't real. On other days, the treatments would leave him so tired he could barely speak. It got to the point where I dreaded walking in to see which Brian I'd be visiting. Seeing him just lie there without much interaction felt like I had lost a day with him each time."

Edward and Jan were a bit taken aback to hear Maggie talk so openly about Brian. In fact, she had never talked to either in this level of detail before. They didn't know how to respond, so they sat silent.

"Guys, come on. It's been long enough. I appreciate you not prying until now, but you don't have to walk on eggshells if I bring Brian up. It was hard, but I also have realized I don't want to avoid talking about him as if it didn't happen. That's not fair to his memory."

"No, it's cool, Maggie. Thank you for being real with us. I didn't know Brian, like Jan did. It's nice to get to know that part of your life," Edward responded.

"Well, believe me, it wasn't perfect. I don't want to give you the impression that we lived a fairy tale, but he changed me. He will always be important in my life. I just need to figure out what to do with the rest of my life."

"Don't we all," Edward agreed.

"Oh yes, you told me you were going to tell me about your latest dating adventures. No time like the present."

"He did?" Jan beamed. "I'm ready!"

"Wait, wait, wait. I said I *might* tell you about the latest dates over a few drinks at dinner. So maybe if you behave yourselves you'll get to hear about the latest batch of also-rans."

"Ugh, I have to wait until dinner?" Jan asked. "But we

have 2 hours in the car. It'll give us something to talk about."

"Believe me, it'll be funnier over wine. There isn't much to hear anyway. Besides, this way I know you won't stand me up for dinner."

"Edward, if I've said it once, I've said it a dozen times. You're an ass," Maggie said wryly.

"Thank you," he responded cheekily. "What should we listen to?"

The ladies noticed the abrupt change in subject, and neither pushed it.

"I have satellite radio, we can connect Pandora, or we can listen to someone's iTunes. It's up to you, Edward. Since you're riding shotgun, you can be DJ," Jan said.

"Cool, let's try Pandora. I like the surprise of not knowing what's going to play next on a road trip. Hmm what would be a good station for a road trip? How about Tina Turner?"

"Tina Turner?" Maggie said unbelievably. "What are we? 70?"

"Hey now. Let me prove you wrong. It's a great Pandora station. You get everything from the 60s and 70s to the 80s and 90s because her career was so long."

"Fine, but you've got 30 miles or 8 songs to prove me wrong, whichever comes first. Then we're ditching our Ensure to get something a bit more modern."

"Fair enough. Here we go."

As Edward hit play, the opening bars of Tina Turner's Proud Mary started to play. All he heard from the back seat was, "damn it!" The rest of the drive was uneventful with a lot of bad car singing and bickering between Edward and Maggie. Jan refused to play referee, but she was happy to see them engaging so freely without the tension of the previous week. They arrived at the hotel at 6:20 pm, slightly ahead of schedule. Maggie was starving having skipped lunch.

"Hey since we arrived early, would you mind if we grabbed dinner at 6:45 instead of 7:00? I'm really hungry!"

"I'd love that!" Edward responded. "I'm really hungry too. Plus, I wouldn't mind getting to sleep early tonight. It's going to be a long couple of days."

"Sure. I'll see you both at 6:45 then," Jan agreed as she walked toward reception.

Edward wasn't in his room 3 minutes when his phone rang.

"Hey, Mom, how are you? I was going to text you that we made it safely. Tell me you're not checking up on me already!"

"Hi, Edward. No, no. Nothing like that. Actually, I was going to leave you a message. I didn't think I'd get you. I won't keep you. I just wanted to let you know that I visited Grandma today, and it wasn't a very good day for her. I just wanted to say that if you haven't visited her lately, perhaps you should go soon."

"Mom, I just saw her yesterday. It wasn't a great visit, but nothing out of the ordinary. Is there anything in particular wrong today? Should I be concerned?"

"Oh, I'm so glad to hear that. I didn't realize you visited yesterday. Edward, she's getting tired. Nothing new necessarily. I just didn't know when you went to see her last. She couldn't remember."

"Really? I was just there yesterday. Literally 1 day ago. She couldn't remember?"

There was a silence on the other end of the phone.

"Mom?"

"I'm here."

Edward could hear her sniffling. He knew she was trying not to cry.

"Mom, you know she has good days and bad days. I've been making a concerted effort to go almost weekly now. We have our Saturday morning coffee. This week's visit wasn't great, admittedly. She was pretty tired. So that would explain why she couldn't remember me being there. Perhaps you should take her to the doctor. Make sure there's not something else going on."

"Yes. Agreed. I made an appointment for her this week. Hopefully if there's something going on, they can help address it. If not, well, we know she isn't going to be with us forever. We just have to be grateful for the time we have."

"I know, but that's not easy for me to comprehend. I can't imagine my life without her."

"Me either, Edward. Me either."

"Ok, enough of this somber talk, Mom. Thanks for letting me know. Keep me posted if you find anything out this week. I need to go meet my co-workers for dinner soon."

"Love you."

"Love you, too. Bye."

Edward sat on the edge of the bed and looked out the hotel window. Being in the hotel reminded him of the trips they would take growing up with Eltz joining the family as the built-in babysitter. She didn't mind. She loved time with her boys. Tears welled up in his eyes. The thought of losing Elsie always instantly brought tears to his eyes.

Edward stood up and let out a deep breath trying to shift his focus. He looked at his watch. He had five minutes before he needed to be back downstairs. He couldn't meet them with red, puffy eyes. He went into the bathroom and hurriedly splashed cold water on his face. He knew he was short on time. "Ok, I think I'm ready."

By the time Edward made it to the lobby, Jan and Maggie were already waiting.

"Geez, who's the girl? What took you so long, princess?" Maggie asked sarcastically.

"Sorry guys. My mom called. Let's go grab some food. I'm starving," Edward responded without much emotion.

They opted for the hotel restaurant, as it was the easiest, and no one would need to drive home if they chose to have a few drinks. They were seated quickly.

"Hello, welcome to our steakhouse. What can I bring you?"

Jan excitedly answered first. "I'd like one of these Coco Loco's with an extra piece of pineapple please," she said to the waitress.

"I don't get out much, guys. I'm getting a specialty drink!"

"Oh, Jan. I've missed traveling with you! It's been too long," Maggie said as she smiled at her before asking for a glass of Pinot Grigio.

"And I'll have a Malbec please," Edward said somberly.

"Edward, what's your deal? It's like someone let the air out of you. You're deflated!" Jan said with a furrowed brow.

"I'm sorry. My mom called to tell me that my grandma wasn't doing well. Well, not even that. That she... I don't know. Nothing new happened. It's just..."

Maggie touched Edward's arm. "It's ok. If there's one thing I know for sure, the slow process of death is never easy. You have to focus on her living, not her dying."

Edward smiled slightly. "You're right, Maggie. Besides, I've been looking forward to this dinner. I don't want to be a downer. Let's celebrate."

They raised their glasses and toasted.

"Maggie, I've been wanting to ask you all week, but I never knew how to bring it up. Forgive me if you don't want to talk about it, but what happened this week when Steve asked you to stay behind after the brainstorm?" Edward asked with Jan leaning in and nodding approvingly at the question.

"Oh, I don't mind. You could've asked me that day. I have to tell you. I've replayed that moment over and over in my head. He said that I had been short with him and that he didn't appreciate being put on the spot in the meeting. He said he understood I had been going through a lot, but he still expected a level of respect. I can quote almost verbatim what I said to him.

"Steve, I have gone through a lot. Indeed. More than anyone should ever have to. And for almost a year, I was caring for Brian while working tirelessly here to grow this business. I've waited for a promotion you had said was coming never arrive. And today, for you to be late to both meetings that you had asked for without credence to our time and all the work this team is trying to deliver, was unacceptable to me. So, I'm sorry if you feel disrespected. I will look to better provide this feedback to you in a more constructive manner going forward."
I walked out before he had a chance to respond."

"Maggie! Are you serious? Are you trying to be public enemy number one for him?" Jan asked concernedly. "You know he does not take kindly to having his authority questioned."

"Jan, I hear you, and I know you're right. But I can't go on acting like nothing is wrong. He *is* going to hear me. He showed up to every meeting after that on time, didn't he? I can't be concerned about losing my job anymore. I lived in that prison while Brian was dying. If he fires me, so be it. Maybe that'll be the catalyst I finally need to go do something else."

By the time Maggie was done talking, they all were on to their second drinks. Edward could tell Maggie was fired up, so he decided to lighten the mood.

"Ok. Ok. Enough work talk. We'll have enough of that over the next few days. So as promised, I will tell you about my latest misadventures in dating."

"Alright! The main event!" Maggie said very loudly. She was already buzzed.

As Edward began, the waitress brought Maggie her third glass of wine. She was about to be one drink ahead of Jan and Edward. Edward looked at Jan as if to ask if they should cut her off, but Jan just shrugged. They both knew she needed to unwind.

"Well first of all, let me begin by saying online dating is terrible. It's like having another job. You have to log in daily. If you're not responding to previous conversations, you're looking at new matches. It's exhausting. And heaven forbid you should not log on in any given day - people will think you're not interested if it has taken you more than one day to respond. I've only been doing it for a couple of months, and I'm already over it."

"Anyway, let me tell you about the latest. Emily. Our first date was so terrible, I felt like I was talking to myself. Every question I asked, she answered with just a few words. *'Yeah.' 'Ok.'* It was the most awkward conversation I ever had. At the end of dinner, when she offered to pay for herself, I figured we both thought it awful. Instead, she says she had a great time. Great time? She barely spoke to me!"

Maggie looked confused. "That's it. You had an awkward first date."

"Hold your horses! It turns out she's a James Bond fan of all things, and we go see a classic Bond film that was showing."

Maggie looked even more perplexed. "Hold on. You had a terrible first date, and you agree to go out again? Why?"

"Because she's hot."

Jan and Maggie both groaned loudly at his honest answer.

"Hey now. At least I'm honest. I figured that since she was attractive and educated, I'd give her the benefit of the doubt and try again. Is that better? You wouldn't want me to be so callous as to rule out a lovely young woman that wanted the pleasure of my company again," Edward said devilishly.

"Oh no, we wouldn't want that. Heaven forbid you should deprive poor Emily of the opportunity to spend more time with you," Maggie said as she slurped down the last of her third glass motioning the waitress for number 4.

"Good. I'm glad you agree. Anyway, she was so attentive and flirty during the movie. I thought perhaps I had judged too quickly. I decided to ask her out again. Date three proved that I had been right, unfortunately. It was another date where I talked so much I thought I was filibustering. I knew that would be it for me."

Jan hadn't said much, but she was enjoying the dynamics. When Edward stopped, it was as if someone had turned off a show she was binge-watching on Netflix.

"Wait, that's it? How did you end it?"

"So...," he paused.

"Oh no, spill it, Mr.," Jan insisted.

"Ok, well she invited me back to her place."

"You didn't?" Jan asked as her eyes grew bigger.

"I had no intentions to! I was going to see her home. Maybe make out a little. That was it. But it turns out this boring little accountant was a nymph! I wasn't there but 30 minutes, and she was already rubbing her hands on my leg up toward my crotch. Hey listen, I put up a good fight, but that girl wanted sex!"

"You're a pig, Edward," Maggie said as her buzz grew stronger. "Was she good?"

"Did you really just ask me that?"

"What? You've gotten this far. Spill it."

"Well, again, for a boring little accountant, she was amazing. However, not amazing enough to go out again. I could only take so much. I knew we weren't a good fit."

"So then how did you end it?" Jan asked.

"I'm not proud of this. Ok, maybe I am a little, if for no other reason than its poetic irony. As I was leaving, she asked if I wanted to go out again. I just answered, 'Yeah' and haven't spoken to her since."

Jan and Maggie started laughing, which made Edward laugh. The alcohol was clearly working. Edward looked at his watch, and it was already 9 o'clock. He didn't realize it had gotten so late.

"Should we get the bill?" Edward asked.

"Hold up. You promised a dating story, and what you gave us was some boring chick that you banged. She was educated and beautiful, but boring. Call the Enquirer. We have a hot lead... not," Maggie said sarcastically, feeling no inhibitions after 4 glasses of wine. "I'll tell you a dating story."

"So, my friend, Renee. Edward, you met her at the funeral home. She decides that I need to get back into the dating scene. She has a co-worker that has a friend. Had she met him? Nope. I should've known that was a red flag, but she's so damn persistent."

"Was I ready to date again? Probably not. But I had been in purgatory for over a year, so I took a chance. He shows up in a skin-tight t-shirt and khaki shorts. His arms are amazing, and you guessed it, he has a tattoo going around his arm at the bicep. He's nothing short of a 'bro.' I wouldn't exactly say my type, but attractive nonetheless."

"In shorts and a t-shirt, I figured we weren't going to a high-end restaurant. Nailed it. We went to his favorite restaurant, Applebee's. Now I'm not hating. I crashed a few Chili's for some rum and diets after Brian's death. But let's be honest - he wasn't exactly trying hard here to make the best first impression."

"They knew 'Nick' by name when we walked in. I wondered if he brought all his dates here. Was I a showpiece in a long list of ladies he was proving he could bag? The thought crossed my mind. What was I doing? Better yet, what had Renee gotten me into? I owed her for this one. When we sat down, the cute, young 20-something waitress brought Nick a Miller Lite on draft, his usual. She was flirting heavily, and he wasn't minding. If he thought this added attention was making him sexier, he should've considered his audience better. I ordered a double rum and diet. I figured if I was going to make it through this, I better go strong."

"The conversation started normally enough. What do you do? Hobbies? Places you've traveled? Yada yada yada. However, this is where it got weird. The travel question led him to tell me everywhere he's traveled in the world when he was in the military, which certainly explains his physique. He was ripped. *God damn!* He then proceeds to tell me in the military is where he developed his love of masturbation that continues to this day. I kid you not. I almost spit out my drink. It was like one of those cartoon moments where my eyes bugged out, I swear. I didn't know how to respond. He told me how he needs to relieve himself 2-3 times per day. The whole time I'm thinking *is this supposed to be an aphrodisiac? Or am I on Candid Camera?*"

Maggie stops what had become her monologue to take a drink of her wine. Jan and Edward are too busy laughing at this point to interject. Maggie can only shake her head at the absurdity of her story before she begins again.

"At this point, I'm already thinking we're probably not a fit, but I have to make the best of it. We had already ordered dinner, and I was hungry! So, I tried to change the subject.

"You were in the military? What branch?"

"The army. I got out 4 years ago. Now I'm left with only *one* branch. Do you think you could keep up with my needs?"

"I couldn't hold back any longer. I started to laugh. He had a confused look on his face as if this discussion typically worked with most women he had dated. He then continued the absurdity."

"Come on, baby. Don't be like that. You don't have to play shy."

"He called me 'baby.' I probably would've left at this point, but I wanted my hamburger damn it. If I was going to go to Applebee's, I was going to at least eat something greasy and delicious. As much as I tried to change the subject, Nick kept trying to bring it back to sex and masturbation. He must've mentioned he needed it 2-3 times per day at least 4 times!"

"Hey, at least he's consistent!" Edward chortled.

"Yeah, Edward, if you thought you were dealing with a sex-fiend in Emily, I'm not so sure she had anything on Nick."

"Hey!" Edward said excitedly. "We should fix them up!"

"What?"

"Yeah, from the sounds of it, Nick never stops talking. And Emily wouldn't say, 'shit,' if she had a mouth full of it. And they're both big sex hounds. Let's introduce them!"

"Edward, I don't make a habit of talking to past dates, especially bad ones. What would I say? 'Sorry you were too crass for me, but I have a much better piece of ass for you?'"

"Come on. Not exactly. We had a couple of bad dates. So did they! If we know there are 2 people out there that are potentially a good fit, why shouldn't we try to introduce them?"

"Um, at the risk of looking crazy, Edward. That's why."

"You're overthinking this. Maybe they're not interested. Maybe they don't take us up on our offer. Big deal. But we have a chance to help two people find each other."

Jan had been quietly sipping her drink for the last 20

minutes, but she was quickly running out of steam. She looked at her watch, and it was now well past 10 pm. It was time to call it a night.

"Hey, Chuck Wooleries. Why don't you save your game of Love Misconnection for tomorrow? It's past 10, and we all need to be bright eyed and present by 8:30 am tomorrow morning. I'm going to get you both some water to go. You should probably both drink a few more when you're back in your rooms. It's been fun, but it's time to call it a night."

− −

As Edward packed up his laptop bag after a grueling few days, he was amped for how well the sessions went. He had to give Steve credit - having thoughtful and forward-thinking ideas about where the businesses could go was a brilliant idea. It became clear as the days unfolded which agency partner had come prepared. Despite how well the sessions went, Edward was spent. He was ready to be home for the weekend. He worried Steve would ask him to ride back with him, which he didn't really want.

"Hey, Jan, have you seen Steve? Did he say what his plans were?"

Jan laughed. "Oh Edward, sometimes I forget you're still new. Steve's gone. He left immediately following the last session."

"Well I guess I don't have to worry about him asking me to ride back with him then! Have you seen Maggie? Are you both ready to go? I'm so tired."

"She went to use the restroom before we leave. She said she'd meet us at the car. We're both beyond ready as well. I'm drained."

The first 45 minutes or so in the car were pretty quiet on the drive home. There didn't seem to be much energy to socialize. Finally, Jan broke the sequence of occasional one-off comments. While she was equally as exhausted, she didn't want to miss the chance to debrief while it was still fresh in their minds.

"So, what did you guys think?" she asked.

"About?" Edward responded instinctively without much thought.

"About the last few days. What else! I just figured it would be helpful to discuss while it was still top of mind."

Maggie started. "Well, I think it became clear pretty early on that we were the most prepared, at least to our clients. Sheila even pulled me aside after lunch on the first day to say how thankful she was we were there."

"No way! Sheila actually said that? I didn't think she knew how to say anything nice," Jan said surprised.

"Which one was Sheila?" Edward asked.

"She was the tall, polished woman. Black woman with graying hair. Pretty purple blazer. She's the Marketing VP of all of Crandon's brands. She was in and out throughout the last few days," Jan responded.

"Her? She said something nice to you, Maggie? Wow, now that's impressive! Actually, I was going to say, Maggie, that you really rocked it the last few days. Not only do the clients respond well to you, but so do all the other agencies. You were like Miss Congeniality," Edward said sincerely.

"During each of the activities, you knew when to jump in. I picked up a few things from you about this client. So, thanks."

"Edward, thank you. That's really very nice of you. I guess having been on this client for so long, I take for granted that I just know almost everyone. We've all been in the trenches together for most of the last 7 years. Heck, even Sheila tolerates me. At least seemingly more so than some of the other agency leads. Funny thing is - Sheila let it slip to me once that she is not a big Steve fan. Called him inauthentic."

"Maggie, Sheila does more than tolerates you. You're the Sheila whisperer. You're the only one she likes. I think she sees a bit of herself in you. She is a workhorse too," Jan said.

"Hey, whatever the reason, I've always been thankful. She's never ripped me to shreds, and I've been present at a few of her tirades. I've even seen she and Michael go toe to toe. That. Was. Epic."

"No...really? What happened?" Edward asked, curiously wondering what happens when the Joker battles the Riddler.

"Well, first let me say, Michael didn't know I could hear. I think he'd be embarrassed if he knew I saw him handled like that. We were at a planning meeting similar to this early on, and since the account was relatively new, Michael decided to join us, despite the fact that he hates sessions like these. He has no attention span for it. I had left the room to use the bathroom, and when I came back, I could hear Michael and Sheila. The tone said I should probably wait outside. Michael made the mistake of raising his voice first. He quickly adjusted after he realized this wasn't a lowly coordinator, but it was too late. I'm surprised we didn't lose the business right then and there."

"What did she say?" Jan asked surprised she had never heard this story before.

"To paraphrase, she basically said this was his one and only warning that if he ever spoke to anyone on her staff in that manner again, not only would their business relationship cease, but that she would be happy to discuss with anyone whom asked why the relationship ended. Michael apologized again, but Sheila said that it was probably better if he didn't make further trips. That's when Michael appointed Steve to run the account. Sadly, I was already on the business and leading the day-to-day activities, but Michael wanted someone more 'senior.' I still think it's because Steve was a man. Steve's been promoted twice since, and I've done the work without a promotion."

There was an awkward silence in the car. Jan and Edward knew Maggie had been screwed over, and they didn't need to ask why she tolerated it for so long. With Brian dying, she couldn't be without work, and it was just easier to continue on.

"What do you think Sheila thought about me?" Edward asked out of curiosity.

"She didn't say. I will say, though, if she thinks you're one of Steve and Michael's cronies, you have a bit of a hill to climb."

"Maggie, why do you think then she doesn't just fire us, if she doesn't like Michael and Steve?" Edward asked.

"Probably because of the amount of work we handle. We process so many projects at a relatively lower rate than the other agencies based out of New York or Chicago. I'm sure part of it is the economics. We do good work, and we do it at a fairly competitive rate," Maggie answered.

"And because Sheila adores Maggie. Maggie, that's nice of you to be so humble, but let's be honest, if not for you, I'm fairly sure we would've already lost this business. I'm actually surprised Sheila hasn't pushed to have you promoted," Jan said.

"Well, thanks, Jan. That's nice of you, but you kept moving while I was out. Business is business."

"Speaking of business, we're almost home! We shouldn't think about it again until Monday. We've earned this weekend off," Edward said as they exited the freeway on the final leg home.

Ten

Edward relished the opportunity to have a weekend with no plans. Since he had been out all week, he hadn't coordinated any dates. He was frustrated with online dating anyway. He considered deleting his account for a while. The challenge was how would he meet anyone otherwise. He was too old to cruise the local bar scene and too young to want to hit the cougar hotspots around town.

In a moment of boredom, he logged back into the dating site. He saw Emily was logged in as well. His face got flush from embarrassment. He chided himself at the ridiculousness of it.

"She can't actually see you! If she reaches out, deal with it then, crazy man," he said to himself.

Edward still felt bad for how he treated her. While he knew that was the world of dating, and that men often would have sex and not call, it wasn't his style. He then thought back to Maggie's date, Nick. It really did sound like they could be a potentially good match. He made a mental note to bring it back up to Maggie Monday over coffee. Really, what could it hurt?

Edward logged off quickly before anyone poked, prodded, or smiled at him. He didn't have the energy to deal with it. He decided since he had no other plans, he'd go see Elsie today.

Like always, Edward walked in with 2 hot coffees in hand. Elsie's face responded with a wide, sly smile.

"Well, Eddie. Nice of you to make time for me."

"Eltz. You know I don't just make time for you. How've you been?"

"I'm ok I guess. It could be worse I suppose. I listen to some of these women struggle to even remember their names. It would be hell to lose your mind. So, all in all,

I'm lucky to have my faculties. I have my stories and the Game Show Network, so at least I have entertainment."

Edward laughed. 'Her stories.' She had been watching Days of our Lives for as long as he could remember. He could tell he had caught her on a good day. Her sense of humor and awareness were both sharp.

"Eddie, how are you?"

"Eltz, I'm hanging in there. It was a long week at work. We were visiting a client for the entire week."

"How am I ever going to be able to go to your wedding if you're always working? You're never going to meet anyone. You told me you weren't going to focus so much on work anymore."

"Gram, I've tried. It's not so easy. Dating isn't much fun."

"Oh, hogwash. It's all about perspective. You don't have to marry everyone you date. You go out and have fun. Meet new people. For every pot, there's a lid. For every Jack, there's a Jill. You just have to keep putting yourself out there."

"I know, and I will. I promise. I keep hoping that it'll happen organically, and I'll just meet her somewhere along the way. I hate online dating."

"Online dating? What's that?"

"Oh. I suppose you wouldn't know. It's where you create an online profile and try to connect with people whose profile you like. You can add a picture and information."

"Well, hell, Eddie! No wonder you're struggling. It's dating. It's about human interaction. It's not about catalog shopping. It's not Sears Roebuck!"

Edward laughed. "Eltz, Sears is almost dead."

"Eddie, so am I!" she answered emphatically before laughing. "I'll use what I know, and don't change the subject. You need to meet friends of friends, or volunteer, or heaven forbid, go to church once in a while."

"I love you, Gram. I know you're right. As always."

"Eddie, I just want to see you happy. You deserve someone nice. Don't just go for the pretty ones either. Pick someone that will take care of you and vice versa. Pick someone that, when you're old, you want to have a conversation over breakfast. As you age, that's way more important. I still long to have coffee and toast with your grandpa. I miss him so much, but I'll see him soon enough."

"I miss him too, but not too soon! I won't be ready for you to see him for at least another 15 years."

Elsie wrinkled her nose at his comment, as if to say he was crazy.

"Eddie, I'll go when the good Lord calls me home. When it's our time, it's our time. Not for me to decide. But good heavens, 15 years? What are you trying to do to me?"

Edward took her hand. "I know, Eltz. I just won't ever be ready to let go."

"We've gotten off course. Tell me more about this catalog dating. Do you filter by big knockers and small waist? Is that how this crazy crap works?"

"Boy, I've caught you on a good day. You're full of piss and vinegar."

"Hey, I know how most men operate. Remember, I was young once too."

"Well women can filter too, you know."

Elsie howled with laughter. "I don't even want to know how they filter. Is there a built-in ruler they use?"

Edward's jaw hung open. "Elsie Wagner!"

"Edward, take my advice. Get off the computer, and get out in the real world."

"How about I do a mix of both? I've got to spread a wide blanket to find the one so you can attend my wedding. If I don't have 15 years, I better hurry."

Elsie smiled at the thought of seeing her Eddie get

married. "Nothing would make me happier young man. Nothing."

"Well, if it'll make you happy, I need to prioritize it. I guess that means I have to keep trudging through."

"Young man, I can barely walk. My trudging days have long since passed. What I wouldn't give to be able to go dancing or for a malt with a handsome young man. It's all about perspective."

"You're not going to let me have this one, are you?" Edward replied sheepishly.

"Eddie, I didn't allow you to win at cards when you were younger, and I'm not going to allow you to win now!"

"I wouldn't have it any other way."

Edward took a long sip of his coffee, relishing this time with Elsie. He sat quiet for a moment collecting his thoughts. He looked at Elsie, who had started to nod off again. He glanced at his watch. He had already been there over an hour. Some days an hour can feel like an eternity. Today, it seemed to race by. He felt blessed to have today's visit - it was like rewinding the clock 10 years. He knew these visits would be fewer and farther between, which is why he was sad to have to go. However, she needed to rest. He stood quietly, turned off her table lamp, and pulled up her afghan to cover her hands. He leaned over to kiss her forward.

"15 years isn't that long…"

Edward's drive home was filled with mixed emotions. He drove in silence as a few tears streamed down his face. He talked with *his* grandma again today. Some days he saw her body, but she wasn't the same spit-fire he knew. But today, he saw the spirit of his grandma again, vibrant and alive. This strong, proud woman had the desire to still live life to the fullest, but her body was tired. Edward knew he couldn't freeze time. The realization felt like a punch to his stomach.

Yet he felt better about dating after their talk. It was about having fun and going out. So what if Emily wasn't the one. She clearly wanted to have sex. He didn't pressure her. And Jessica made for an entertaining story - wanting nothing more than her M. R. S. degree. He really didn't have to marry everyone he dated. He just needed to have fun.

When he got home, Edward logged back in to see if he could set up a date for this week. He decided to narrow his filter to a 5-year age range, hoping fewer selections would make it less daunting to manage. He found an interesting profile of a woman two years older than him, Sami. She was educated, a teacher, and liked sports. She was moderately attractive, but certainly didn't jump off the page. She only had one picture, so he had nothing else to go on. They had talked one time before a few weeks ago before he met Emily, so he hadn't continued the conversation. He sent her a note asking if she'd like to get coffee this week.

He wondered if Maggie would continue dating. She had tried it because of Renee, but was she really ready? He figured she'd be happy to hear about his misadventures. He was hoping by Monday he could tell her he had a date this week. He wasn't quite sure they were friends, but they had found at least a level of mutual respect. They had come to understand each other - both losers in love, back in the dating game, and trying to make their jobs manageable.

By the time Monday morning rolled around, Edward did indeed land a date - Tuesday after work. Edward waited to get coffee until Maggie arrived.

"Hey, Maggie, how was your weekend?"

"Well, good morning to you too. It was glorious. Admittedly, I slept and watched Netflix most of it, but it felt good not to have anywhere to go or anyone to take care of."

"Do you want to go get coffee?" Edward asked.

"Yes! I have a feeling it's going to be a three-cup day. What did you do this weekend?"

"Well, I went to see my grandma. We had a great visit. We talked dating interestingly enough. She had a good perspective that I just need to have fun with it. Despite all the crazies out there, that's what I'm going to do. Just continue to put myself out there and try to have fun. In fact, I have a date Tuesday."

"What? You do? Ok, we need to grab our coffee and discuss."

They grabbed their coffee and headed back to Edward's desk to chat. Edward's work area, while still a cubicle, was large enough to fit a small table. Unfortunately, they had to almost whisper because there wasn't any privacy.

"So, Edward, tell me about your date?"

"Not much to say. We chatted a few weeks ago before Emily, and I sent her a note this weekend. I've only seen one picture. She's a teacher. How about you? Any dates coming up?"

"None. I'm not sure I'm ready. Nick was a reality check that dating isn't for the faint of heart."

"Oh... speaking of Nick. I saw Emily logged in online this weekend. She's clearly still out there trying to date. Please let me try to connect them. Why not?"

"Why are you so set on doing this? Usually matchmaking is a woman's thing."

"I don't know. Maybe it's part guilt for how it ended. Maybe it's part hopeless romantic. But we have two single people that we can help connect. Why not? And if dating is going to suck so badly, at least I can try to make a pastime out of it."

Maggie laughed. Edward liked to see her smile. He hadn't seen much of it over the last few months since she returned to work. They hadn't sat and talked one-on-one much until recently. He was struck again by how much

Maggie's eyes reminded him of Kate - beautiful, big, bright. Edward hadn't thought much about Kate in several months. He felt relieved to know maybe he was finally ready to move on. Perhaps he was, in fact, ready to tackle dating head on.

"I tell you what, Edward. I'll give you Nick's contact information. You handle it from there."

"Deal. I know you said you're not ready, but have you considered online dating? Just to dip your toe in the water?"

"Ugh. I have. I'm just not sure. It seems like a lot of effort."

"Well, I'd love to tell you otherwise, but it is frankly. However, you're too young, smart and pretty just to spend the rest of your life alone. Why don't you do online dating with me? Then we can compare dating horror stories. We can set up your profile today!"

"Edward, did you just compliment me? And I think I'd be capable of setting up my own profile without any help, thanks."

"Don't get a swelled head, *Mags*," Edward said as a humorous barb.

Maggie smiled again, not protesting as she normally had at the nickname. She was starting to appreciate Edward. She had misjudged him. He was kind and funny, but also seemed to have her back on the team. She felt relieved considering she probably had two strikes against her with Steve. She took a sip of coffee and considered his offer. She still wasn't sure she was ready. Conversely, this way she wouldn't have to go it alone.

"Fine. I'll set up a profile and start online dating," Maggie said trying to sound exasperated while masking her hint of excitement.

"Boom. Let's do this. Try to get a date for this week, and we can compare notes the next morning. We can brighten our weeks with coffee and our dating sagas."

Before Maggie could answer, Steve walked up to Edward's desk. He was a bit surprised to see Maggie sitting there. He had a puzzled look on his face.

"Oh, sorry to interrupt. Hopefully you're planning how we can capitalize on the momentum of last week already. Great job, Edward. You did great for your first multi-agency meeting. Could you set up some time with me later today to touch base?"

Maggie's face turned red, and again, she had to bite her tongue. Not only did Steve not acknowledge her efforts last week, especially with Sheila, he didn't even acknowledge her period. She tried to remain calm. She just smiled at him as if he had no effect on her.

"Sure, Steve. Happy to. I'll look to connect this afternoon."

Edward turned back to look at Maggie after Steve walked away. He could see she was visibly upset. He didn't know what to say. Should he discuss what just happened or try to lighten the mood by going back to discussing dating? Thankfully, Maggie spoke first.

"Don't worry about it. You don't have to say anything. You and Jan both acknowledged my contributions last week. Clearly this is my issue with Steve now, and I'm going to have to figure it out. I should get back to work."

Maggie walked back over to her desk. She looked at her phone. Renee had texted her *good morning* with a kiss emoji. It couldn't have come at a better time. She smiled and texted Renee that she was going to try online dating. Renee just replied back with *???* and *We need to discuss later!*

Edward felt awkward. He didn't know how to best handle the Steve situation. He didn't want to cause tension with Maggie, but he also couldn't avoid his boss either. He hated office politics. After setting up the meeting with Steve for the afternoon, he decided he'd take a mental break before digging into work. He shot Maggie an instant message, *So what's this Nick guy's email or phone number? No time like the present!*

Maggie responded right away with Nick's phone number but with no other comment. He logged in to see if Emily happened to be online. By chance she was. He opened an instant chat with her:

Edward: *Hey Em... how are you?*

Emily: *Edward? I'm surprised to hear from you after several weeks.*

Edward: *I know! I'm surprised to be reaching out myself, truth be told. But life is funny. I wanted to run something by you.*

Emily: *I don't think after how it ended I'd be interested in starting up again.*

Edward: *Well, Em, you're in luck! I think I've found you someone better.*

Emily: *You messaged me to try to set me up? That's weird, Edward.*

Edward: *Listen, I get that this is odd. However, I wanted to introduce you to a guy named Nick that I think you'd really like. Knowing what I know about you and him, I would be remiss if I didn't at least introduce you. I think you'd enjoy each other's company.*

With that, Edward sent Emily Nick's phone number and name. The conversation ended as quickly as it began, as Edward mentioned he needed to get back to work. After logging off, Edward opened his email to see one from Maggie to the team recapping last week. She was a good partner and teammate. He didn't want there to be any tension between them.

He sent her another instant message. *Hey are we ok? Yes* was all she responded.

Maggie knew rationally not to blame Edward. She had created this environment with her own attitude, but she couldn't help but be frustrated with him. Why couldn't he have said anything positive about her to Steve? Yet that was an emotional reaction. She tried to remind herself that he didn't belong in the middle. She was already ready for 5 o'clock, and the day had just started.

Maggie wasn't ready to delve into her project list just yet. She sent Edward a message:

Maggie: *What dating site are you using?*

Edward: *Match.com*

Maggie: *Ok, thanks.*

Edward: *Wait... does this mean you're creating a profile?*

Maggie: *Yes, and don't hit on me when you see my profile, weirdo. LOL*

Edward felt better after receiving Maggie's last instant message. Maggie did not. She stared at her blank profile. She thumbed through her phone thinking about what picture she should make her profile picture. She hadn't felt particularly attractive lately, nor had she really tried. Thankfully, the stress of Brian's death had served as a good weight loss program, and she was 15 pounds thinner than she was at this time last year. She settled on a recent picture of her and Renee clinking glasses at a wine bar. She hoped it would give the illusion that she was fun. She wasn't sure if she even was anymore. Maggie did the bare minimum to activate her profile. She figured she could finish it later.

She wasn't sure if it was more her disdain for Steve or her curiosity of Edward, but she couldn't help but click on his profile. She clicked through the 6 pictures he had uploaded. For the first time, she noticed how attractive Edward really was. She read his profile description and again felt she had misjudged him. He talked a lot about his love of family, travel, and being optimistic. Maggie hoped she could write a profile that read as well.

Maggie heard a ping on her computer. It was an instant message from Edward.

Edward: *Like what you see?*

Maggie: *What?*

Edward: *You're checking out my profile.*

Maggie: *No, I'm not.*

Edward: *Maggie, it tells you when someone is reading your profile. I can see that you read it.*

Maggie was mortified. She felt her face instantly get hot and flush.

Maggie: *Oh, well, fine. You caught me. I was looking for some inspiration on what to write. Don't get overly excited. You're not my type. The Boss's Ass Kisser isn't what I'm seeking. ;)*

Edward: *Ouch... low blow, Cruella.*

Maggie: *Well you'll have your chance to critique mine soon enough.*

Edward: *I feel like I have to now that you've skewered me.*

Maggie: *We need to get back to work. Plus, you have to meet with Steve. Lucky you...*

Edward did wonder what Steve wanted to discuss. Since having started, Steve hadn't put an extraordinary amount of effort into coaching, developing or getting to know Edward. And since meeting Steve, Edward sensed the guy was not to be trusted, so he didn't seek him out either. Considering that the meeting last week seemed to be successful, he wasn't concerned it was bad news. When it was time to meet with Steve, Edward begrudgingly headed toward his office. Edward knocked as he poked his head in.

"Hey, Steve, still a good time?"

"Absolutely! Come in. Come in. Please shut the door behind you."

"How was your weekend?" Edward started with small talk not knowing where to begin the conversation.

"It was fine. Family stuff, you know? Listen, I wanted to connect on last week. Great stuff, bud! I was particularly impressed with how comfortable you were working with the other agency partners and the clients. They all seemed to genuinely respond to you. I couldn't be happier. Do you feel good with how the meeting went?"

"Yes, for sure. I think you were spot on, Steve, to push us to do the pre-thinking. I appreciate that recommendation. As you know, we're heads down driving the current workload, so earmarking time to do that was key. I think the team did a great job helping us prepare, and I think Jan and Maggie did a great job too."

Edward wished he had been more on his toes to give them all credit earlier, so he wasn't going to miss the second opportunity. He did, indeed, feel like it was a good meeting, but he wasn't sure why Steve was gushing over him. Edward did not feel as if he stood above Jan or Maggie.

"Edward, that's exactly why you're a strong team leader, and why Michael and I have been discussing your career. You understand you need to develop and credit your team. After last week, I've put you on Michael's radar. We're going to continue looking for opportunities to let you shine. I just wanted to let you know that. How does that sound?"

"Well, first, thanks, Steve. I appreciate the vote of confidence. As you've probably figured out, I'm about the work. I come in, put my head down, and look to get it done. I give credit when it's due, because that's the right thing to do. Beyond that, I look for opportunities to grow the business. No secret formula for success."

"And perfect attitude to boot. No immediate changes. Keep on keeping on, my friend. But I really believe good things are coming for you. I just wanted to let you know that."

"Great, thanks, Steve," Edward said as he got up to leave. 'My friend?' Edward thought the newfound chummy terms and friendly tone were strange. It all seemed to be such an extreme about face, none of which alleviated his distrust of the guy.

<u>Eleven</u>

The day didn't progress any faster for Maggie. She did her best to focus, but she continued to wonder what and how much she should include in her profile. How much information is too much? It all seemed so foreign to her. Yet the prospect of going to a bar seemed worse.

Finally, at 5:00 pm, she texted Renee, *Free tonight? No time like the present to make me feel incredibly inadequate and out of my zone. Let's create my dating profile... Barf!*

If you're really doing this, I will make time! Renee texted back.

Ok, I'm leaving work now. I'll be there in 15. Don't rush. I'll let myself in and pour a glass of wine in agony... I mean anticipation.

Sounds good.

Maggie thought about Brian on her drive. It was so easy when they met. There were no awkward profiles or selfies. She regretted not having enjoyed those early days more. It seemed like they had raced to married mediocrity quickly. Yet now she missed him terribly. An average day with him seemed so magical now in retrospect, but she knew her lens had been tinted. It wasn't so happy during. Perhaps she just liked the stability she admitted to herself.

Maggie let herself into Renee's apartment. Renee lived about 15 minutes away from the office. She had a beautiful apartment overlooking a lake on the complex's grounds. Maggie poured a glass of wine as promised and sat out on the patio. She considered starting her profile but figured why stretch out the torture of it all. Instead she just stared in silence. She wasn't quite sure how to start again, even if she did meet someone she liked. A year ago, she was on autopilot focused on her career and ignoring her marriage. She recognized the irony now that a short 12 months later, she hated that same career and was forced to focus on her personal life to move on. As she sipped her wine, she tried not to think about anything at all, staring at the reflection of the sunset on the water.

About 20 minutes later, she was startled out of her daze when Renee came in yelling, "are you ready to do this, chica?"

"Hey, Renee," Maggie replied over her shoulder as she continued looking out in the distance. "Pour yourself a glass of wine and come join me."

"Hey you. What are you doing out here? It's getting chilly. Where's your coat?"

"I'm ok. The wine is keeping me warm. I don't know. The fresh air just seemed nice. I needed to escape my thoughts."

"About Brian?"

"About everything, Renee... I just never pictured myself starting over in my 30's. I'm not sure if I should be looking for a boyfriend or a new job. I'm not sure which is the bigger priority."

"Oh, Mags. What happened? Has it gotten that bad?"

"Honestly, I don't know. I'm not sure if it's that bad, or if anything has even changed really, besides my own attitude. All I know is I go to work dreading it, and I leave hating it more. When I'm working I can tolerate it, but that's because I focus on my clients and my team. I'm just not sure I can reset mentally there. Perhaps losing Brian was a wake-up call. Before, work was my salvation from my shitty marriage. Now I'm alone with my thoughts when I leave work, and I'm becoming my own worst enemy."

"Damn, girl. You've been doing some major self-psychoanalyzing. No wonder you needed wine." Renee reached over and hugged Maggie and kissed her neck.

"You've been through more than anyone should have

to go through in the last year. You've spent a lot of time thinking about this. This drum has been beating over and over in your head. That's why I was excited to get your text today. It's time to start playing a different song. I don't want to see you like this. I'm not saying it's easy. I'm not even saying I can relate. All I'm saying, Mags, is I love you, and we've got to help you move on."

"I know, Renee. I know."

"Ok, great. No time like the present! Let's set up your dating profile! But come inside. It's getting cold out here, and Lord only knows how long it's going to take us to finish this."

Renee grabbed her laptop and set it up on the dining room table. They still had a nice view of the sunset over the lake, as Maggie closed the sliding glass door behind her.

"So, Mags, have you decided which dating site you're going to join?"

"I think match.com."

"Any particular reason why Match and not eHarmony, Ok Cupid, or a different one?"

"Is one better than another?"

"I don't know. I was just curious, Mags."

"Well, not to sound lame, but if I'm being honest, it's because this is the one Edward showed me at work."

Renee started laughing with a sly look in her eye.

"Don't even say it, Renee. I know what you're thinking."

"What? That I'm curious if you have a thing for this guy. I wouldn't dare."

"I don't. I'm not even sure I like him yet. He's growing on me, though. He's not as bad as I thought."

"So, he has a profile on here, hey? Let's look!"

"No, don't! I already made that mistake today, and he called me out for looking at his profile. How embarrassing."

"Did you like what you saw?"

"Renee… enough! I'm not into him. I was curious as to how he described himself vs. the guy I knew in real life. I'm new to this. I was searching for a little inspiration."

"And?"

"And, he had 6 really cute pictures, and his profile was charming. Fuck him."

Renee laughed again. She wasn't convinced Maggie didn't at least like him a little.

"That's ok. You couldn't date him anyway."

"Why?"

"Because remember what a bitch I was to him at Brian's funeral? It would be too awkward for *me*."

"Gee, thanks, Renee. Always putting my needs first."

"You're welcome!" Renee answered sarcastically. "Now let's get down to business. Have you created your login information and password already?"

"I have."

"Care to share so I can pull this bad boy up?"

"Um… AdLady05, and my password is brian2016"

"Ok, no. No, no, no! Maggie, what the fuck? You set up your profile as AdLady? You want to be known as AdLady? You just said you hated your job and were considering starting over."

"It's what I could think of today at work while I was hating my boss and procrastinating from working."

"Well, we're changing that shit, right now. And what the hell kind of password is brian2016?"

"It's what I could remember. Brian's the reason I have to do this, and I lost him in 2016."

"Girl, this is pathetic. You don't think it's a tad ominous to use your dead husband's name as your password in your search for your new Mr. Right?"

"I hate this already, and I'm sort of hating you at the moment."

"You love me. And at the moment, you need me. Or

AdLady is going to attract LoserMan and live in Deadendsville, population 2."

"Renee, you're really making me enjoy this experience. I'm already down, why don't you just kick me some more?"

"Ok. Pour another glass of wine. Pull the stick out of your ass. We're going to have fun with this. We're going to find you a fun date. We're going to get you laid. And we're going to help you move on. Got it?"

Maggie looked at Renee with a mix of contempt and love. She did, in fact, need her. She couldn't have gotten through without her. She wouldn't let her totally fall apart, and now she was helping her get back up.

"I really do love you, Renee Michele. I couldn't have done this without."

"Oh God. Don't go getting soft on me now just because I gave you a kick in the ass."

"Way to kill a moment, Renee."

"Fine. I love you too. Is that what you want me to say? That it has killed me to watch you go through this and feel helpless at times in the process. That there were times in the last year that I wanted my best friend back. That I needed you too, but I knew it would be too selfish to call you out on it."

"Renee, I had no idea. I'm so sorry. I guess I have been sort of wrapped up in my own shit to look around me."

"See? This isn't getting us anywhere. We're totally fine. This is water under the bridge. I get it. And when I help you get some, maybe I'll get my friend Maggie back. Now pour us some more wine, and let's get AdLady a new profile name."

Renee logged Maggie in. She was surprised to see 2 guys had already checked out her profile. Not surprisingly, no one had sent a message considering there was no picture, and barely any information.

"What do you want your profile name to be?"

"Ad Queen?" Maggie answered snarkily.

"Enough with the ad crap. There's more to you than work."

"There is? Since when?"

"If not, we're going to make it up, because nobody is going to find you interesting because you sold an extra can of soup or household cleaner along the way. What about StartingFresh16?"

"Ew, no, Renee. I don't want to have to explain to every guy why I'm starting fresh. Because my husband died of cancer suddenly leaving me a miserable widow."

"Ok, moving on. Um…" Renee sat looking at Maggie quizzically. They sat there for a few minutes before Renee offered, "Cool Chica?"

"Renee. Dear friend. Cool Chica? Am I a freshman in college?"

"Ok, smarty pants. Let's see you do better. AdLady was such literary brilliance."

Maggie sat with a grimace on her face. This was as painful as she was expecting, and they hadn't even started answering questions yet.

"Maggie, this is ridiculous. We're going to be here all night. How about MagsAgain?"

"Well, I don't love it, but it's what we're shooting for. I'm going to be Mags again, so let's do it."

"All right! Now let's really get this party started. Ok, so first up is headline."

"What do you mean, headline?"

"You know like what's the first impression you want to give people. Your 5-second elevator pitch, AdLady," Renee answered as she laughed at her own wittiness.

"Forced into doing this by my best friend, come help me."

"Hey now, maybe you'd score a fireman with that headline. Then you'd really have to thank me if he came rushing over here with his… *hose*."

"I just don't know, Renee. Click on one of the guys that looked at my profile. Let's see what his headline is."

It read, "Romeo searching for his Juliet. Will searching for his Kate."

Maggie rolled her eyes. "Are you kidding me with this crap?"

"What? I think it's sort of cute. We're reading his profile more thoroughly later. You may be saying hi!"

"Ok, how about this? Figuring out dating in the digital age. Help me take this offline."

"Woah, Mags. That's not bad. You must work in advertising."

They continued filling out her profile for another 30 minutes or so. The basics were easy - eye color, body type, education, ethnicity. As the wine flowed, Maggie's answers got punchier, but she didn't care. Perhaps it was truer to form of the old Maggie, a bit biting but smart. She needed a guy who could handle that. Then Renee asked, "Status?"

"HIV-. I haven't had sex with anyone but Brian since we were married, and I was tested then."

"Are you kidding me right now?"

"What?"

"You damn goofball! I meant what do you want me to list as your marital status. Widowed or Single?"

"Oh…" Maggie sat and thought for a while. Widowed would be the most honest, obviously, but single would require much less discussion about what happened. As she thought, though, she also didn't want to be disrespectful to Brian. She quietly answered, "widowed."

After Renee was satisfied that they had built a sufficiently great profile for Maggie, she clicked back on Romeo's profile.

"All right, Mags. Let's find you a date! Let's look at ol' Romeo's profile again."

"Ugh, no. Not that guy. 'Will looking for his Kate.'

Are you serious?"

"Maggie the guy is clearly searching for more than just sex. Let's just look at his profile. It's not going back to his house. Besides, you do realize, this is your new norm, right? If you're going to do this, you're going to have to review profiles and be responsive."

Renee started reading. He was an engineer that was looking for a long-term relationship and potentially kids.

"Mags, he sounds like a nice guy. Should I send him a note?"

"May I at least look at his pictures please?"

He just had one posted. He wasn't bad looking. He was athletically built but starting to show his age with receding hair cut short. Maggie couldn't really tell if he was her type, but based on what was in his profile, it was worth at least saying hi. After thinking for a moment, Maggie took the laptop and started typing her first message to a guy on a dating website.

Renee had a look of surprised delight on her face. She knew what a big step that was for Maggie, although she was a little disappointed she didn't get to write the message herself.

"So, what did you write?"

"I just said hello and that I liked his profile. It seemed that we were at a similar place in life and that I'd appreciate getting a chance to chat more with him."

"Look at you, already moving from Dating 101 to 201! How do you feel?"

"I don't know. I guess that was the easy part, right? I put myself out there into the abyss, but I haven't had to interact with anyone yet. Remember how my last awesome date went? Nick? The oversexed macho man that took me to Applebee's?"

"Oh, yes. Well just look at it as getting the bad one out of the way."

Renee and Maggie poured another glass of wine each

and continued laughing as they shared other bad dating stories. By now, Maggie could feel her face flush from the alcohol as her buzz grew. Her face had a look of panic on it when she heard the computer chime.

"Oh, my my my, Ms. Mags. Look who has already responded!"

"What do I do, Renee?"

"Back to 101! You read it and respond!"

Maggie grabbed the laptop from Renee and read the message:

Hi, Maggie. Thanks for sending me a note. I'm happy to see you've filled out more of your profile. It's nice to read more about you. I'm Bob. As you may have read, I'm an engineer by trade seeking someone special. I think it's hard to get to know someone typing 3-4 line messages, so would you like to grab a coffee?

"Renee, he already asked me out. Is that weird? How soon is too soon? I mean we've only really just exchanged pleasantries."

"Mags, you're going to learn this sooner or later. From here on out, there are few norms. Dating really is the wild, wild west now. Some guys will chat with you for weeks, and you think you've got a pen pal instead of dating potential. Others, like this guy, will want to meet right away to avoid prolonged chit chat. If you think it's worth your time, I'd say meet him for the coffee. What could it hurt?"

Maggie started to type her response. Within 5 minutes of back and forth messaging, she had a coffee date for the next night. She was a little taken aback by how fast it all was happening, but at the same time, relieved that she wasn't being ignored either. She looked at Renee and wondered if she'd linger in the dating scene like her best friend.

Maggie woke up the next morning on Renee's couch. She could smell the coffee already brewing.

"Good morning, dating diva. How'd you sleep?"

"Hmm, I don't even remember falling asleep."

"Well, let's just say by the time you got up from setting up your first date, you were in no condition to drive. I helped you to the couch, and you were asleep within 2 minutes. I covered you up and went to bed. How do you feel?"

"Late! I have to get home, shower, and get ready for work!"

"Nonsense. Shower here and wear something out of my closet. No big deal. That'll save you at least 30 minutes and get you to work on time."

"Bless you. Now pour me some coffee please. I feel like hell."

Maggie grabbed her coffee and headed toward the shower. She had never taken a mug of coffee into the shower before, but today was a special circumstance. She needed to kill two birds with one stone. As she was shampooing her hair, Maggie realized she had no makeup, and tonight was her coffee date. *Well that'll be one hell of a first impression,* she thought to herself. She decided she'd run home at lunch to put on her makeup, but that meant she'd face the Monday morning status meeting with the team au naturale. She felt like she'd be the subject of a new Dove commercial, but instead of Real Beauty, her campaign would be titled *Real....Life.* She laughed to herself as she thought perhaps AdLady really was an appropriate profile name.

Despite how great the hot shower felt and how good the coffee tasted, Maggie felt completely disheveled. She was hungover, and while Renee's clothes fit, they were one size too big. She felt like she was wearing her older sister's hand me downs. When Maggie arrived to work, she tried to hurry to her desk as to not see anyone. She didn't know why it would matter. She was going to look like that until she could run home at noon. She'd have to face the team sooner rather than later this morning. She could only hope Steve didn't come to this week's meeting.

"Good morning, Maggie."

Maggie looked up from her desk to see Edward looking over her cube wall. She couldn't help notice how professional and dapper he looked today, perhaps because she was comparing it to her own appearance. His jaw was square and strong and his eyes a warm brown. She had never really taken stock of just how handsome he really was, which made her feel even worse about herself at the moment.

"How was your night? Want to grab coffee?"

She didn't really want to. She felt like burying her head in the sand. She wondered why she didn't just go home and arrive late.

"No thanks. I'm not quite ready yet. I just got here, and I want to look over my email quickly, but thank you."

That was an out and out lie. She wanted coffee desperately, but she didn't want to walk with Edward to look even worse by comparison. Why did he have to come dressed in a sports coat today? Maggie decided she would wait a few minutes before heading to the kitchen to allow Edward time to get back to his desk.

"Here you go. Cream, no sugar just how you like it."

Edward sat down in Maggie's cube handing her a cup of coffee. Maggie was at the same time touched and annoyed.

"Thanks, Edward. You didn't have to do that."

"I know, but I get the sense that perhaps you're not at your finest today."

"Excuse me?" Maggie snapped sharply.

"Hey, I don't mean anything by it. I'm just trying to help. I wanted to be nice and bring you your coffee. I've been working with you now for several months, and I've never not seen you wear makeup or look absolutely stunning."

Maggie was taken aback by the compliment. Just when she wanted to smack him, he throws that at her.

"Well thank you, I guess. Admittedly, I feel like I look today, as much as I'd like to tell you you're wrong. Renee and I had a bit too much wine last night."

"What was the occasion?"

"Honestly? I needed some liquid courage to finish my dating profile. As much as I hate it, I need to put myself back out there and move on. And, Edward, it's really hard."

"Maggie, I know. I get it more than you know. But hey listen, that's awesome news about your dating profile."

"I suppose, and I already have my first date tonight."

"Maggie, no offense. You may want to postpone. I know you've been out of the dating scene for a while, but first impressions still matter," Edward laughed as he shot her a wicked grin.

"First, you're an absolute ass. Way to kick a girl when she's down. Second, I'm going home at lunch, and you've just given me motivation to come back looking even more stunning than you've ever seen me. You sir, will wish you were the lucky gent who gets to accompany me this evening."

"Maybe so…. Maybe so. Fortunately for me, I also have a date tonight."

"Oh? Did you also meet on Match?"

"We did. I'm not sure what to make of her quite yet, but I figured I'd give it a chance."

"Actually, I feel the same about Bob."

"Bob?"

"Yep. Bob the engineer. I'm going on my first online date tonight with Bob the engineer."

"I want to see him!"

Edward bounded up to go get his laptop before Maggie could object. When he logged on, he noticed he had a new message. It was Emily.

130

Despite the fact that I thought it was weird as hell, Edward, for you to reach back out and try to fix me up, I have to admit, I'm really enjoying getting to know Nick. He's sexy as hell, and we have explosive chemistry. I guess you're not such a jerk after all. -Em

Edward had to laugh. 'Explosive chemistry' because they're both sex fiends. One can't get enough, and the other can't stop talking about it. Luckily for Emily, if Nick is talking, she doesn't have to.

"Maggie, look at this. Nick and Emily hit it off. Look at us matchmaking with our dating leftovers."

"You're kidding. The guy that couldn't stop talking about masturbating found someone before me?"

"Indeed. He found a sex addict that barely talks, so they're a real fit!"

Edward flashed that wicked grin again, and Maggie laughed, playfully smacking Edward's knee. For a moment, she forgot that she looked like hell, as she was drawn to him by his humor.

"Well, Edward, since you were so spot on last time, perhaps if our dates tonight bomb, we can fix them up."

"Let's hope we find some quality somewhere, and not just misfits that we match with other misfits."

"We'll see tonight, won't we?"

"I tell you what, Maggie, I'll see you back here in 24 hours, and we can report over our morning coffee how the dates went."

"Deal."

Twelve

Edward awoke the next morning wondering exactly how he'd describe his date to Maggie. He wished he hadn't announced he had yet another date, and he certainly wished he hadn't agreed to share details. He hoped Maggie's date went as poorly so she would commiserate, but he felt bad knowing all Maggie had been through. He had laid in bed an extra 15 minutes thinking over the events of last night - analyzing it and positioning the story. Finally, he decided to get up, determining the best strategy was to not bring it up and hope that Maggie would be too busy to chat or had just forgot.

When Edward arrived at the office, he decided to go straight for coffee without stopping at his desk to drop off his things. He figured if he could just slink in once with coffee in hand perhaps he could be covert enough not to be noticed. It was a failed strategy. As Edward approached his desk, he could see Maggie sitting in his cube waiting for him.

"Where have you been? You never arrive this late. Does that mean you were out to all hours of the night enjoying yourself? I thought perhaps you were standing me up for our coffee date to discuss our dates!"

Edward didn't answer right away. He set down his coffee and took off his jacket. As he was opening his bag to dig out his laptop, Maggie shot him an incredulous look.

"Um, hello? Are you just going to ignore me?"

"I kinda, sorta wanted to yes... well not ignore you necessarily. Avoid you would probably be more accurate."

"Why? Did I do something?"

"Oh no. It's just my date. It was pretty disastrous. I was planning to just avoid the topic today, but that doesn't seem to be in the cards."

Maggie laughed as she smacked the top of Edward's desk.

"No worries, there, buckaroo. Mine was equally as disastrous. What a shit show. If my first online date is a sign of things to come, I'm going to call time of death as, last night, 9:45 pm."

Edward smiled with relief. He felt like an asshole for being grateful Maggie's date wasn't a rousing success and even more grateful that he wouldn't have to sit and listen as she described a great evening.

"Alright, so I'm going to need details," Maggie said as she sat back taking a sip of her coffee.

"So, you're really going to force me to discuss, hey?"

"Oh absolutely. Misery loves company, and last night was miserable. This should be fun. Renee keeps telling me dating is fun. I personally haven't experienced that yet, but maybe the sharing of the bad dates will be the fun part."

Edward sat down. He exhaled before taking a drink of his own coffee. He sighed before beginning.

"I guess maybe my expectations were too high. I'll say that to begin. I'm not sure why - we really hadn't talked that much. In reading her profile, it seemed like we had a lot in common. She was educated, athletic, and we liked a lot of the same things. So, I was hopeful."

"Oh man, Edward, she sounds just terrible. I'm feeling really bad for you."

"Maggie. Are you going to let me tell the story, or should I start going through my emails now?"

"Fine…"

"I had offered to pick her up. She declined. I had suggested a nice restaurant where we could sit and chat over a good dinner, but she said that was too formal for her. All this despite my normal approach being just coffee or a drink for a first date. See? I was hopeful. Anyway, she picked a local tavern. I had heard they have good burgers,

133

so I thought why not. She was already seeming pretty cool."

"I got to the restaurant a few minutes late. I had texted her to let her know I was running behind because of traffic, and she let me know she was already there. Now, Maggie, I had only seen one picture of her. Admittedly, it was a bit distant, but she had longer hair done well with makeup and earrings. It was a pretty good pic."

"And your point? That you're shallow?" Maggie laughed.

"No, but we work in advertising! There should be truth in marketing."

"That bad?"

"Maggie, she was wearing track pants and a t-shirt. Tennis shoes. Her hair was cut in a short bob. No makeup or jewelry of any kind. For a first date, I was just a bit shocked that she seemingly put no effort in at all."

"Yeah that does seem a bit odd, if her one picture showed her looking completely different."

"From what I hear, welcome to dating in the digital age! Five-year-old pictures and sketchy lighting. In this case, I think it was an Olan Mills glamour shot because in reality, it looked nothing like her. How do I know? Because after the date, I logged back on to look to make sure I wasn't crazy!"

Maggie couldn't help but laugh as she listened to Edward. He was normally very polished and polite at work, and she was seeing a different side of him this morning. He was snarky and irreverent. She wondered if the first few months working together would've been different if she hadn't had walls up and been dealing with Brian. She was happy that they were starting to build a friendship. She smiled as she continued listening.

"Now, wanting to give her the benefit of the doubt, I introduced myself politely and figured maybe she wanted to see if a guy would like her for more than her appearance. So, I went with it. I was already there. I might as well enjoy a good burger and hope for a decent conversation. Our waitress came over to greet us. That's when it started getting interesting. Our waitress had a v-neck t-shirt on, and I kid you not, I think I saw my date checking out her boobs. If her appearance didn't give me a clue, I'm pretty sure that sealed the deal. I think I was on a date with a lesbian."

"Oh, Edward. That means nothing. Girls check out each other's boobs all the time. We're not obsessed with them like men, but we certainly compare and notice."

"Fine, but do you ogle? If it's that obvious to the casual observer, I'm pretty sure it wasn't a quick comparison."

"Ok, fair point, but still you don't know."

"You're right. I didn't know definitively, but the evidence was piling up. She drove a Subaru. She was raised in a very religious family. And, she hadn't been in a relationship with a man in several years."

"Why do you think she would want to go out on a date with you then? And why go through the trouble of creating an online dating profile?"

"Hell if I know! I've asked myself that question a few times. Maybe she's bi? Maybe she hasn't come to terms with her sexuality yet? Or perhaps she just uses it as a cover to get her parents off her back? I don't know, but let's just say there probably won't be a second date. Again, it's not like she was unpleasant. I guess it was just the discrepancy between my expectations and reality and feeling like I'm starting over again."

"Aww starting over again? Did your spouse just die? It's all relative," Maggie said disparagingly.

"How many times are you going to play the cancer card? The husband just died trump card?" Edward said sarcastically.

Maggie didn't know whether to be shocked or impressed by the speed of his wit. They both started laughing simultaneously.

"Ok, your highness. Please bestow upon us the tales of your bad evening."

"Ugh, Bob. So, Bob is an engineer. I think I may have told you that. That was reflected in pretty much everything about him. He drove a gray Toyota. He wore a solid blue button up. He spoke in virtually one tone all evening. The guy was just beige."

"Maybe he was just nervous. Engineers are often introverts. If he was a good guy, perhaps you may want to give him a second chance."

"Again, ugh. Bob spent much of the evening just talking about what he was seeking in a life partner. We were on a first date! He would ask me about how many kids I wanted. If I saw us living in the suburbs or the city. It was all too much too fast. I just got the sense that the guy had a biological clock of his own. It was weird. I think the only interesting thing about him was his extreme comb over. Edward, you should've seen this thing. Now in all the pictures I had seen his hairline was receding, but he kept his hair short. It was pretty much buzzed. Then I arrive, and it was this obvious ode-to-Donald-Trump-thing. I couldn't believe it. Unlike your lesbian, I think my guy was trying a bit too hard to make a good first impression."

"Wait, this guy was pushing hard for a wife?"

"Yeah... you could say that. I was worried he was going to pull out a ring at any minute. Or that I'd find one lodged in my baked potato."

"Do you know what this means?"

"There won't be a second date with him either?"

"No! Our leftovers matchmaking services are still alive and well. Do you remember that girl Jessica I went on a date with a while ago? She was ready to graduate with her M-R-S degree within 30 minutes too! If we had success with Nick and Emily, why not Bob and Jessica? We have better match rates than Match!"

Maggie rolled her eyes. She was about to discredit the idea again, wanting to focus on her own frustration, but then she thought why not. It would give her and Edward even more to talk about.

"Edward, I say let's do it. Let's get Jessica and Bob to the altar! Do you think we'll get invited to the wedding? If so, can we tell everyone that we fixed them up?"

"Hey, if we're going to continue to put ourselves out in this shit storm, the least we can do is help a few lost souls with some umbrellas along the way."

"So, what's your plan then, Edward?"

"What do you mean? I'll probably just text Jessica Bob's contact information."

"No. I meant are you going to go out on another date soon? Take a bit of a break?"

"Oh. I guess I hadn't really thought about it. I suppose I'll go out on another date soon, or at least try to. Your story reaffirms that dating today is hard for everyone. I guess I'll have to log back on tonight. It's my new part-time job."

"And I guess I'll have to do the same."

Maggie looked at her watch and realized they had already been talking for almost 40 minutes. She motioned to Edward that she needed to go. She was already late for her first meeting.

He sent her an instant message. *Don't forget to send me Bob's contact information.*

Maggie hurried into Jan's office to review first round creative concepts for her upcoming spring campaign.

"Good morning, Jan!"

"Boy, you're in a good mood considering you're 10 minutes late. You hate being late."

"I know. I'm really sorry. I was catching up with Edward, and I lost track of time."

"Edward? Since when do you catch up with Edward? I

didn't realize you had moved past being civil work partners. It's not as if you have any shared projects. You've split the business."

"You're going to find this funny, Jan, but we've taken to discussing our dating woes together. It's commiseration amongst the undeft digital daters."

Jan had a disbelieving look on her face as she listened. She had known Maggie a long time, and if she didn't know any better, she would guess that Maggie had a crush on Edward. Maggie has no poker face. She's too honest, wearing her emotions on her sleeve. Jan could almost hear excitement in her voice as she discussed her chats with Edward.

"Maggie, how long have you guys been chatting?"

"What do you mean? Since he started, silly. We've always talked."

"Maggie Jenkins. Check yourself. When that man first started, you called him a douchebag. Now you're acting as if you have been friends all along. What's the real story?"

"Jan, you never have been one to not call me out, have you? I guess you make a fair point. I suppose chats about dating are relatively new since I joined Match recently."

"Oh, Maggie! I'm so happy for you. You've decided to put yourself back out there. I have been hoping you would be ready at some point. I know Brian's death took a lot out of you. I was worried, friend."

"It's hard, admittedly. I think that's why Edward and I have connected recently. It's nice to have a friend that can relate to the nightmare that is dating these days."

"Maggie, have you considered going out with Edward?"

Maggie had a look of shock at Jan's question, as if the thought had never crossed her mind.

"Jan, no. We just work together. I can admit that I was wrong about him at first, but I don't see Edward like that. He's handsome yes, but I don't see him like that."

"If you say so…"

"What's that supposed to mean?"

"Nothing. Ok, we have only 15 minutes until my next meeting, and I need to go over these three concepts with you. So, let's focus."

Maggie's schedule had her in meetings most of the morning. By the time she got back to her desk, it was almost 1 pm. She saw Edward's message, and smiled instinctively. She sent him Bob's contact information and was about to walk to the kitchen to get her lunch when he responded.

Edward: *Guess what!*

Maggie: *What?*

Edward: *I logged back on to Match after our chat. I wanted to see if I had any new messages.*

Maggie: *And?*

Edward: *And I have a date tonight! I wasn't expecting that, but she seems really cool. She's a vet.*

Maggie: *Oh!*

Maggie's first reaction was a hint of jealousy. She was surprised herself. She had just told Jan she wasn't interested. She rationalized to herself that it was more that Edward was so comfortable putting himself right back out there, when the thought of logging back on in search of a date turned her stomach. She could understand how he could so easily get a date. He certainly was charismatic.

Edward: *Having learned my lesson on my lesbian date, I only offered up getting a drink.*

Maggie: *Good idea. Where are you meeting?*

Edward: *She said she's not a big drinker, so we're taking her golden retriever to a dog park tonight and going for a walk. How cool is that? I'm pretty stoked. Why do I let myself get my hopes up like this? I'll report back tomorrow!*

Maggie: *Damn you! That means I have to log back on and try to chat more. Ugh! ;)*

Edward: *You can do it! Gotta run.*

Maggie considered logging on herself, but she had too much work. She hadn't even eaten lunch yet. Maggie locked her computer and headed to the kitchen. As she passed Jan's office, she saw Edward meeting with her.

"Edward, so what's this I hear you and Maggie are sharing dating diaries. That was an unexpected turn."

"I know, right? It's fun. Well, back up. To be honest, it was stressful and unpleasant before our conversation this morning."

"What happened this morning?"

"I tried to avoid her, first off! I was so embarrassed by my latest date with a woman I'm pretty sure was a lesbian that I dreaded having to compare war stories."

Edward had Jan near tears from laughing as he told her the story of his latest date and how he tried to dodge Maggie.

"I'm just happy her date was equally as bad. We're talking ugly-comb-over-seeking-wife-by-second-date bad. From there, we just sort of agreed to support each other as we try to find the one. This isn't easy.

Jan took the opportunity to ask Edward the same question.

"Have you considered asking Maggie out?"

"Jan, what are you talking about? Maggie is just a friend. Besides a few weeks ago she could barely stand me. I'm just happy we've found a solid working relationship and now have this in common to help build our rapport."

Edward didn't have the same affectionate lilt in his voice when he spoke about Maggie. She believed him when he said there was no interest there. The same couldn't be said when Maggie responded. That had her worried about her friend.

"Just be careful when it comes to Maggie, ok? She's been through a lot, and she's still grieving and Steve-ing.

140

She can't handle much else."

"Be careful? I'm trying to help Maggie and support her. That's what I've done since I found out about Brian."

Jan decided to change the subject before she said too much. Edward was oblivious to what she meant, and it was probably better that way. She'd have to take it upon herself to keep an eye on Maggie.

As the day wore on, Edward still hadn't had time to reach out to Jessica. Finally, just before 5:00 pm, he sent her a text with Bob's contact information saying he thought she'd really enjoy meeting him. Much like Emily before her, her first response was one of disbelief. And much like he did for Emily, he persuaded her to give Bob a chance. He asked her to keep him posted.

"Good luck on your date tonight."

Edward looked up to see Maggie with her coat on and work bag on her shoulder ready to leave.

"Thanks. We'll see how it goes. If you see me slinking in tomorrow morning trying to avoid you again, you'll know it was another certified disaster. But hey, it makes for good stories!"

"Indeed! And quite frankly, inspiration for me. It gives me courage to keep going if a charismatic charmer such as yourself is having trouble, then it's par for the course."

Edward laughed, overlooking Maggie's compliment. Instead he heard the frustration in her voice, and assumed that's what Jan was referencing earlier.

"Maggie, you'll find someone. You've got to give it time. You literally just started putting yourself back out there. I'm right there with you. We will go through this together."

Maggie warmly smiled at Edward's graciousness. She nodded before heading out for the evening.

Edward looked at the time. He needed to be at the dog park in 45 minutes, so he decided to shut down so he could grab a quick dinner before meeting Annie. By the time he drove to the general area of the dog park in rush hour traffic, he would only have time to do drive through, which wasn't the healthiest. He decided to wait to eat until afterward. He arrived at the dog park about 10 minutes early as a result. He sat on a bench near the front of the park hoping there weren't any other entrances. He didn't have her phone number to text her, so he waited impatiently.

After a few minutes, Edward decided to check the headlines on his CNN app. He was so engrossed in an article about a Syrian refugee family that he didn't hear Annie approaching until he felt a dog lick his hand. Startled he looked up to see a smiling brunette with big, beautiful brown eyes. She had a soft smile and spoke with quiet warmth.

"Look! He likes you already. He's usually an excellent judge of character, which is why I bring him on my first dates," she said jokingly.

"Hi, I'm Edward. Apologies for not seeing you coming. I was reading."

"I noticed. About Syrian refugees. Do you always end your days digesting such heavy stories? By the way, I'm Annie. Nice to meet you."

"Not always, no. Besides, I like to think of that article as a human-interest piece. It was more about a particular family and their plight after moving to Germany. Both triumphant and sad actually."

"Triumphant and sad. That could be the title of my dating life."

They both laughed and shook their head in agreement. Edward stood up to give Annie a hug. She smelled amazing, and her hug was as inviting as her smile. As he embraced her, his heartbeat quickened in excitement.

"This is Bruno. I named him after Bruno Mars. Corny I know, but I'm a big fan. When I first got him, I was playing Uptown Funk non-stop, and he would, I kid you not, jump in unison to the beat. So, he's now Bruno, my best buddy. Aren't you, boy?"

"Nice to meet you too, Bruno," Edward said as he knelt down to pet him. Bruno licked Edward's face this time knocking him onto his butt.

"Oh boy, does he ever like you! You must have a good energy about you. I had one date that met him, and all Bruno did was low-growl. I'm so sorry. Here. Let me help you up."

Edward looked up at her and smiled. He had just met her, and he was already having a great time. As she reached out to help him up, he playfully acted as if was going to pull her down instead. Before he could get up, Bruno jumped in Edward's lap.

"Bruno, buddy. You're going to have to give me space. You're preventing me from getting to know this beautiful woman. Maybe that's your game plan. Prevent me from getting to know her so you can have her all to yourself. Who could blame you?" Edward said as he wrestled the dog off his lap so he could get up.

Annie tilted her head and smiled at the affectionate way Edward interacted with her dog. She was half-joking about Bruno being a good judge of character, but she also knew she wanted someone that was good with animals, considering the role they played in her life. She noticed how handsome he was right away, but in a few short minutes, she was already drawn to him. As Edward stood up, she grabbed his arm so they could stroll through the park.

They walked together in the park for the better part of an hour before the evening chill set in. They talked about everything from family to work and anything in between. Annie collected magnets from the places she had visited around the world, and Edward was impressed with how often she traveled. She was touched by the way he spoke of his grandma having moved home to be closer to her.

"May I walk you and Bruno to your car?"

"Of course. Thank you for a lovely walk. I hope we can go out again, Edward."

"I'd like that as well. Listen, what are you doing now?"

"Going home. Why?"

"I haven't eaten dinner, and I wondered if perhaps you'd like to extend the evening."

"Um… sure. Actually, that sounds nice. I wasn't ready for it to end anyway. I just have to drop Bruno off at home, and then I can meet you. Where should we go?"

They agreed on a Thai restaurant, and after Edward said his goodbyes to Bruno scratching under his chin and accepting a few more doggie kisses, Annie took the opportunity to give him a quick kiss herself. Edward raised his eyebrows in surprise. He grabbed her hand and lightly squeezed as he gave her another kiss himself.

Thirteen

Edward entered the office whistling quietly to himself as he approached his desk. He continued to whistle as he unpacked his notebook from his bag and took off his coat. He switched to humming as he grabbed his coffee cup and headed toward the kitchen. By the time he got back to his desk, Maggie was already waiting for him at his table with her own cup of coffee.

"Boy, you're in a good mood today. It must've gone well, hey?"

"Maggie, you have no idea. Right from the moment we met, it was so easy. There was no awkward silence. No nervous laughter. It was just comfortable."

"What did you end up doing?"

"Well, we met at the dog park like I mentioned. She has the cutest golden retriever named Bruno. After an hour or so of walking and talking, we decided to keep hanging out and grabbed dinner."

"Oh, it's like 2 dates in one."

"No! It was like 3! Because after dinner, she invited me back to her place to spend some more time with Bruno and continue talking."

"Tell me you did not sleep with her on your first date."

"It would've been our third date," Edward said slyly before admitting they had not.

"We just talked. I can't believe that after almost 4 hours together, we still could find things to talk about. And Bruno is just awesome. We were sitting on the floor of her apartment in front of her fireplace, and he came up and just put his head in my lap. She said that he had never done that - that he must really like me."

Maggie's pang of jealousy returned. Her first instinct was to be sarcastic about his wonderful evening, but she didn't want to appear resentful. Instead, she opted to listen intently and offer up a few questions to allow him to elaborate, as well as statements of support.

"So, when will you see her again?"

"Soon I hope. We haven't set anything up definitively, but I have her number and certainly plan to call her today. And Maggie, to top things off, she's beautiful."

Maggie looked down to take a sip of her coffee so he wouldn't see her roll her eyes. She hated that she felt that way. She felt frustrated in almost every aspect of her life. She had no interest in dating, but being alone sounded worse. The situation with Steve could only be described as tenuous at best. She considered that if not for Sheila, he may have already fired her. And while she and Renee remained best of friends, she also knew she had just taken in the last year without providing much in return. She was so thankful for Renee, but also felt extreme guilt about being a shitty friend.

"Maggie, guess what. Jessica already texted me last night that she and Bob are going to go out. How cool is that? Maybe we'll go 2 for 2!"

Maggie remained silent as she took stock of her life. She hadn't really heard what Edward just said.

"Maggie? What's wrong?"

"Oh, nothing. I'm sorry - I just got lost in thought there for a minute. I'm really happy for you and what's her name."

"Annie. But I just said that Jessica and Bob are going to go out. Cool, right?"

"Oh Lord. Is their first date wedding cake tasting or venue inspections?"

"Very funny! You sure everything is ok?"

"It will be… thanks," Maggie said as she smiled and walked back to her desk. She didn't want to feel this tangled ball of emotions anytime someone else had something good happen in their life, especially Edward.

He was turning out to be a decent guy, and she wanted him to be happy. She pulled out her phone to text Renee.

Maggie: *Day off to a shitty start. I can't get the blahs every time someone has good news. I'm turning into Debbie Downer.*

Renee: *Well good morning to you too, sunshine. It's a phase, don't worry.*

Maggie*: Let's grab dinner tonight. My treat. I owe you an undivided ear so I can hear what's going on with you. Love you.*

Renee*: That sounds great. I'd enjoy that. Love you too, AdLady ;)*

That put a smile on Maggie's face. She knew no matter what, Renee could always cheer her up, even if she weren't trying. They had been through a lot over the years. They had met in college. Renee was seeking part-time work and decided to check the campus bookstore, as it had a help wanted sign in the window. Maggie was the shift manager during the afternoon, and upon seeing Renee's Delta Zeta sorority t-shirt, lied and said the position had already been filled. They didn't become friends until a few years later when they were in the same book club, which eventually turned into a wine and whine girls' night. When Renee put it together how she recognized Maggie, after a few glasses of wine, Maggie admitted she lied about the job opening because Renee was a sorority girl. Renee has never let Maggie live it down.

Despite that, they became fast friends. Maggie was Renee's rock when she was date raped in her twenties. Renee moved in with Maggie for a few months because she was afraid to be alone. It has affected her relationship with men ever since. That time together cemented their loyalty. On some of the toughest days during Brian's decline, Renee would recall how much she leaned on Maggie, and how she needed to stand up and provide the same in return.

Maggie was happy to shut down right at 5 pm to meet Renee for happy hour. She had been looking forward to a glass of wine all day.

"Good night, Edward."

"Leaving already? Wait. Do you have a date tonight?" he said excitedly.

"I, in fact, do. With my bestie. Better than any man, and certainly more reliable!"

"Ok. Ok. You go have fun. I'm actually meeting Annie tonight myself. I reached out a bit ago, and we were both so anxious to hang out again we decided why wait."

Maggie just smiled and waved as she turned to leave. She had been looking forward to seeing Renee all day, and he just had to go and overshadow it with another date. As she got in her car, she tried to think about something else, but she found herself mimicking him, "I've got another date. Blah, blah, blah. We were so anxious to hang out. We're so great together. We already share the dog because he loves me so much. Blah, blah, blah."

Maggie got to the restaurant about 10 minutes before Renee and had no issues starting in on her first and second glasses of wine without her. She was hoping Renee was right - that this was just a phase. Being single in her mid-thirties was never part of the plan. When things were shitty before, she at least had work to throw herself into. She no longer felt an incentive to work harder to make Steve look better.

"Hey, beautiful girl. How are you? I see you didn't waste any time on your first drink."

"Second, Renee. It's just been that kind of day."

"What's up? What happened today?"

"Oh Edward. He had a good first date, and he was so happy and mushy. Everyone loves him at work. He's so happy all the damn time. He's charismatic and handsome. And now he went out and had a good date. At least before, he was a single loser like me too. I held onto that."

Renee couldn't help but laugh, which made Maggie sneer at her.

"Why are you laughing?"

"Because you sound ridiculous, and only your best friend can call you on it. A guy you work with, whom up until recently you couldn't care less about, had a good first date, and it has affected you this much? What's up with that? Do you have feelings for this guy?"

"God no! It's just that everything seems to be going so well for him, while my life just keeps stalling out. I guess because all I do right now is go to work, that people I work with are what I have to compare against. I know I shouldn't do that."

"Especially to someone you don't care about. Forget that guy. So what? He had a good first date. Good on ya, mate! Live long and prosper. It has no impact on you. As for us, we're going to have a kick ass ladies' night!"

Just as Maggie was about to cheers to Renee's statement with her now third glass of wine, she couldn't believe what she saw across the restaurant.

"No, it can't be."

"What is it?"

"Oh my God, it is. That couple over there that just walked in. I think that may be Jessica and Bob."

"Who the hell are Jessica and Bob?"

"Um… well… they're two people that Edward and I went on dates with separately that we fixed up together."

"You what? So not only does this guy's life affect you, but you're playing matchmaker together? Correct me if I'm wrong, but the last time I knew, you weren't too keen on this guy. What gives?"

"Eh, he has turned out to not be that bad. And since we're both dating at the same time, we have found that some of our leftovers are actually matches for each other. Case in point, Jessica and Bob. Well, I know that's Bob. I can't be sure that's Jessica. I'm going over to say hi!"

"What? Why would you do that?"

Before Maggie could answer, the wine had lowered her inhibition enough to start toward their table.

"Bob! It's so nice to see you again. Who's your friend?"

Bob was taken aback to see Maggie. He didn't figure he'd ever see her again based on how their communication fizzled, let alone that she'd approach him in a restaurant.

"Hi, Maggie. This is my date, Jessica."

"I knew it! Jessica, how are you?"

"Pardon? Have we met?"

"No, but you know my co-worker, Edward. That's how Edward knew about Bob. You see Bob and I went out recently. When Edward told me about you, I figured you'd be a good fit for Bob."

Jessica and Bob both had a look of confusion mixed with horror on their faces. They didn't know whether to be thankful that these two people had set them up, or offended that they were date-hand-me-downs.

"I'm so happy that you two decided to go out. It sounds like you have a lot in common. We're rooting for you."

"We're?" Bob asked incredulously.

"Oh, Edward and I. You see, we are trying to help people find love. Just because our respective dates didn't go well, doesn't mean we don't want to see good people find their happy."

"Oh, is that so?" Jessica asked rather sharply. "Well, you'll be happy to know then, that Bob and I are getting along great. We do want the same things, and we've already decided that we're going to go out again."

This last statement didn't surprise Maggie. She was surprised Bob hadn't already proposed based on how fast he moved. Maybe that would be on the second date. However, the next statement did catch Maggie off guard.

"Maggie, since you and Edward seem so keen on seeing us happy, why don't you join us for dinner soon?"

While the dinner invitation seemed polite, Jessica's face said it was an act of awkward retribution. Before Maggie could decline, Jessica insisted. All Maggie could do was politely nod in agreement before wishing them a lovely evening.

"Renee, you're never going to believe what just happened?"

"They called the psych ward to come pick up the buzzed, crazy woman that just interrupted their date?"

"I wish! That would be preferable to the dinner I'm now going on with Jessica, Bob and Edward."

"What the fuck? You're now going to have dinner with Edward and your dinner date rejects? That's messed up, Maggie."

"Listen, you're the one that told me I should be dating again. I'm out dating!"

"I told you to date - what you just described is not dating. Because as far as you've told me, you're not interested in Edward nor Bob. And I'm assuming you don't want Jessica's puss, unless you're trying something new I don't know about!"

"Renee Michele!"

"Oh. I'm sorry. Am I the crazy one now? As far as I knew we were meeting to celebrate us, and I believe as you said, you'd like to hear what's been going on in my life. Since I arrived, all I've done is hear about Edward."

Maggie looked down solemnly at the bar. She knew Renee was right. She honestly didn't know much about what had been happening in Renee's life. When they had created her online dating profile, Maggie was already buzzed when Renee arrived home, and she had fallen asleep right after finding her first date.

"Renee, you're right. I don't know what to say. I haven't been a very good friend of late. I'm not going to make any excuses, because by now, I need to have found a new normal."

"Mags, I'm not saying you need to be over Brian. Or finished grieving. Or even that you shouldn't be interested in Edward if you are. I'm saying that I want my friend back. I need you too."

Maggie leaned over and gave Renee a hug as tears rolled down her cheek. Renee felt 2 tears hit her neck.

"Ok, girl. Pull yourself together. Mulligan. Let's start over."

"Deal. So, Renee Michele, what's been going on with you?"

"Well, you may have noticed, but I'm down 12 pounds. I've also started meditating. I decided I didn't want to just be an also-ran. I was tired of making excuses for myself. Maggie, it's been a while, but I feel back in control. I have to say, as much as I have missed you, needing to be emotionally self-sufficient lately has forced me to step up."

"I noticed when you walked in. Your boobs look amazing. Well done, my friend. Have you been seeing anyone?"

"No, and for the first time in a long time, I haven't wanted to. I need to work on me before I'm ready to date again. Maybe that's why I haven't had much luck in the last few years."

"Wait... then why did you push me to return to dating?"

"Because you were spiraling downward so quickly, I was afraid I wasn't going to be able to help you. I figured dating would give you a distraction and force you to leave your house."

"And it has! Now I'm hosting the NewlyWon't Game, fixing up my bad dates."

"And going out with them and their new date. Don't forget that!"

They both erupted into laughter. It had been a while since they had felt their old chemistry with each other.

They continued to talk and laugh for another hour before Renee decided to call it an evening.

"I need to head out, mi amiga. I have been committed to getting more sleep as I invest in myself. I also have been hitting the gym in the morning, and if I'm not in bed by 11, it's nearly impossible for me to get up."

Maggie dreaded leaving because it meant she was that much closer to having to explain to Edward she obligated them to go out with Jessica and Bob. Plus, she would have to hear about his date with Annie. She wondered how she could get out of it. Surely, Bob would understand. Maggie decided to send Bob an email apologizing for interrupting his date and graciously decline the invite to dinner. As she crawled into bed, she felt a little better about embarrassing herself tonight, at least she felt more connected with Renee.

In the morning, Maggie picked up her phone to check her email. She was surprised to already see a response from Bob:

Maggie - I must say it was a surprise to see you again. Jessica and I talked after you left, and as awkward as it was hearing how you came to set us up, the reality is, you still helped us. We really hit it off. So don't be silly - we are excited to thank you and Edward over dinner.
Bob

Maggie's face turned flush with embarrassment. Why didn't she listen to Renee and leave well enough alone? At least the sentiment in Bob's note seemed authentic and not one of reparation like Jessica's face indicated. Or perhaps, he was just being polite, and they would return the favor over dinner. Maggie knew she had to tell Edward before Jessica reached out. She dreaded it all the way to work.

Maggie could hear Edward humming well before she heard his footsteps. She closed her eyes and sighed. She knew that meant he had another good date she had to hear about.

"Good morning, Magdalena. How are you this fine morning?"

"Magdalena? What the hell? You know we don't do nicknames, and it certainly won't be that one!"

"Oh, Maggie. Lighten up. It's a great morning, about to get better with caffeine. Let's grab some coffee."

His cheeriness irritated her. She needed caffeine to endure. As they walked back toward their cubes with their coffee, Edward asked, "How was your night with Renee?"

Before Maggie could respond, he continued, "my evening was really great, Maggie. Annie is just so real. It's so easy to talk to her. It feels like I've known her for years, not 2 dates. It's so comfortable. Since Bruno had been home alone all day, we decided to do take out and a movie to stay with the big guy. The three of us cuddled. We've already set up our next date too. Sorry was too excited. So how was your night?"

"Well, Edward. I think it can only be described as interesting. Do you remember Jessica?"

"Of course."

"Well, I met her last night, when she and Bob showed up to the same restaurant as Renee and me."

"Were they already married?" Edward laughed amused by the coincidence.

"Funny you should ask. While they weren't married yet, they had already planned for more dates. And here's the funniest part, they want us to join them on one."

"Come again?"

Maggie sheepishly smiled. "Well, Edward, I may have indicated that we had discussed fixing them up after we had gone out with them respectively."

"You told them they were leftovers!"

"I said we were rooting for them! I think it came out wrong."

"How does it come out right?"

"Without the wine?" Maggie said shrugging and

wincing simultaneously.

"Oh, Maggie. Tell me you said no, right? There's no way we're really going to hang out with 2 people with whom we've already had bad dates with."

Maggie grimaced and shook her head yes.

"Maggie, I'm not doing that. That's lunacy and awkward. Plus, I'm seeing Annie. How would I explain this nonsense to her?"

"Edward, I know all of this. I emailed Bob last night to decline, but he already responded saying they want to thank us. They understand it could be awkward, but they're really wanting to show their appreciation."

"Gift cards. Greeting cards. Hell, even playing cards would work. Those show appreciation. I don't need to sit through dinner with two people we barely know. I'm not doing that," Edward said with increasing annoyance.

Maggie's faced turned red as she looked down and shook her head.

"I know you're right, and I'm sorry, Edward. I should've left them alone. I don't know what came over me. I'm sorry for putting you in this position. I'll reach out to Bob to let them know it'll just be me."

"You're going through with this?"

"I don't want to! I'm hoping if it's just me, they'll decline, but I made this mess. I have to accept it."

Her face turned from embarrassment to remorse. She wished she hadn't relied on wine so frequently of late. She wished she hadn't gone over to speak to Jessica and Bob last night. Most of all she wished she didn't feel so alone. Edward saw the look on Maggie's face. He could see the sadness and emptiness. He remembered that feeling all too well when Kate left. Seeing Maggie hurting was like a punch to Edward's stomach. Against his better judgment, he reconsidered.

"Ok, Maggie. I'll go with you, but it's a one-time deal. We can have dinner with them, but schedule it sooner than later. I'm not dragging this out any further than we have to."

Maggie's face lit up. She was relieved she wouldn't have to endure this train wreck alone. She looked at Edward, seeing the compassion and warmth in his eyes, and again felt that she had misjudged him. As much as he sometimes annoyed her, his smile was one of the few things that made her days bearable at work anymore. She was about to ask him when she should schedule when he got a text. It was now Edward whose face beamed. He responded right away, laughing to himself at what he typed. This time, it was Maggie who felt like she had been punched in the stomach. Without a word, she headed back to her desk. He didn't notice.

Maggie shook her head in disbelief. She couldn't believe she was so affected by other people's lives. She didn't even feel like herself anymore. Renee was right. She can't live a life of comparison. It was making her even more unhappy. Yet she was. Maggie decided she needed to try again to cancel the dinner with Bob and Jessica. It had moved from inane to embarrassing.

Hi Bob - the saying is right. Small world indeed. It was lovely to see you last night - you and Jessica make a great couple. You should focus on your budding courtship. No need to thank us. Seeing you happy was thanks enough. Dinner isn't necessary. Wishing you all the happiness. - Maggie

Maggie opened her work email to start her day. She needed to be productive today. She felt like Steve was watching her more closely lately, and while projects were meeting deadlines, she knew she wasn't fully dedicated. She had 4 new emails, one of which was from Sheila. The subject line just read *Campaign Launch*. Maggie's stomach dropped. Maggie recently led the marketing launch of a new product on her biggest brand, and she feared the worst if Sheila was emailing.

Hi Maggie. I'm writing to thank you for your team's help on the launch! We could not be more pleased with the early results. Since launching, we've seen strong interest online beating our original KPIs, as well as higher than expected sales. Your team did an excellent job, and once again, you, Ms., have proven why I value your partnership on my business. -Sheila

A wave of relief washed over her, and she instinctively started to cry. The team had worked very hard on the launch, and while she recognized the work was strong, she also knew she hadn't poured her soul into it like previous efforts. Guilt had joined the other dozens of emotions she had been wrestling with for weeks. For a moment, she felt proud of herself again.

Dear Sheila - what great news to start the day! The team is really proud of the work, and it's great to hear that it's resonating in the market as well as we felt it would. And personally, thank you for your continued support of my leadership on the team. I can't tell you how much it means to me. -Maggie

Just as Maggie was about to compose an email to the team congratulating them on the success, her cell phone chimed with an email.

Maggie, don't be silly. Jessica and I are really excited to take you and Edward to dinner. I can't tell you how well it's going, and we would not have met if not for you. So please accept our invitation. We're really looking forward to it. How about Thursday? -Bob

Maggie rolled her eyes in disbelief. Talk about highs and lows. She messaged Edward.

Maggie: *Is Thursday after work open for dinner with Bob/Jessica?*

Edward: *If it has to be... yes. :(*

Maggie: *It has to be. I'll buy your dinner to thank you.*

Maggie and Edward didn't discuss dinner further over the next few days. In fact, they hadn't really talked much at all. Since Edward was completely smitten with Annie, he no longer was regularly checking Match. Maggie didn't want to discuss her dating woes, as there wasn't much to discuss anyways. They peacefully coexisted in staff meetings exchanging pleasantries and smiles. Jan took notice.

"Maggie, are you ok?"

"Living the dream. Yes, I'm ok. Why do you ask?"

"Well, for a while, you and Edward were becoming very friendly, and now it seems like it has reverted back to when he first started."

"Oh, well Mr. Charming has started dating. Frankly, it's a bit much for me to hear about. And no, it's not like when he first started. I can tolerate him now."

"Tolerate? Two-weeks ago you were on the precipice of friendship. Are you jealous?"

"Why does everyone keep asking me that? No, Jan, I'm not jealous. I'm frustrated and lonely. Those are markedly different emotions."

"First, lose the tone, Maggie. I'm asking because I care. We've been friends a long time. I'm just trying to see what's going on with you."

"I'm sorry, Jan. You're right. You don't deserve my attitude. Steve does, but you don't. No, I'm not jealous. I'm really not. What Edward does is his business. I just wish I didn't feel so alone. At least when he was in the dating pool, I had someone to commiserate with."

"Maggie, you just started dating. It takes time. Do you have any dates upcoming?"

"Does going out with Edward and two of our leftovers we fixed up count?"

"Maggie, no… That isn't going to help your situation. Was this another of Edward's bright ideas?"

"I wish it were. Unfortunately, this was all me and Mr. Pinot. I had too much wine and approached them when I was with my friend Renee."

"When is this shit show happening?"

"Tonight, after work. It'll be fast. It'll be ok. They want to thank us for fixing them up. After that, I don't have to see them anymore, and I don't have to deal with Edward except at work."

"Good. Because Maggie, you need to focus on you. I have to run to my next meeting, but I want details tomorrow!"

Jan sounded like Renee. They both say focus on yourself. Put yourself out there. Don't worry about Edward. It all proved easier said than done.

Despite hearing Edward working at his desk, Maggie messaged Edward instead of stopping to chat.

Maggie: *What time should we plan to leave work tonight? Dinner is at 6.*

Edward: *Well it doesn't take long to get there. So 5:45?*

Maggie: *Ok. I'll meet you there. I think I may go a bit early to grab a glass of wine. I think dinner will be easier to take with a drink already in me.*

Edward: *Sounds good. If I get finished early, I'll join you.*

Maggie kept looking at her phone throughout the afternoon hoping that Bob would email making some last-minute excuse to cancel. She hoped that was the ultimate plan of revenge. Alas, the email never came. At 5:30 pm, Maggie again chose to message Edward instead of talking to him. She simply noted, *I'll see you there.*

Maggie didn't know what to expect for the evening. Jessica had been so snarky the last they interacted; Maggie was still surprised she'd be ok with this dinner. Maggie also wondered how she should deal with Edward. Was he going to be distant? Was he going to try to leave as quickly as possible? For a dinner with no real consequence, she felt a terrible amount of nerves building.

When Maggie got to the restaurant, she texted Renee quickly for moral support.

Maggie: *I'm here. Really nervous. Feel stupid that I am, but I am!*

Renee: *You're already there. Consider it a funny life experience. You've got no skin in the game. Just have fun.*

Maggie: *I came early for a pre-game glass of wine. That should help.*

Renee: *Because it helped you so much last time. You should consider slowing down on the wine. Text me if you need a ride. Love you.*

As always, Maggie felt better after talking to Renee. She got out of her car, exhaled, and walked into the restaurant hoping that Bob and Jessica didn't arrive early as well. She hoped to have a single drink to herself. As luck would have it, the bar was virtually empty. Maggie ordered a Pinot Grigio, as she took out her phone to catch up on the latest BuzzFeed stories.

Maggie only had a few sips when she heard, "Hey! Glad I arrived before they did."

She looked up to see Edward smiling ear to ear. He quickly approached her and gave her a surprise hug. She felt his stubble against her cheek and could smell his cologne. Her pulse surprisingly quickened.

"Have you heard from them? Do you think they'll actually show? How was your day?"

Maggie was still a bit taken aback by Edward's about face from when he first accepted the dinner invite. He was so cheery and energetic. His smile was one of warmth, and his body language showed no signs of tension.

"I haven't heard from Bob. I was somewhat hoping he'd cancel, and we could forego this evening. You didn't seem too thrilled by the prospect."

"I know. I'm really sorry. I didn't react well, but I was talking to Annie about it. We had a good laugh. She made me realize that if their intentions are true, and if they really just want to thank us, then we should meet them reciprocally and enjoy dinner."

Maggie stopped listening the minute he mentioned Annie. She took a long drink of her wine and let him finish, acting as if she were paying attention. Her body language betrayed her.

"Something I said, Maggie? I thought you wanted me to join you. Should I leave?"

"No, no. I just had something on my mind. Don't pay attention to me. I'm glad you could join. You should order a drink, and we can toast to another successful match."

Edward didn't quite believe her. Since they had started talking more regularly and enjoying coffee chats in the morning, he had come to understand Maggie better - better than she realized. Edward knew something wasn't quite right, but he decided not to press.

"Cheers, Maggie. To helping people find true love, and finding love again ourselves…"

Maggie raised her glass, but she didn't say anything in return. She was finishing her first glass as Edward was just starting his. She ordered another.

"Hey, strangers. It's so good to see you both. I'm glad we could find a time to reconnect," Bob said jovially as he approached them in the bar.

Maggie was surprised to hear him speak with such emotion, as she remembered him a bit more dry. His comb over was just as bad as she remembered, though. She took another long drink of wine to keep from laughing.

Jessica followed closely behind with no real expression on her face. Maggie smiled and nodded at her and received a lukewarm smile at best. Maggie wanted to ask her what her deal was, but decided not to start the evening on the wrong foot.

"Jessica, you look just as lovely as I remember. Thank you again for inviting us to dinner. We're thrilled you and Bob are doing so well," Edward charismatically said as he gave her a hug. Again, Jessica just smiled meekly.

Bob did the majority of the talking for the two of them during dinner. Maggie listened and wondered why he hadn't been that engaged or interesting on their date. She considered that perhaps she was going to have to give people more of a chance to get past their first date jitters, but then she looked at his hair and remembered that was a significant strike. The other being that he was already talking marriage on the first date. She took another long sip of wine. By the time dinner ended, Maggie had finished 5 glasses of wine. She was about to order another when Edward interceded.

"We should probably start winding down," Edward said as he nodded to the waiter indicating no more. "Does anyone want dessert?"

No takers. The conversation had hit a bit of a lull as they waited for the bill. Maggie, having moved past buzzed around drink 4, looked at Jessica seriously.

"So, Jess, Jessie, what's the deal? You invited us to dinner, and you've barely spoken a word to us."

Edward closed his eyes and sighed at Maggie's faux pas. The table had another awkward silence.

"I didn't invite you. Bob did. He's excited to go out with anyone, and clearly, I mean *anyone*, that can see us as a couple. And please don't read me wrong. I'm happy with Bob. Thrilled in fact. But this dinner was awkward from the minute you suggested it last time you were *drunk* with us in a restaurant. We were clearly your bad date scraps that you thought you could connect for what? For shits and giggles? I don't want to be a part of that, but I'm here for Bob. You were so keen on the idea apparently that it took you how many glasses of wine to make it through dinner? No wonder you and Bob didn't work. He's too good for you. Bob, I'll be in the car. Edward, thank you for being a gentleman as always. I hope you and Annie continue to do well."

Maggie sat quiet for a moment, her face red with

embarrassment. Edward tried motioning for the waiter to speed up the process, but he couldn't get his attention.

"Bob, I'm so sorry. I really am happy to see you doing well as a couple. I'm so embarrassed."

"Maggie, I'm sorry, but you should be. Admittedly, Jessica was a bit chilly this evening, but she was at least polite. I just wanted to truly thank you both for helping us find one another. I view it differently than Jessica. I don't think you saw us as scraps. I think you saw two people who were better fits for one another. And I'm glad you did!"

Edward nodded furiously in agreement. "Yes, Bob. That was our intention. This was in no way some experiment. Maggie and I have had similar paths to finding ourselves back in the dating pool, so we've been sharing our experiences. When we discussed our dates with you and Jessica, it just sounded like you both wanted the same things, and it's proving true. So, thank you for inviting us to dinner."

"Bob, again, I'm sorry. Let me at least buy dinner since I ruined the evening. Please give Jessica my best."

Bob left shortly thereafter. Maggie knew she most likely would never see him again. She turned to Edward to try to explain, but his stern face was unwelcoming. He had pulled out his phone. Maggie could see he was texting Annie, most likely to describe what a debacle the evening turned out to be. She paid the bill quietly without saying another word, knowing the large dinner bill was suitable punishment for her behavior.

Maggie got up to go, as Edward continued to text. She just wanted to slip out.

"Where do you think you're going?"

"Home, Edward. I think it's time for me to go."

"I couldn't agree more, but you're in no condition to drive."

"Please, let me go. I'll be fine. I don't live that far from here."

"Maggie, this isn't up for discussion. You're not driving. I was just texting Annie that I'd be a bit late, as I needed to get you home safely. So, let's go," Edward said sternly as if reprimanding a child.

The mention of Annie and needing to report on when he'd be home, especially because he needed to take his drunk co-worker home, mixed with his tone, enraged Maggie. She didn't respond. She just started walking toward her car.

"Maggie, I'm not letting you drive," Edward said as he followed close behind her.

"Why don't you just go home to Annie? Perfect Annie."

"What the fuck is that supposed to mean?"

"Nothing. Good night, Edward."

Maggie tried to open her car door, but Edward moved quickly in front of her, closing the car door behind him. He was now leaning on her car.

"Move, Edward. I'm not your problem. I can handle myself."

"Oh, yeah, that really showed tonight. You handled yourself beautifully."

"Fuck you! You have no idea what I'm going through."

"No, of course not, Maggie. No one understands what it's like to lose the person you love most in this world. To have to start over. To have a shitty boss. You're the *only* one. Well fuck you too. I get it!"

"And you've moved on."

"Is that what this is about? That I've started dating someone. Do you… do you have feelings for me?"

"Not unless you count contempt at the moment."

Maggie reached again behind Edward to try to open the car door, but there was no way she was going to move him. She fell into his chest. She tried to stand up, but the alcohol was impairing her balance. Edward held onto her to make sure she didn't fall. She could feel the hair on his arms against hers. She looked into his dark eyes, and his look of annoyance had turned to concern. She just stared at him for a moment, again smelling his cologne. Instinctively, she leaned in and kissed him.

Fourteen

Edward didn't sleep much that night. The events of the evening kept playing in his mind, and the thought of how to deal with Maggie weighed heavily on him. He considered if he should've held strong and just skipped dinner, or if he could've contained Maggie to only 3 glasses of wine. Then maybe none of this would've happened. It was no matter now. He couldn't change it. He looked at the clock and knew he had to get ready for work, although he was far from rested. As he sat up to put his feet on the ground, Edward put his face in his hands confoundedly, as he said to himself, "why did you have to let the kiss linger? Why didn't you just stop it immediately?" He wondered if she thought he returned the kiss.

His shower was no more relaxing. As he felt the warm water hit his face, his mind continued to reel. At least the kiss helped control the situation. When Maggie realized what she had done, she was so mortified that she no longer fought Edward on driving home. She needed the situation to be done as quickly as possible. She agreed to let Edward drive her home, but not a word was spoken. She just walked meekly to his car. Before he could ask for directions, she allowed her phone's map app to narrate the way. As he pulled up to her house, she just got out without looking at Edward. She closed the door behind her, again without uttering a word. Edward waited to make sure she got inside before driving away.

Edward got dressed wondering what he should say to Maggie this morning. He considered that perhaps she would try to act like nothing happened to save face, but should he accept that approach? In his last few social interactions with Maggie, she drank heavily, and Jessica mentioned she was drunk when they had seen her as well. Yet he couldn't see Maggie as an alcoholic. Was he fooling himself? Should he try to intervene? Even without addressing Maggie's drinking, he didn't want it to be awkward at work, for either them or the team. They had finally reached a solid working team dynamic. He just felt befuddled. Edward kept trying to figure out why Maggie was acting this way. It didn't align to the woman he first met. He remembered her reaction to mentioning Annie, and again considered if she had feelings for him.

"Fuck it. I'm not going to figure this out. I'll never understand women. I'll just wait to face Maggie at work and see what happens."

He'd have to wait another few days. Maggie didn't show up to work on Friday. She had sent an email that morning to the team saying she was sick. Edward figured that based on how heavily she drank that may actually be true. He was relieved upon seeing her email. He wasn't ready to deal with any of it. However, as the day wore on, his feelings changed to one of concern.

"Hey Jan, have you heard from Maggie today?" he said as he popped his head into her office.

"No, Edward. She emailed this morning that she was sick. Why?"

"Ok. Just curious."

He walked away quickly before Jan could ask more questions. Jan was confused by the question. Edward would've been copied on Maggie's email that morning. She wondered what was up, but based on an impending deadline, she chalked it up to him having a work question and let it go.

Edward had a strange mix of emotions as he sat back at his desk and thought about Maggie. In one sense, he felt responsible for letting her drink that much without interceding. He even felt a tinge of guilt for how well things were going with Annie. He knew neither were merited emotions, but rationality didn't preclude emotions. Having been blindsided by Kate and his world turned upside down, Edward had sincere empathy for Maggie. On his worst days after Kate left, he just wanted to stay on the couch and not talk to anyone. Maggie lost her husband, and she didn't just shut down, although she had turned to drinking. He wondered which was worse.

Edward stared out the window pensively. He was frustrated that so much of this was out of his control. As he had done for most of his life, when he felt things spiraling, he wanted to talk with his grandma.

"Hey, Mom," Edward greeted his mother as she picked up his call.

"Hi, honey, why are you calling me during the workday? Is everything ok?"

"Oh yeah. I hope I didn't alarm you. Everything's ok. Just juggling a few things. I was hoping to go see Gram tomorrow. Will she be there? Or are you taking her to any of her appointments?"

"Edward, she would love that. She's been asking about you."

"Mom, I saw her not too long ago. Maybe two weeks back. It hasn't been that long."

"Edward, I didn't mean anything by it. You know she'd love to see you every day if she could, but I have to warn you she's been struggling of late."

"Struggling? What does that mean? I just saw her not that long ago. She seemed the same as she has been for a while. Certainly not gaining strength, but stable."

"Edward, she's tired. She's just tired. I've talked with her, and she says she's ready to go when the good Lord calls her home. But you know she's a firm believer that 'when it's your time, it's your time,' and not before."

"So, are we talking days? Weeks? How should I treat this visit? Am I saying goodbye?"

"You should treat this visit like it's special, like all of

your visits should be. Don't take it for granted. I can't say she will live another year. I can't say she'll live another week. I don't even know if she'll be awake when you visit her. But I do know she has been wanting to see you, and I'm happy you have time tomorrow to go."

"Mom! Why didn't you call me and tell me to go see her? What have you been waiting for?"

"Edward, she asked me not to."

"Mother, that's ridiculous. Why would she ask you not to, and why would you listen?"

"Edward, if you ever have a family and kids and have the privilege of growing older maybe you'll understand. She didn't want to burden you. She wanted you to come see her because you wanted to - not because she was frail. No one wants pity. She's a proud woman. You always tell me we guilt you - the one time I don't, and you're upset. You can't have it both ways, kid."

Edward sat silent knowing his mother was right, but felt frustrated anyway.

"Edward, are you still there?"

"I am. Sorry. Just add this to the list of my frustrations lately. I'll go see Eltz tomorrow - just not feeling as good about it as when I first planned. I wanted to talk to my Elsie. I need her still. I just don't know if my Elsie still exists. It's not fair of me to expect her to listen to my problems at this stage of the game."

"Edward, shame on you. Of course she still exists! She'd give or do anything for you and your brother. You know that. Her soul and heart have not been diminished solely because her body is weak. Perhaps feeling needed will give her a reason to keep going."

"Thanks, Mom. I see the Queen of Guilt has returned from her vacation. How was the stay?"

"Go see your grandmother, smart aleck. Call me and tell me how she is. Love you, bye."

Edward looked at the time on his phone as he hung up.

4:45 pm on a Friday. He knew it was futile to try to get anything more done today. Between his exhaustion from last night, his concern about Maggie, and now his sadness about what he would find when he visited Elsie tomorrow, he didn't have much more to give. Although he missed Annie, he was happy she had a work event tonight. Edward grabbed take out on his way home. He was enjoying an early, senior citizen dinner by 5:20 pm. He was asleep by 8 pm.

When Edward awoke the next morning, his mind didn't go instantly to Maggie. In fact, for the first time in a while, she didn't even cross his mind. His thoughts centered around Elsie and what life will be like after she's gone. He didn't want to start his day with tears. He just had a dull longing in his stomach at the thought.

"Hey, come on now, Edward. Don't go visit her feeling like this," he said to himself. "Go enjoy seeing her. Just don't take it for granted."

Edward left his house shortly after, feeling a bit better. He was off to get his two hot coffees. When he walked into the assisted living facility, the nurse greeted him with a smile. The staff had all come to know the many visitors Elsie received. On a weekly basis, at least 3 people normally would stop to see her. The staff had come to love Elsie too, even though they're trained not to get too attached. Based on how lovely her family was and how often they frequented, the nurses recognized a life well lived.

"Good morning, Edward. She's still sleeping. She's been sleeping more lately, and I didn't want to wake her. I checked on her this morning. She seemed comfortable. Have you talked to your mom?"

Edward knew that last question meant everyone is preparing for what's to come. His mom was Elsie's listed primary caregiver. The dull ache returned to his stomach.

"Thanks. Do you mind if I sit in her room for a while?"

"Of course not. You're more than welcome. Please let me know if she wakes up or needs anything."

As Edward headed toward her room, he wondered if this, in fact, would be his last visit. He stopped as a single tear rolled down his cheek. He didn't want to go in feeling like this nor did he want Elsie to wake up to see him emotional.

He took a few moments to compose himself in the hallway before going into her room. She was still asleep. Lying there sleeping in her nightgown, she looked frail - more frail than he realized. He normally saw her after she had already been dressed for the day. Her arms barely had any remaining musculature, and he could clearly see her spine as she laid on her side. It was a far cry from the stout grandma he remembered from his childhood.

He walked to the easy chair in the corner of her room. Normally, he may have opted to come back at another time, but another time wasn't guaranteed. He sat back, put up his feet, and pulled out his phone to read the morning news. After 20 minutes or so of reading in the quiet morning solitude, he nodded off.

He was awakened to a soft, yet stern, "young man, you're in my chair."

Elsie's voice startled Edward awake, but when he looked at her, she welcomed him with a warm smile. The nurse was wheeling her back into the room after getting her bathed and dressed.

"Good morning, Eltz. How are you? Wait. How are you already up and around? I just nodded off a few minutes ago. What time is it?"

"It's already 11 o'clock. I slept so late I missed breakfast. Good thing you brought me coffee."

"11 o'clock. You're kidding me! That means I was asleep for a good hour."

Edward noticed that Elsie seemed as attentive as she had been for his last few visits. She wasn't dozing off mid-sentence. He was comforted to see her stable. Perhaps his mom had just been overly concerned.

"You must've been tired. Eddie, tell me what has gotten you so weary."

"Oh Eltz, it's just been a crazy few weeks, but that's not important. I want to hear about you. How are you doing?"

"Eddie, I haven't left this place, except for a few doctors' appointments, in weeks. Nothing has really changed here since your last visit. But when my handsome grandson comes to visit me and falls asleep without waking up to me being pulled out of bed and put in a wheelchair, I want to hear what's going on in his life. Clearly you have more going on than me."

"Fair enough." He knew better than to argue.

"Eltz, I don't even know where to begin. I've started seeing this wonderful woman, Annie. From the time I met her, it has just seemed so easy. She's beautiful and smart. She's successful. She's a veterinarian, and she has this great dog, Bruno, that I can't get enough of. We take him to the park. The three of us hang out and cuddle. It's just going really well."

"And this Annie, is she the one keeping you up at all hours?" Elsie asked curiously.

"Oh Gram, I wish!" Edward said wryly.

"Is she the one, do you think? Should I be meeting her soon?"

Edward hadn't yet considered introducing Annie to his family, let alone to the person he most cherished. It was all too new. However, he realized time wasn't on his side if he wanted Annie to meet Elsie.

"Honestly, Eltz, I really like her. It's too new to say if she's the one, but I'd like to think there's enough potential to say maybe. If things continue going well, then yes, I certainly hope you can meet her."

"Don't wait too long, Eddie. I don't think I'm in it for

the long-game."

Edward's smile sank on his face. He took Elsie's hand and gave her a warm half-hearted smile as he looked at her.

"I'm not ready to say goodbye...." Tears welled in his eyes as he stroked her small, bony hands.

"We never are, Eddie. We never are. You have a lot of life to live. You have love and children to look forward to. I've lived my life. I've known great love. Don't be so focused on letting go. Go focus on living."

He looked down at his lap. He couldn't bring himself to look at her in that moment. He didn't want her to see him cry.

"I'll do my best, Eltz. I'll do my best."

She heard the pain in his voice and had the presence of mind to change the subject.

"Eddie, tell me what's been keeping you up."

"Gram, do you remember the woman, Maggie, that I told you about from work?"

"Hmm, I think so, but remind me."

Edward knew this meant she couldn't remember but didn't want to hurt his feelings - a trick she had used most of his life. His mother was right, glimpses of his Elsie were still quite alive.

"Well she's the one who lost her husband a while back. We have a similar job at work."

"Oh, yes. The one that was mean to my Eddie when you first started."

Edward laughed. "Indeed, she was!"

"Is she still mean? Is that what's keeping you up? If so, I'll cuff her one good."

"Simmer down there, Eltz! No, she hasn't been mean. In fact, we had been getting along quite well until late. We both had found ourselves unexpectedly back in the dating pool in our 30's, and we could relate to each other because dating has changed so much since we were in our early

20's. We were sharing our dating stories. We had found a nice common ground that spilled over in our work. We really started working well together."

"So, then what is it, Eddie?"

"Well, Gram, lately, she seems to be drinking heavily, and it's causing her to not be herself. She embarrassed herself at dinner the other night. Then when I tried to take her keys so she wouldn't drive drunk, she got mad, and even more belligerent when I mentioned Annie. To top it off, she went and kissed me out of nowhere. Then she didn't speak to me at all."

"Edward, it sounds like this young woman has feelings for you. Or at least, is confused by you."

"Gram, that's just it. I considered that, but I don't think that's it. She has never shown any level of interest prior to the other night."

"Oh, Eddie, you should know by now that women are terribly unpredictable and difficult to read."

"Truer words have never been spoken!"

"You said her husband died? She may not yet be able to process what she feels about him, about you, about the situation."

"Gram, she took 3 months off after he died. I carried almost all of her workload. We're going on just shy of a year now since he died. She needs to get it together."

"Edward. You listen to me, young man! Grief has no timetable. You can't prescribe how long someone is allowed to grieve. Until you go through it, you should not claim to understand it."

"I do understand. I lost Kate."

"No sir. That's a different situation. You can't compare the two. Her husband died. You and Kate broke up. There's a marked difference."

"Gram, Kate just up and left. No warning. No real explanation. It felt like she died. I was crushed."

"Edward, I wish there was something I could say to

make you understand. I know Kate broke your heart. However, as you processed that break up, you could come to terms with the fact that she left. Get angry. You could fall out of love. When someone dies, you don't stop loving them. If anything, that love freezes at that moment, and in some ways, grows as you mainly remember the reasons you fell in love. This woman had to learn to live again, and now she's trying to love again. That can be very confusing. Throw in a handsome, smart boy like my Eddie, and it's damn near mayhem. No wonder she's a mess."

"So, then what do you propose I do?"

"Do you have feelings for her?"

"No, Eltz, I honestly don't. I hadn't ever really even considered her as much beyond a co-worker until she kissed me."

"Eddie, if you don't have some sort of feelings for her, then why is she keeping you up at night? Why does she weigh heavily on your mind?"

"I guess I have compassion for her. Again, I can relate to being back in the dating pool. I understand starting over. I figured I'd try to help her where I can."

"Edward, just as women are complicated, men are basic. If a man is interested, he'll call; he'll write; he'll show up. For this woman to have this level of impact on you, I just don't believe you don't care."

"I do care for her. I want her to find happiness, and I certainly don't want her to fall into the abyss of drinking."

It was Elsie's turn to grab Edward's hand. She tried squeezing it for effect, but she barely had any strength in her hands. Her tone grew even more serious.

"Eddie, I'm happy to hear you're excited about Annie. And if she's the one, then I hope it works out for you. More than anything, I want you to know the kind of love your grandpa and me had. But if you and Maggie have this much in common, she weighs on your mind, and you're genuinely concerned about her, then perhaps you're not being honest with yourself about your own feelings."

"Thank you for the advice, Gram, but I'm telling you, it's strictly platonic."

Before Elsie could argue the point, her nurse interjected.

"Hello, I'm sorry to interrupt, but since Elsie missed breakfast, we need her to join us for lunch. We have to keep up her strength."

"I'm not hungry. I'm visiting my Eddie. I'll eat dinner later."

"Now, Elsie, you know you have to keep up your strength. You must eat something."

"Come on, Gram. Let's get you lunch. I've bothered you enough with my life for today. I'll be back soon to give you an update. Love you."

"Ok, but you never could bother me, young man. Will you push me to the table?"

Edward was more than happy to help push Elsie to the table. He leaned down and kissed her on the cheek.

"I love you, Eltz. I'll see you soon. You remember I'm not ready to say goodbye."

"I love you more. I do hope I see you soon. And you'll never be…"

Edward smiled faintly and walked quickly out of the facility before he started crying again. As he got in his car, he took a moment to think about this visit. Elsie was perhaps even more aware and attentive than she was during his last visit. He still couldn't understand why his mom had been so ominous when they spoke. Edward decided to give his mom an update.

"Hey, Mom. I just left seeing gram."

"Oh good, honey. How was she today? She was pretty weak, right? Are you ok? Was that hard for you? I tried to prepare you the best I could."

"No, Mom, that's what I wanted to tell you. She was

more alert than I had seen her in my last few visits. We visited for a good hour, and she didn't doze off once while we spoke. She didn't slur any of her words. It was like I was visiting with the Elsie I grew up with. It was a pretty special visit."

"Oh..." his mother responded before a long pause.

"What? It's a good thing. She seemed stronger today. I think perhaps you were a bit too worried, Mom."

"Edward, you're quite possibly her favorite person. I don't think we're fooling anyone by acknowledging that. It's not uncommon in these situations to have our loved ones use up their pools of energy to have a wonderful visit before letting go. She certainly wasn't going to let the opportunity pass to visit her Eddie."

"Mom, I'm not going to think that way. She looked decent, and she was responsive. She was alert. I took her to lunch myself so she could eat to keep her strength. I'm going to stay optimistic."

"As you should. I'm not ready to say goodbye either, honey, but she is. She's told me countless times she's ready to meet the good Lord. I just want you to be prepared is all."

"I'll look at a time this week to go back and visit. Today was wonderful. I'm not ready for it to be my last visit."

"That sounds great, honey. Let me know in advance if you figure out when, and maybe I'll join you."

"Sounds good, Mom. Talk to you later."

Edward hadn't started his day thinking about Maggie, but the conversation with his grandma had him revisiting the subject. As he drove home, he was even more unsure of what to say to or do about Maggie.

Fifteen

When Monday morning arrived, the pit in Edward's stomach returned as his alarm went off. Even after 2 extra days of weekend, he still wasn't prepared to face Maggie at the office. Despite needing to address the growing tension, he somewhat hoped she would try to pretend nothing happened. That may be an easy way out for both of them.

Edward arrived at the office to find another email from Maggie to the team stating that she would again be out sick. If she were trying to avoid him, how long could she stall by calling in sick? Edward considered that perhaps she really was ill. Then he felt guilty for thinking she was faking to avoid him. He recognized how much time he was spending thinking about this situation. He shook his head in frustration. He walked to the kitchen to get coffee in hopes the caffeine would help him focus on his work.

"Good morning, Edward," Jan said before taking a long sip of coffee. She beat him to the first cup.

"Good morning, Ms. Jan. How was your weekend?"

"Lovely - spent much of my time outside either in the garden or with my dogs. Hey, did you see Maggie's email? I'm starting to think I should be worried."

"It's probably nothing. It's only been 2 days."

"Nothing? Why would you say that? It's now been 4 days if you count the weekend, and this is absolutely not like Maggie to call in sick unless she were really sick. I'm a bit concerned. I think I'll call her today."

"Jan, maybe she's just dealing with some things. Why bother her? She'll be back when she's ready."

Jan had a skeptical expression on her face as she looked at Edward. She wondered why he was so intent on downplaying this. If Maggie weren't sick, she certainly intended to ask her what was going on when she called today.

"Indeed, she will. But until then, I'm going to call to check on her."

"Suit yourself. Let's just hope she's sick, and it's not something else that's keeping her away."

"Let's hope she's sick? Ok, what's wrong with you? What's going on between you and Maggie now?"

"Huh? Nothing. I'm just saying that with the Brian situation and her drinking, let's hope it really is explainable just by a minor stomach bug or something."

"Her drinking? Come again?"

Edward's face went white. He looked down at his shoes and tried to ask Jan about her garden, but she just gave him a puzzled look. There was a long, awkward silence in the kitchen as Jan waited for Edward to answer her question.

"Good morning, team. I hope you enjoyed your weekends," Steve said as he entered the room.

Jan's nose curled up in frustration as she looked at Edward. Her look told him this conversation was not yet over.

"I have good news for the team. I was going to stop by your status meeting this morning to tell the larger team, but I will tell you both now as a preview. I heard from Sheila late Friday during our quarterly business review. She was ecstatic about the latest launch performance numbers. She's really happy with the greater team's work. I was pretty pumped to hear this myself. She mentioned that she had reached out to Maggie last week. I wanted to connect with Maggie as to why I didn't get the update sooner. Is she here yet?"

Jan looked at Edward as she lifted one eyebrow. She didn't know what they should say to Steve considering Maggie's tenuous relationship with him. She hoped Edward would get her subtle facial cue and not say anything negative about Maggie.

"Steve, Maggie's a bit under the weather today. Hopefully, she'll be back tomorrow. If you need anything in the meantime, please let me know. I'm happy to handle. Maggie and I meet regularly now since her return to review the status of our projects, so I'm pretty up-to-speed. I think the team would love to hear the positive feedback straight from you at our status meeting. Please do join us."

"Edward, we're so lucky we found you. How do I find about 3 more of you for my other teams? I should be good for today, but I do need to connect with Maggie when she's back. I'd also like to connect with you this week too, Edward, when you have time. Put some time on my calendar."

As soon as Steve had walked out of the kitchen, Jan grabbed Edward by the arm.

"We need to talk as well. You're lucky I have a meeting, or we'd hash this out right now. This isn't over."

Edward watched as Jan walked out of the kitchen. He sighed in frustration as he poured a fresh cup of coffee wondering if he was doing right by anyone lately. He headed back to his desk to text Annie. She was the one bright spot of late.

Edward: *Hey good morning.*

Edward wondered if she would be with a patient, but thankfully she responded quickly.

Annie: *Hey! GM. How are you?*

Edward: *Ok. Anxious to catch up with you. ;) When are you free?*

Annie: *Anxious to see you too! I have late clinic nights today and tomorrow. Free later this week.*

Edward: *How about Thursday? I hate that we have to wait that long.*

Annie: *Sounds good. And me too!*

It had been a few weeks now since he had first met

Annie. Despite their busy schedules, they had managed to have about two dates per week. Edward had only told Annie a little about the drama with Maggie. Considering it was all so new, he didn't want to disrupt the strong connection that was forming. He did feel like he was hiding it from her, though, and it was starting to bother him. He didn't like to compartmentalize in that manner, especially with someone who he was starting to have feelings for. Instead, he tried to talk to her about his grandma and the difficulties he was having in processing letting go. Surprisingly, that was the one topic Annie seemed to avoid. She would often respond by trying to change the subject or keeping it surface level. It had surprised Edward, but he thought perhaps talk of intimate family dynamics was too fast for her. He was happy to stare at her beautiful face and discuss whatever she liked.

Edward considered texting Maggie to see if she were ok. He stared at his phone for several minutes contemplating whether to reach out. On one hand, he could break the ice and perhaps lighten the situation so Maggie felt comfortable returning to work. On the other hand, he felt like the discussion would be better in person. He was torn. He wished he didn't care. He asked himself why he did care so much considering how badly Maggie had treated him in the past and how erratic she had been. He thought back to their conversations, though, when she was the most honest with him, and he knew at the core of her being, she was a good person. Considering all she had been through, he wanted to give her the benefit of the doubt. Besides, they bonded over their mutual distrust of Steve, and he gave Maggie credit for her judge of character. And at her best, she was wickedly funny.

As Edward stared at his phone deliberating, he noticed the time. It was 9:15 am. He had burned almost an hour since arriving at work. Edward decided it was best to just leave it be for now. As his mind raced, he wasn't sure how he was going to focus on work. He decided to start with an easy task. He opened Steve's calendar to see when he may be able to connect. Edward wondered what he wanted to discuss now. He hoped he wouldn't put him in the middle of the Maggie situation. He had enough to handle with her, without feeling like he was playing middle man with their boss. Steve's calendar was almost completely booked solid for the next three days, and Friday was marked out of office. Edward picked 1:30 pm today. He really didn't want to meet with Steve so soon, but it's what was open. Edward was instantly annoyed with Steve's request. Why didn't he just say, "make time with me today as I'm full the rest of the week?"

Edward wondered if Jan knew what Steve wanted to discuss. He knew better than to seek her out right now, though. He was starting to feel alone. He wished he could deliberate with Maggie about the Steve situation. He recognized that he came to rely on their conversations more than he realized. She had been a strong sounding board.

Edward's morning continued to drag on as he couldn't get Maggie off his mind. Mainly, he convinced himself, he was worried about her well-being. When it came time for the staff meeting, Steve showered heavy praise on the team, including Edward, for the success of the recent launch campaigns. Even that felt hollow for Edward. He would normally have loved to congratulate and thank his team for strong work, but in his heart, he knew Maggie should be there both receiving the praise for her leadership, as well as providing it to their team. He worried Maggie's relationship was too far gone with Steve to truly correct. He wondered if she even wanted to. Yet, he considered that perhaps drinking had clouded her judgment on her professionalism.

While Edward sat pensively, Jan tried to get his attention. She wanted him to speak up for Maggie, to give the deserved credit in front of the team, since Steve hadn't. Edward remained in his own head. Despite the fact that he was thinking about Maggie, Jan only saw his silence. As Steve was about to leave, she interjected, smacking her hands loudly on the table as she stood up. This snapped Edward out of his daze.

Jan looked right at Edward with a look of sincere annoyance as she proclaimed, "I'm sure Edward will agree that this celebration wouldn't be complete without recognizing the efforts Maggie had put in to make this a success. I wish she could be here today to hear the great client feedback, but we hope she's better soon. We need her back at the helm."

As the team clapped softly for Maggie, Steve had a blank expression on his face.

"Yes, Jan, you're right. We also need to give Maggie credit for this strong work. I have to run to another meeting, but thanks again team for a great job. I'll make sure Michael knows of this success."

Jan again shot Edward a look of disgust. Based on the respect Steve had developed for Edward, Jan had hoped Edward would better support Maggie. Jan had worked with Steve for many years. He wasn't one to quickly change his opinion of someone once they pushed him too far. She recognized that Maggie's job may be in trouble. This worried her - Maggie made their team better.

Edward tried to approach Jan after the meeting to explain himself, but she was evasive. For the second time today, he felt overwhelmingly alone. Despite the recent stresses, Edward wasn't worried about his relationship with Jan. He knew she was just protecting her friend, and he respected her for that.

The look on Steve's face when she mentioned Maggie weighed heavily on Jan's mind. She feared Maggie's job was truly in jeopardy, so she texted Maggie to encourage her to come back as soon as she could.

Jan: *Hey, Maggie. I hope you're feeling better. Text me when you get this. Thanks!*

Jan hoped she would hear back quickly so she could confirm when Maggie would be back and move on with the rest of her day. Thankfully, Maggie responded within a few minutes.

Maggie: *Hi, Jan. I am feeling somewhat better thank you. What's up?*

Jan: *I wanted to see how you're feeling. Also, we really need you back here! Hope you can come back tomorrow.*

Maggie: *Did something happen? What kind of fire am I walking back into?*

Jan: *Oh no. Nothing like that. I just think it would help smooth everything over with Steve if you came back soon. He wanted to talk with you today.*

Maggie: *Oh. Him. I'll deal with that when I'm back. Thanks for the head's up.*

Jan: *Will you be back tomorrow?*

Maggie: *TBD.*

Jan didn't respond further. She was now irritated with Maggie as well. Both of her team leads were acting like petulant children, and she grew tired of trying to corral them. As much as she tried, it was too draining to worry about. She had a creative department to lead, and that was more than enough work without tending to the office drama. She decided to back off following up with Edward for now. He'd probably want to talk after his meeting with Steve anyway. Jan pulled up Edward's calendar to see when he had scheduled it. She was surprised to see it was happening soon.

Edward wished he knew how to better prepare for his meeting. He couldn't fathom why Steve would want to meet without Jan and Maggie. He took the little time he had to put together a brief executive summary on the business as precaution. When Edward walked into Steve's office, he handed him a copy of the summary.

"Hi Steve. Here's an overview of the business. I figured we could review…"

Steve put up his hand and stopped him mid-sentence.

"Edward, this is why we love you. Thank you for this. I'll review this afternoon. Not surprising that you again went above and beyond. I actually didn't call you in to discuss the status of the business necessarily."

Edward sat stone-faced. If he didn't want to discuss business, what was left? Steve was notorious for not discussing his personal life, and Edward certainly didn't want to discuss his with his boss. Edward started to become nervous that it wasn't good news.

"Michael, myself, and the rest of the agency's leadership committee have been discussing our recent growth and how we're going to restructure to support the growth. Michael has asked me to focus less on Crandon and start to oversee a few new pieces of business as well."

"Oh congrats, Steve. That's great news for you."

"No, Edward. That's great news for you. The reason I wanted to chat with you today is because Michael and I agree that we want to promote you to senior director on the Crandon business. While you've been with us, what, just a little over a year now, you have consistently exceeded all our expectations in leadership, account service, creative. I couldn't be happier with your work."

Again, Edward sat stone-faced. The news took him by surprise.

"I have to say, Edward, this wasn't the reaction I anticipated. You're awfully quiet. We're giving you a promotion - you should be excited!"

"Thank you, Steve. You've just caught me a bit off-guard with the news. As you can see by the summary I put together, I assumed you wanted to get tighter to the business since you mentioned this morning wishing Maggie would have filled you in sooner."

Edward stopped himself. He didn't want to say anything else that may paint Maggie in a negative light. In that moment, he also realized he would now be a level above Maggie at the agency.

"Well, Edward, yes and no. Of course, I want to be up to speed on the business when VP clients like Sheila are involved, but moving forward, I won't be as engaged in the day-to-day. I'm passing that baton to you. As for Maggie, now that you'll be leading the Crandon team, I can be candid with you. You probably already have noticed that there's some friction that has existed between us lately. I wish I could pinpoint why it started, but something changed after she came back from her leave."

Edward thought to himself, *yeah, she wasn't willing to put up with your shit anymore.*

"I recognize that Maggie is adored by your team. She has been a consistently strong performer for the agency. Making you team lead will have Maggie reporting into you, so there is a level between us. I'm sure she'll appreciate not having to deal with me as much."

Edward recognized already that he would be a level above Maggie, but hearing that she would report to him concerned him, although he couldn't divulge to Steve all that had transpired.

"So, Edward, congratulations. We're very proud of your work and happy for you. Any questions?"

"Yes. I actually have two. First, how will the news be communicated to the team and to Maggie? And second, how will my compensation change? Regarding the first, Maggie has done an outstanding job for this team. I know she's been leading it much longer than I have. I want to make sure that we message this correctly, as well as continue to make sure we do what's right for her career."

Edward was sincere in his concern for Maggie's well-being. While he was honored by the agency's faith in him, he also knew Maggie was as deserving, if not more so, of the promotion. He felt confounded.

"Ah, both great questions. I will tell Maggie when she's back, and the greater agency will learn at this Wednesday's town hall meeting. This is a great opportunity for you, and most likely will mean you will have more interaction with Michael, which should also set you up for long-term success here."

Edward heard "more interaction with Michael" and "long-term" in the same sentence and wasn't sure they could co-exist. He had been thankful to date that he hadn't had to deal with Michael's belligerence more since starting. The idea of having to deal with him more made Edward wonder about his tenure at the agency. This was only going to be a *job* for Edward so he could visit Elsie more. He certainly didn't expect to be promoted within a year.

As Edward thought about the news, Steve droned on about Edward's compensation change. Edward heard the numbers but wasn't fully present. He shook his head to feign listening as he continued to think about having to manage Maggie going forward. When Steve had finished talking, Edward stood up, shook his hand, and left without any further discussion.

As Edward walked back to his desk, he passed Jan's office. She was working alone, so he had the opportunity to stop in and give her the news. He didn't know what to say, and he didn't know how she would react. Of late, she was much more concerned about Maggie, so he wasn't looking to fight with her right now. He smiled and kept walking. Jan, having had her fill of the situation also, wasn't sad he didn't stop. She figured he would connect when he was ready. Her thought was if it were big news, he would tell her right away.

Monday proceeded without any further altercations, mainly because everyone retreated to their respective corners. Having already had the staff meeting in the morning, Jan and Edward chose to avoid each other and work independently for the rest of the day. Edward began Tuesday with yet another pit in his stomach, for he feared having to deal with Maggie on both the fallout from the kiss and now additionally the new reporting structure. There was still no need to worry. Maggie emailed in sick yet again. This marked the third straight business day and would mean 5 straight days of sickness including the weekend. It was starting to appear suspect.

No one seemed to notice, though, except Jan and Edward - Jan, because she was worried for Maggie's job, and Edward, because he knew he had to address the entire situation. Luckily for Maggie, Steve's calendar was too booked for him to seek her out, and Maggie wisely didn't copy Steve on her email to the team about her absence.

Jan decided to make one last effort to convince her long-time friend it was time to come back to work. She had known Maggie for years, and never in their entire working relationship, had she taken more than a single day off due to sickness. She knew there was something larger at play.

Jan: *Maggie... It's now been five days since you've been in the office. Tomorrow is our town hall meeting. Everyone will be present, and people, including Steve, are going to notice if you're not there.*

Maggie: *Hey, Jan. Thanks for looking out. I should be better by tomorrow. I'll see you at the town hall.*

Jan read the last text and was satisfied she had done her part to help. Shortly thereafter, Michael emailed the agenda for the town hall, which included a line item for *Team Changes & Updates*. Jan normally knew heading into town halls of any team changes, because often they affected her creative team as well. This time, however, she wasn't aware of any impending changes, nor had she heard any rumors. This made her incredibly nervous. Jan didn't like to be caught off guard with surprises, because she had no poker face to speak of. She wasn't fond of letting her team see her real-time reaction to agency news without first having time to process. While she still wasn't quite ready to be chummy again with Edward, she sent him an instant message to try to find out what he knew.

Jan: *Hey... yt?*

Edward: *Yeah, what's up?*

Jan: *Did you see Michael's email he just sent?*

Edward: *yep - should be a good town hall. We've had a lot of solid agency wins lately. Looking forward to seeing some of the creative presented.*

Jan rolled her eyes at the last message. While Edward's intent in responding was to be light and positive so he and Jan could begin communicating well again, Jan read it much more negatively. She wondered if Edward had drunk the Kool-Aid. In reading it, she could hear Steve's voice almost saying those words. Her trust of Edward continued to shrink. Still, she wanted to find out if he knew anything.

Jan: *Cool. Did you see the last line item about team changes? Know anything?*

In fact, he did. Edward took a minute to think about how he should respond. Normally, under different circumstances, he'd happily tell Jan about the promotion and getting a chance to take on a greater role leading the team. They had worked so well together in growing the business. He also knew that with their recent disagreements, Maggie issues, and over IM no less, this wasn't the time or opportunity to discuss. Yet, he didn't want to lie.

Edward: *Somewhat. No extreme changes to our team. More realigning resources to support the agency's growth. Our team remains you, me and Maggie at the helm. :)*

Jan felt appeased for now. As long as there were no major changes happening to the Crandon business, she could manage her reactions during the town hall tomorrow. Still, Jan felt it suspect that after such a short time at the agency, Edward already was in the know about personnel changes. Jan started to wonder if Edward was more ambitious than he had let on, if all this time he was playing both sides to get ahead. She sighed in frustration not knowing what to believe anymore. She knew her own career at the agency was inhibited by her unwillingness to play the political game under Michael's dictatorship. Jan did, however, worry that perhaps Maggie would be impacted by this and that's why Steve hadn't discussed it with her.

Jan tried not to let the town hall news impact the rest of her Tuesday, but different scenarios kept popping into her head. Each scenario was coupled with Jan's own brand of detailed implication analysis. Under Michael's Law, no one was ever truly safe, regardless of how good you think your work is, except for perhaps Steve. He had gained the Golden Boy moniker almost since day one. If teams were merging, new leadership was changing structures, or something else, it may mean trying for cost savings - aka headcount reduction. If history repeats itself, Jan's mind wouldn't truly be at ease until after the town hall meeting.

Thankfully, the town hall meeting was scheduled for early in the day on Wednesday, so Jan wouldn't have to endure the entire day. Jan walked into the office on Wednesday ready for three things: her coffee, the town hall, and with Maggie back, for things to return to normal. The first thing Jan did when she walked into the office was to walk to Maggie's desk to see if she were there. Jan had expected Maggie to get in somewhat early after having been out for several days now. Still no Maggie. Jan shook her head in bewilderment as she walked toward the kitchen.

As Jan approached the kitchen, she could hear Michael and Steve talking. She didn't particularly want to interact with either of them, and certainly not first thing in the morning before her caffeine. She waited outside the kitchen, out of view. She pulled out her phone so that if they walked out, she could feign distraction.

"It's pretty exciting these days, hey Steve? It feels like when we first opened again. Landing new business and getting to grow teams. I can't wait to get to work in the morning."

"I couldn't agree more. I'm excited to be spreading my wings beyond Crandon. I think I can better help the agency working on several accounts."

Jan didn't wait to hear anymore. She walked away in a huff. So, the big personnel change was that Steve was getting yet another promotion to multi-account VP? She couldn't believe it. She hoped Maggie could contain her disgust for appearance sake at the announcement. Jan knew Maggie had been working for a promotion for quite some time, and this may just be the final straw for her. As Jan sat back at her desk frustrated at both the news and her lack of coffee, she then began to wonder why Steve had told Edward already. Before she could give it much more thought, Maggie walked into her office.

"Good morning, Jan!"

"Boy, are you a sight for sore eyes. How are you feeling? I'm so happy you're back."

"Jan, I won't be coy. We've worked together over a decade now. You know I've never let a sickness slow me down. Last week was a low point for me. Probably the lowest since Brian passed, and frankly, I needed to take a mental health break. That's why they give us sick time, and I needed to use it. So, to anyone who inquires, I was, in fact, sick. How's Edward been?"

Jan's suspicions were confirmed, although she was happy to hear her friend was taking care of herself. Jan thought it was odd, though, that Maggie's first question was about Edward.

"He's been fine. A little distant. Did something happen between you two? He was acting weird last week wanting to check on you, but I told him to leave you alone."

"Nothing to speak of. And thank you. I absolutely needed some time away. I should be ready to go now. I'm going to try to get through a bunch of emails before the town hall. I just wanted to stop and say hi and thank you for your continued support. I'm going to be ok. Promise."

Maggie looked out of Jan's office both ways, as if she were going to cross a busy intersection. She then scurried to her desk and quickly sat down. Jan didn't know if she were avoiding Steve... or Edward. Either way, it was clear Maggie was not ready to face them. Jan looked at her clock. The town hall would start in an hour. That was just enough time to finish her needed two cups of coffee. She hoped Michael and Steve had returned to their respective offices by now. Jan laughed to herself. She had avoided them like Maggie was avoiding Edward and Steve. Jan shook her head at what a soap opera this place had become. She wondered how they made money, as they broke most organizational best practices.

As Jan headed toward the kitchen, she saw Edward as he was taking off his coat at his desk. She wanted to wait to see if there would be an awkward interaction between him and Maggie, but she knew standing and gawking would be too conspicuous. She instead headed toward the kitchen in hopes Maggie would be more open after the town hall.

For his part, Edward wasn't aware Maggie would be back today. In fact, he wasn't sure when he'd see her again. He was, thus, unprepared to be face to face with her as he rounded the cubicle wall to head toward the kitchen.

"Oh, hi," Edward said a bit flustered. He wasn't sure why he felt awkward. He hadn't done anything wrong, except try to help her.

"Hello, Edward. How are you?" Maggie responded

exceptionally composed, having had a few days to gather herself.

"We should probably plan to catch up later. After the town hall. I think it would help to be on the same page," Edward said more calmly, recognizing that Maggie wasn't conveying a sense of nerves.

"Edward, I think we're good for now. I just need to dig out from being out the last few days. Perhaps we can catch up early next week."

Edward, of course, was implying a need to talk about the new team structure, but he couldn't tell her that. He was counting on Steve to have that discussion with Maggie. Maggie assumed Edward wanted to rehash the events of last week, which she had decided she was going to simply move on and pretend didn't happen. She couldn't change it, but she was damn well not going to talk about it at length.

Edward just shook his head in response, preferring to placate Maggie for now. As he walked away, he looked at his watch, which read 9:15 am. Town Hall would start in 45 minutes. He hoped Steve would stick to his word and talk with Maggie, even if just briefly. In fact, Edward was so adamant about Maggie finding out first, he turned around and sent Steve an instant message that simply read, *Maggie is back. Please talk to her before town hall.*

By the time people started gathering in the center of the agency's large atrium for the town hall, the creative team had already started putting up boards showcasing their latest work. When Edward arrived, he looked at the series of 5 creative campaigns that would be shared today, one of which was the Crandon team's new product launch. He acknowledged that their agency really did do strong work. Despite having accepted the job as simply a way to move home, he was proud of his team. Even with his hesitation about being a leader in this particular organization, he was excited by the opportunity. As the last few people shuffled in, Michael kicked off the town hall.

"Welcome everyone. Nice to see everyone gathered today. We've had an exciting few months since we last gathered. I continue to be proud of this agency and the work we're doing. Based on the new business we've been winning, it's being recognized in the marketplace."

Edward marveled at Michael's Jekyll and Hyde personality. How could someone be so warm and charismatic in one moment and a crazed, yelling maniac in the next? He wondered how he was able to build such a strong business with that leadership style. Yet Edward couldn't deny Michael was right - they were winning strong new business and producing very high-quality work.

For the next 30 minutes, each creative team lead, including Jan, reviewed the business objective provided by the client, the insight that led to the creative idea, and the final campaign creative. By the time the last campaign was shared, the audience was growing restless, as people started playing with their phones.

Michael was annoyed by this when he returned to the mic. "Ok phones away. We allocate this time to learn from each other. I'm hoping you're responding to clients, and that's why you couldn't wait 15 minutes before looking at your phones. I'm realistic that's probably not the case. Geez guys. Come on!"

Unfortunately, that was a hard transition to personnel news. Michael's tone was a reminder to the agency that they worked in an environment of tyranny. At this point, few people were excited to hear about team updates.

"Ok, thank you for putting your phones away. I wanted your full attention because I have exciting news for our agency. We just went through all this great creative work. It shows how strong we are together. That strength has led to a few recent business wins. I needed to look more broadly across our company to see how we should support this growth to make sure we're still well positioned to deliver the quality our clients expect. Therefore, I am moving Steve to be a group VP over Crandon and 2 of the new pieces of business. He'll be responsible for executive engagement at these 3 companies and look for ways to organically grow these accounts. Please join me in congratulating Steve."

There were blank stares as people looked at each other confused. They clapped softly and politely, but it certainly wasn't a thunderous response. Steve had just been promoted within the last few months. It was yet another reminder that the Golden Boy would be rewarded for the work of the serfs. Maggie looked at Jan with a look of complete disgust and contempt, for which she made no attempt to mask. Jan could only respond with raised eyebrows. She knew she would probably have to cool Maggie down after the meeting. Steve approached the mic as the dull clap subsided.

"I want to thank Michael for this opportunity, and I want to thank the hardworking Crandon team, which I've been proud to lead over the last few years. I'm excited to be taking on a few new challenges, while still working with my Crandon team to grow that strong business. As you just saw when Jan reviewed our recent product launch creative, that client is beyond thrilled with our work. They're seeing strong sales results, and that's because of this team. I'm hopeful that I can take that team recipe and grow our new businesses, but I didn't come up here to talk about me."

"Change creates opportunities for multiple people, so as I take a step away from the Crandon business, Michael and I are excited to promote Edward to senior director leading that business. Since joining us, he has shown exemplary leadership in the face of multiple curve balls thrown his way, from leaves of absences to growing workload as the client gave us new work. He has risen to

195

every challenge presented to him. We're confident he'll continue to grow the Crandon business. That team will remain the same, just reporting into Edward now instead of directly to me. Please give Edward a round of applause. Thank you everyone. With that the town hall has concluded."

Jan couldn't believe it. That's why Edward had known what was happening. She felt betrayed and lied to. Edward hadn't mentioned anything about this. It was official - he was a Steve crony.

Maggie! Jan looked over to where she was sitting, but she was already gone. Jan hurried to Maggie's desk. When she got there, Maggie's face was beat red. Maggie looked up at Jan and simply said, "I'm done."

"What do you mean?"

"Today is my last day. Effective immediately. I don't need this bullshit anymore. I've worked here how long? Growing this business to what extent? That creative today... that was ours, Jan. That was my part of the business, and my team's product launch. To give Edward credit for that is sickening."

"Well, that's not exactly what Steve said, Maggie," Jan said trying to cool her friend down.

"Don't, Jan. I don't want to argue semantics. I've been vying for a promotion for over a year to lead this business, and to give it to Edward who has been here for a year total? And for me to find out like that? Utter bullshit. They have no respect for me. Misogynistic assholes! Michael never saw me as part of his leadership team. It's a sausage club. To that I say, they can suck my *dick!*"

Jan couldn't help but laugh at that. Maggie shot her a look of disdain.

"Jan, I'll miss you. And I'll miss this team, but it's clear I'm not part of the future here."

"Are you sure you want to be this hasty? It is easier to look for a job when you have one. Maybe take a day to

196

cool off?"

"No. They don't deserve me or my work. I have too much self-respect to offer them another second of my time."

"Are you ok financially? Are you sure you can swing this?"

"Jan, thank you for your concern. Truly. But I'm going to be fine. Fortunately, or unfortunately, I have Brian's life insurance money. That buys me time to figure this out. It also buys me a one-way ticket to never have to deal with that fucking weasel, Edward, ever again."

Edward had approached his desk just as Maggie was calling him that. He shook his head expectedly.

"Maggie. Can we talk?"

Maggie slapped her hands down on her desk furiously, but before she could say anything, Jan intervened.

"Not now, Edward. You got what you wanted. You got what you played us for. Congrats. You won. But it's too soon for your victory lap. Now go away."

"What are you talking about?" Edward said confused.

"Fuck you, Edward," Maggie hissed.

"It seems we all need to get on the same page. Cool our jets. Let's grab a conference room and discuss this professionally."

"There's nothing to discuss, Edward. I quit. Effective immediately. You clearly used my personal situation to angle for a promotion. Well, kudos to you. My husband dies. I take a leave, and you get promoted. Well *this* is all yours now. I hope you're proud of yourself. I hope you and Annie have a real good laugh about how stupid I am tonight."

That last comment angered Edward. It was purposefully personal and pointed. He responded in kind.

"That's not how this played out at all, Maggie. I've done nothing but try to help you for the last few months since you've been back, and you were beyond help. I tried my damnedest to curtail your spiral. So, if you're feeling bad about this, you have no one to blame but yourself."

Maggie grabbed her purse and ran out of the office leaving all of her stuff beyond. She didn't want to give Edward the satisfaction of seeing her cry.

Jan punched Edward in the arm. "You're a real jerk!"

"Hey, how is this all on me?"

"You're kidding, right? Do you see what you've done to her?"

"Jan, you don't know the whole story."

"I know enough, Edward. You have your promotion. Congrats. And since I can't afford to quit myself, we'll find a way to work together. But just know the trust is gone. We're co-workers that's it. You've driven a close friend and a strong teammate away. I hope you're proud of yourself. As leader of the team now, you can explain this to the team because I'm not."

Jan walked away leaving Edward feeling shell-shocked. He had anticipated Maggie being upset, but it was clear she wasn't made aware of the change before the town hall. His face turned red in anger. He went to Steve's office and closed the door.

"Not now, Edward. I'm in the middle of something."

"Steve, did you tell Maggie about the changes prior to town hall as you had promised me?"

"Unfortunately, I didn't get the chance. I was in meetings all morning, and I hadn't seen her. But Edward, that does not give you the right to barge into my office."

"Well, Steve, she just quit. Effective immediately. I hope you're happy. Is this what you wanted all along? To push Maggie out?"

"Edward, I'm going to give you the benefit of the doubt here, but bud, you're way out of line. You need to leave my office and remember you don't talk to me like this. We're done here."

Edward shook his head in anger and walked out. He

felt like the fall guy. He stormed back to his desk, his chest heaving. He had expected a rocky reception from Maggie, and perhaps he should've anticipated this reaction. Yet, he truly believed Steve would honor his word to tell Maggie beforehand. Now both Maggie and Jan think this was his plan all along. Edward slammed his fists on his desk in anger. He was a man of principle, and if he had been so cunning that would be one thing. But it cut him to his core that Jan and Maggie could think that of him. It also confirmed his belief about Steve. He questioned whether Steve ever intended on telling Maggie. Edward didn't believe Steve ever planned on getting his hands dirty.

"Excuse me, Edward."

"What!" he hollered as he turned around. There stood the traffic coordinator, Angela. Her already large doe eyes grew even larger, and her face reddened at his angry tone.

"I'm so sorry to bother you. Should I come back?"

"No, I'm sorry. I'm just having one of those days. I want you to feel you can come to me. I'm sincerely sorry. What can I do for you, Angela?"

"Well, I've been searching for Maggie for the last 15 minutes. We need her sign off to release this art to print, and I can't seem to find her anywhere. It's due out the door by noon, and with the town hall meeting this morning, we're racing to get this to print. Could you sign off on this?"

"Unfortunately, Angela, I don't think you're going to find her anytime soon. Sure. Let me review quickly. There you go. You should be good to go."

"Edward? Has she left for the day? I have a few more things due to release this afternoon."

"Angela, if I'm being honest, I'm not sure when she'll be back. Feel free to route through me for the time being. I'm hoping she'll be back sometime soon."

As Angela walked away, Edward's mind raced. He

wondered if Maggie was really quitting for good, or if she just needed some time to cool down. He didn't want to add to her tailspin. He needed to get Jan's perspective, and despite emotions being high, he didn't want to wait to address this.

He walked directly into Jan's office where she was reviewing a creative brief with two of her junior art directors.

"Excuse me, guys. Sorry to interrupt, but I really need to talk to Jan. It's quite urgent. I wouldn't intervene if it weren't time sensitive. You understand I hope."

"Edward, this is bullshit. No, guys, stay. He can excuse himself and come back later. Edward, I already told you not now. Not today."

The 2 junior art directors looked at each other with utter confusion. They didn't know whether they should stay or go. So, while they had stood up, they hadn't moved further. They had never heard Jan talk to anyone like that, let alone the new senior director on the business.

"Jan, we need to talk. It's not up for debate. Gentlemen, I appreciate it." He ushered them out before closing the door behind them.

"Edward, you mother fucker! I can't believe you just did that. I can't believe you think you can throw your weight around 2 hours after being goddamned promoted. Kiss my ass. We were working."

"I get that you're upset. I can understand why you think you know the situation, but you don't. We're clearing the air. We're clearing the air right now. And when you know the entire situation, perhaps then, you won't be so quick to judge," Edward said tersely and matter-of-factly.

"Ok. So, tell me. Tell me how you didn't screw over Maggie and lie to me."

"Jan, I haven't been telling you everything that has been happening with Maggie out of respect for Maggie. Yet, if I don't, I'm going to be condemned in the school of public opinion. So, you should know, she's been drinking heavily, at least drinking heavily the last time I was out with her. She got sloppy drunk, and you saw it too the last time we all traveled together. She made a complete ass of herself and embarrassed the couple we had dinner with. To top it all off, she kissed me in the parking lot as I tried to stop her from driving. That's why she didn't come to work the last few days. She was avoiding me."

Jan's face registered no emotions. She knew instinctively Edward wasn't lying. She had worried about Maggie the last time she saw her drink. And she remembered thinking it curious that Maggie's first question when she returned was about Edward.

"Fine. Maggie isn't blameless here. She's been in a delicate balance to keep it all together since Brian died. Why did you have to aggressively pursue the promotion and be so deceptive about it? Did you really have to take advantage of her leave for your own gain? Are you that ambitious?"

"Jan. After being in the trenches together for the last year or so, you know me. Do you really think I'm that good of an actor? Do you think this was all part of some grand, elaborate plan? Why won't you give me the benefit of the doubt?"

"Because you lied to me when I asked if you knew anything!"

"If I had answered, yes, Steve promoted me, and I'm going to be running the business over instant message, would that really have helped the tension between us? How would you have handled it, your highness? I'm doing the best I fucking can! Jesus, Jan. Give *me* some credit. I know you and Maggie are close, but you've been alongside me for the last year. Do you really think I did this to hurt Maggie?"

"I don't know what to believe, Edward."

"Steve got promoted. No shock there. We won new

business, and of course Michael bestowed yet another promotion on him. Steve thought it would be better for Maggie to have a level between them based on the tension lately. I didn't ask for the promotion. It wasn't even on my radar. Steve told me out of the blue. If anything, Maggie's attitude doomed her for the promotion. Steve wasn't going to move her up to work even more with her. Jan, I even asked Steve to tell her in advance of the town hall so she had time to process. I wanted to give Maggie that. Of course, the jackass didn't, and I became the fall guy. And here we are. So there. Now you're up to speed. I didn't want Maggie to quit. She's a great asset and partner. I'm not sure after all that has transpired if she would even want to work with me, but Jan, I think we have to try."

"Edward, all I can say is thank you, and I'm sorry. Thanks for bullying me into listening. I'm not sure I would've listened otherwise. And I'm sorry for instantly believing the worst. I guess when it comes to Maggie, my first instinct is to protect her, and I hadn't considered how self-destructive she's been lately."

"Cool. Exhale. Jan, of all people, I don't want to fight with you. Now that we're aligned, how do we get Maggie back?"

"Edward, I don't think she's coming back. I tried to convince her to stay, and she's pretty intent on moving on."

"Jan, that was the heat of the moment. We can convince her otherwise, no? She's great at her job. The clients love her, and frankly, we need her."

"Well I can certainly try. I will call her after work and keep you posted."

Edward got up and hugged Jan surprising her. She wasn't a hugger by nature preferring distance, but as his hug lingered, she knew he needed some solace. So, she patted his back as he breathed deeply. No further words were spoken as he walked out, turning back to bow his head to thank her.

Jan thought for the rest of the day how she'd broach the subject with Maggie. Should she wait a few days to call or try to reason with her to minimize the damage? Her anxiety rose as the day wore on. By the time she got home and settled, her heart began to beat heavily as she looked at the clock on her stove. 6:56 pm. She planned on calling Maggie at 7:00 pm to try to reason with her. She could just as easily call her right now, but waiting until 7:00 pm on the hour just felt like the right thing to do, as arbitrary as it was. Jan was nervous. After years of working together, she didn't understand why, but she was. Perhaps it was because she knew this wasn't the same rational, thoughtful Maggie she had known. This was an impulsive, angry Maggie.

As the clock rolled 7:00 pm, Jan sighed and started dialing. She wasn't sure if Maggie would pick up. Part of her hoped she wouldn't, but that was delaying the inevitable. She needed to talk to Maggie. After 3 rings, she heard Maggie's voice.

"Hi Jan. Miss me already?" Her voice seemed lighter, as if nothing had happened.

"Maggie. How are you? Have you settled down?"

"Jan, I feel great. This is probably the best I've felt in a long while. I had been waiting for something to push me forward, and I guess this was it. It was time."

"Ok, good. I'm happy to hear that. Well, not happy to hear you've left, but happy to hear you're doing ok. You know... I talked to Edward. I don't think it's what you thought."

"Jan, stop. It doesn't matter. I don't care to hear it. What did or didn't happen no longer matters. It no longer pertains to me. Edward can have Steve. They're a match made in hell. Good for them. As I said, it forced me forward, and for that I should be grateful. I don't want to revisit it."

"But Maggie, it's not what you think. Edward..."

"Jan! *Enough*. It doesn't matter," Maggie abruptly cut Jan off. "I don't need to see or talk to Edward anymore. I'm closing this chapter and starting to think about what's next. Well, not right now. I'm going to take some time and then figure it out."

Jan knew there was no further point in discussing. "Ok, Maggie. Final word to leadership is you're done? You're not going to change your mind? Edward is hoping you'll come back."

"For what? To be his whipping post some more? No, I'm good. Final answer: Maggie quits."

Jan continued with some small talk as to not hang up right away, but the conversation died shortly thereafter. Jan wished Maggie the best of luck on the next chapter and told her to keep in touch. Despite all their years together, she wasn't convinced she'd hear from her again considering all that had transpired and Maggie's desire to distance herself from the company. Jan hung up with a lingering feeling of sadness.

Jan opened her email and sent Edward a quick note:
To no avail... she's not coming back. (EOM)

Sixteen

Edward walked into work on Thursday knowing he'd have to call a special meeting with the team. Since the announcement was made that he was new team lead, Edward knew Steve would put forth no further effort on what he would consider a minor personnel issue. Edward did, however, want Steve's opinion on how to handle with the client. Maggie was well-liked, hell loved, by her clients, especially Sheila. Edward wanted Steve's input as to whether he should connect with Sheila, or if Steve wanted to handle it.

"Hey Steve, do you have a minute?" Edward said as he peeked into his office as Steve sat nonchalantly clipping his fingernails.

"Sure, but I just have about 5 minutes before my next meeting. Busy day."

Edward tried to refrain from rolling his eyes, considering he was handling personal grooming instead of actually working.

"Jan connected with Maggie yesterday just to confirm she was, in fact, not coming back. It appears she's officially done."

"Wow, that's pretty unprofessional of her. She couldn't even give two weeks notice. Great way for her to go out on top. It's become par for the course lately, though."

Edward couldn't believe it. The audacity in which this man operated continued to escalate. He wanted to punch his long, gaunt, smug face. Yet he stymied his reaction, mainly because he had to.

"How would you like to communicate the news with the client. Since we have no notice, and emails and calls will be coming in, I need to communicate quickly. I figured I'd reach out to the majority of the team. That's no problem. Do you want to discuss with Sheila? Or should I?"

"Oh… yeah. Sheila." Steve paused for a moment. "Why don't you communicate it. I want to establish you as the new Crandon lead for us, and this is as good of time as any."

"Sounds good. Thank you."

Edward didn't wait around for further conversation. He abruptly got up and walked out. Edward had already expected that answer, so it didn't surprise him. Steve wasn't one that liked to get his hands dirty. Another in a long line of smoke and mirror tactics Steve employed to stay above the fray.

Edward looked at Maggie's calendar first to see which client meetings were scheduled for today. He needed to know which he could attend and which would have to be postponed. He then emailed Sheila asking for time at her earliest convenience to connect. He next drafted an email to Maggie's clients, which he'd wait to send until after he discussed with Sheila. Finally, Edward set up an internal meeting to address his own team. He scheduled that as early as he could. Edward understood then why two weeks notice had become the standard. But who could blame Maggie? He sighed at the shit storm he was in.

Edward gathered the entire Crandon team shortly after 9:30 am. Most people had arrived by then. Edward looked around the conference room. At quick glance, it appeared maybe only 3-4 people were missing. This would have to suffice for now.

"Good morning, team. Thanks for gathering on short notice. We needed to come together because I have news, and I want to be able to answer questions. Unfortunately for us, Maggie has decided to leave the agency. We have lost a great talent, and we'll miss her. We wish her well in her new endeavors. Maggie decided yesterday was her last day, so we do not have the luxury of advance notice. In the short-term, I am going to try to handle as many of her meetings as possible. I will most likely need to reschedule a few based on overlaps with some of my existing client meetings. All work should stick to current due dates. If something is scheduled to release to client, and you haven't heard from me, message me. Right now, we need to help each other be accountable until I can create a game plan and find a rhythm across the entire business. I'm sure it won't be perfect, but I trust this team. We can continue to exceed client expectations with little to no disruption. I know many of you have worked with Maggie for many years, and this is quite sudden. I'll say to you, I'll miss her too. She was very valued on this team. I want to open it up for questions or concerns now, though, so we can all leave here feeling good about delivering against our open projects."

The room fell silent. There were awkward glances and tense shifting as the lingering silence only made the elephant in the room larger. After what seemed like an eternity, a senior art director on Jan's team, Dan, raised his hand. Dan had been on the team for several years, having joined the agency with a storied advertising career already under his belt. For many, this felt like Dan's last ride until retirement. As such, Dan didn't mind speaking his mind.

"Edward, we all have confidence in your ability to take this thing forward. But come on, man. Let's get real. The timing is wholly suspect. Maggie quits the day you get promoted to team lead. That's not our Maggie. So, what gives?"

Edward's face turned red. The room read it as anger toward the question, toward Dan, but it was anger toward what Edward considered being the cause of Maggie quitting. In that moment, he knew people blamed him for losing Maggie, and it pissed him off. He could say that to Jan behind closed doors, but how could he be that open to his team?

"Dan, it's a fair question. If I'm being honest, there are several layers of complexity that out of respect for Maggie, Steve, and our entire team, I'm not going to get into right now. I'll try to be as transparent as I can. As an agency, we're doing very well right now. We're winning new business and growing. Michael made a leadership decision to move Steve forward to lead multiple accounts. Steve made the choice that I would lead this business. I very much wanted Maggie to be part of my leadership team and viewed her as an important asset on our account. She made the decision that it wasn't the right team for her going forward. I have to respect that. What else?"

People nodded their heads with no further questions, as the awkward silence returned. Edward adjourned shortly thereafter with an impromptu "go team!" speech, but even he knew it fell on deaf ears.

When Edward returned to his desk, he had received a response from Sheila indicating that she was available at 10:30 this morning. He acknowledged that it was better to handle early so he could let the rest of Maggie's clients know of the change, but he certainly wasn't looking forward to it. He spent much of the next 45 minutes drafting and editing talking points to be prepared, as he expected Sheila to be tough.

Edward's stomach was in knots as he dialed. "Hello, this is Sheila."

"Good morning, Sheila. It's Edward. Thank you for making time on short notice."

"Sure, Edward. Surprised to hear from you, especially needing to connect so quickly. I have my call with Steve tomorrow."

Edward rolled his eyes and punched the air in frustration. Of course, Steve didn't mention that he'd be talking to her the next day. Edward couldn't believe what an A-1 asshole he was. Yet he still had to play the political game.

"Well, thank you for making time. I wasn't aware you were connecting with Steve. I'm sure he will address with you as well. There's no easy way to say this, but I need to let you know that Maggie is no longer at the agency. Her last day was yesterday."

There was dead air on the phone for a solid 20 seconds before Sheila responded tersely, "Tell me what happened."

"It was Maggie's decision, as she opted to leave for other opportunities. It was not our choice."

"Edward, I'm sure you're just the messenger here, so I'll do my best to spare you, but I'm calling bullshit on this. I've worked with Maggie a long time, and frankly, she's the best I've ever worked with at an agency. I also know her well enough to know she would've let me know well in advance if she were taking another career opportunity. So, thank you for letting me know. I'll discuss in more detail with Steve tomorrow. Take care."

With that she hung up. She didn't wait for further discussion around how the account would be handled. Edward considered giving Steve an update on Sheila's response, but he decided to extend the same graciousness he received from Steve. He'd let him find out on his own. Edward opened his calendar to figure out the rest of his day. Now that he would have to lead the entire account for the agency, as well manage the day-to-day of both sides of the business, he felt overwhelmed by everything. He was due into his next meeting in 5 minutes, but feeling beat down and let down, he just wanted to put his head down. He got through it before, he could do it again he reassured himself.

Sheila's monthly call with Steve was scheduled for tomorrow at 10 am, but she was so livid she couldn't wait another 24 hours to talk to him. Steve saw the number on his phone and considered avoiding it. He also knew Sheila wasn't one to randomly call.

"Hello, this is Steve."

"Steve. Sheila. Why is Maggie no longer on my business?"

"Hi, Sheila. Maggie has chosen to leave the agency. This was her choice. We valued her contributions."

"Why did she choose to leave?"

"Sheila, it came as a shock to us as well. You'd have to ask her as to why she thought this was the best time to pursue new opportunities."

"Steve, I've always been respectful, but I'm calling bullshit. So, cut the crap. If I find out second hand the situation, I'm going to be even more pissed. So, tell it to me straight. Why did Maggie leave my business?"

"Again, Sheila, Maggie was a valued director on your business. We certainly were not looking for her to leave. I wish I could shed more light, but honestly, I have no insight as to why she left."

"Fine. Thank you for your time. Consider this our monthly one on one. We don't need to catch up tomorrow. I'll use that time to catch up with Maggie."

Steve heard the phone slam down. Sheila wasn't one for idle threats. He knew she would pursue Maggie until she had the reason. Steve walked to Michael's office to do damage control.

"Michael, do you have a minute?"

"Always for you, Steve, but just a few. What's up?"

"I just got off the phone with Sheila, VP at Crandon. She's not at all happy that Maggie is no longer working on her business."

"Wait. What? Why? Why isn't Maggie on her business?"

"You haven't heard? She quit yesterday."

"And she didn't have the decency to tell me? She's worked here for a decade, and she couldn't tell me herself? That's disappointing."

Steve jumped on Michael's disconnect with reality. Michael assumed everyone loved working there. He was oblivious to the fact that he was a key source of the problem.

"Agreed, Michael. I was disappointed in how Maggie handled herself. Hell, how she's been handling herself the last few weeks, even months. I know she's had a rough year, but her attitude has been terrible. For the sake of the team, it may be better that she moved on."

"Well, I hate to see her leave on those terms, considering all she's done here, but it was her choice. As for Sheila, what do you think the fallout is? Any risk to the business?"

"I think she'll be upset for a short while but get over it. It's business. I'll talk to Edward to make sure we're exceeding her expectations and over communicating. This will blow over."

"Ok, that's the main thing. We need to protect the Crandon revenue."

Steve nodded in agreement and walked out of Michael's office. He was sufficiently pleased that he covered his bases, should Sheila try to cause any problems. Michael had no problems dealing with upset clients, provided he had forewarning. He hated being caught by surprise.

Steve messaged Edward next.

Steve: *Could you stop over now if you have a minute?*

Edward saw the message and rolled his eyes. Yet he knew he had to go.

"Hi Steve. What's up?"

"I wanted to talk to you about Sheila and Crandon. She called me this morning. She's not happy about this Maggie situation. We need to make this go away. Sheila liked Maggie. Big deal. She's going to have to get over it. Your job, my friend, is to become her *new* best friend. This is your business now. Let me know what you need."

"Steve, I agree. I have to work on my relationship with Sheila. However, don't you have monthly calls with her?

Do you want me to own the relationship going forward?"

"Oh, I'll keep them for now, but truth be told, she cancels more often than not. So as to not cause any more waves, we'll leave things as they are for the time being."

Edward just shook his head in acknowledgement of the plan. He again rolled his eyes as he walked out of Steve's office. Yet another tell-tale sign that Steve really didn't contribute much if most of his executive calls on the Crandon business were canceled. Edward wondered if it was because Sheila really was busy, or if she disliked Steve as much as everyone else.

Edward knew better than to reach out to Sheila today for anything further, let alone setting up future calls. Edward recognized it was best to try to let the dust settle. Sheila had other plans. She asked her assistant to cancel her morning meetings. She then scoured her emails from Maggie in hopes one of them featured her personal cell phone. After a solid 35 minutes of searching, Sheila finally found an email from Maggie she had sent before her impending leave of absence. Of course, Maggie had extended her personal information in the event of emergencies. Sheila shook her head. That's why she was the best.

Sheila dialed immediately. It went straight to voicemail. "Maggie. It's Sheila. Apologies for calling you on your personal cell. Please call me at your earliest convenience. You can reach me at this number. I really would like to speak with you."

Sheila had hoped Maggie would answer but knew that was unrealistic with an unrecognizable incoming number. She had done her part. Now she hoped Maggie would extend one more professional courtesy and return her call. That didn't happen. Several weeks had gone by, and Sheila left at least 3 more messages before conceding that perhaps Maggie wanted to just move past this phase of her life. Still, Sheila considered their long-standing working relationship and found it puzzling Maggie wouldn't respond. It wasn't like her.

Worrying about her friend, Jan also reached out in the weeks following Maggie's exodus. First, she left a few phone messages, and when her calls were not returned, she tried texting, also to no avail. Jan concluded the longer it went without hearing from her, the less likely it would be that she would.

Maggie weighed heavily on Edward's mind as well. He had seen her behavior while drinking. He knew her confidence was shaken and her anger raging. He also wanted to reach out, to try to explain, but knew she wouldn't want to hear from him. Instead, he asked Jan in their next one-on-one if she had heard from Maggie.

"Jan, when was the last time you heard from or talked to Maggie?"

"Edward, out of respect for Maggie, I don't know if I should discuss her with you."

"Jan, I'm not asking you to divulge information about what she's doing now. I just want to know if she's ok."

Jan's face drooped as she bowed her head. "Edward, honestly, I haven't heard from her."

"What? That's crazy! You were so close. Have you reached out?"

"You don't think I've reached out? I feel like I've reached out non-stop. She's not responding. I can't force her to answer. Edward, I don't know what to think."

"Jan, I'm worried. You should've seen her that night. She just looked lost."

"What do you mean?"

"She looked like she was just searching for any answer that would make her feel like it would be ok. I think that's why she had turned to drinking. And now, she's gone off the grid. Frankly, I'm worried about her. I looked her right in the eyes that night. All I saw was pain."

"You really care about her, don't you?"

"Contrary to what you may believe, hell what she now believes, we had become friends. I went out with her that night because she asked me to. I encouraged her to date again. I took my role very seriously here to uphold the good work she did while she was on leave. Yeah, I guess I do care. It pisses me off that she blames me for all this when all I did was try and try."

"I think it's water under the bridge now, Edward. I don't think we're going to hear from Maggie again. I think you have to make peace with your feelings, whatever they are."

"What's that supposed to mean?"

"Well most guys don't let feelings linger if there isn't more there."

"Are you saying I have feelings for her?"

"Of some sort, yes. I'm sensing that maybe you did. That's why this has upset you so much. How often do you think about her?"

"I told you, yes. I do care. I considered Maggie a friend, and I don't want to see her fall apart thinking I purposely hurt her. That's it. I'm dating Annie."

Jan nodded her head to acknowledge hearing him, although she wasn't sure she fully believed him. "How's that going by the way?"

"Great! We get along great. We have fun together. I don't foresee any reason why it won't continue developing. I really like her."

"Does she know that you think about Maggie often?"

"Woah. Stop right there. It's not like that. Yes, she weighs heavily on my mind, but that's because I didn't get closure. And I'm a nice guy. I just hated how it all went down."

"Fine. We can leave it at that, but again, I don't know many guys who spend much mental bandwidth on a former co-worker that quit in a huff."

Edward sighed in frustration knowing they would have

to agree to disagree. "Jan, I have another meeting... with Steve. Joy. Thanks as always for talking."

Jan laughed, "Better you than me!"

"Hi, Steve. Ready for our one-on-one?"

"Sure. Come on in. I have to say, I'm impressed that there has been virtually no further fallout from Maggie leaving. I haven't heard from Sheila again. You must be doing a great job over there. Nice work."

"Thanks. It's been challenging. I'm not going to deny that. With the workload of running the business at the corporate level, plus my businesses and Maggie's as well, I feel like I'm putting in a lot of hours. How is the search for Maggie's replacement? Have we secured headcount for the role?"

"Well, sir, that's the life of a senior director. Welcome to my world!" Steve laughed.

Edward's face burned red. Steve was out the door almost every day by 5:30 pm. To compare himself to Edward's current workload was insulting. Edward looked down and took a drink of water to relax.

"Michael has asked for a hiring freeze for now."

"But we're growing. That's the reason you and I both moved roles. Maggie's role would've otherwise existed had she not left. How can we not have budget to fill that role?"

"We do. It's not that the role is being eliminated. Michael and I agreed that we need to take a step back to look at capacity on some of the new teams to see if we shouldn't shift a manager over. We're trying to balance out teams before we necessarily bring in someone new."

"Meanwhile, my life is anything but balanced. Steve, I can't continue at this rate. I need a timeline as to when I'm going to get some help."

"Edward, can you not deliver?"

That was the final straw for Edward. His face again burned red and his heart raced in his chest. His first

215

instinct was to punch him, but he knew he couldn't. Instead, he took a moment to compose himself.

"Steve, did we not start this conversation on how well I was delivering? I am not going to give my life, though, for work," he said calmly.

"Edward, this is not forever. Again, we're just doing some utilization analysis."

"I get that, but I'd like a timeline so we can agree to expectations."

"I don't have a timeline yet, Edward."

"Steve, that's not an acceptable answer. I've worked 80+ hour weeks since Maggie left. You've not offered to help once. I need to fill that role, and waiting several more weeks isn't acceptable to me."

"It's going to have to be, Edward. I'm not really enjoying this level of pushback. I'm running this business the way I best ·see fit. I'd like a little respect in my decision making."

"Steve, since I've started, I feel like I've given you nothing but respect. It's wearing thin. I'm reaching my limit here. So again, when will that role be filled?"

"And again, I cannot say definitively. Final answer, Edward," Steve said with a level of condescension in his voice.

His tone pissed Edward off. Edward stood up and leaned over to look Steve in the eyes.

"Steve, if I walk out that door, walking in Maggie's exact path, you're *fucked*. Let's get real about that. Enough with the nice guy routine. I'm getting raked over the coals here, and you're holding the rake. So, either you talk to Michael or I will. The role will be filled within the next 4 weeks, or I'm out."

"I don't take kindly to ultimatums, Edward."

"It's not an ultimatum, Steve. Consider this a preview. This could all be yours if you so choose. If you don't think I'm delivering, you can do it all yourself. Thanks for the talk. I need to get back to my desk so I can leave before 10:30 tonight - about 5 hours *after* you'll have left."

Steve hadn't seen Edward that aggressive, but he knew he was right. If Edward were to walk out, he'd have to step up. He tried to change the subject to lower the tension.

"Have you heard from Maggie?"

"No. Why would *you* care?"

"HR has reached out to her several times because I guess there is some lingering paperwork she needs to finish from when her husband passed. When she wouldn't return their calls, they asked me to call her. I knew she wouldn't return my call. I wondered if you had heard from her."

"I haven't. Sorry. I have to get back to work now. If I haven't heard back from you by the end of the week on a timeline for hiring Maggie's replacement, I'll talk to Michael myself."

Edward stopped back at Jan's office.

"Hey, HR has tried calling Maggie several times too. She's not returning their calls either, and it sounds like it's somewhat important. Something to do with final paperwork associated with her husband's passing. Maybe insurance or something? I'm not sure, but now I'm really worried."

"Well, I will try to reach out again. That's all I can do."

"Thanks. By the way, I gave Steve until the end of the week to give me a game plan to fill Maggie's role, or I threatened to walk. Just thought you should know. I may not be far behind her."

Jan's eyebrows lifted in surprise before her face showed just a hint of a sly smile.

Seventeen

Edward had looked forward to Saturday morning all week. He wanted to go for a long run to clear his head. He wanted to get past Friday hoping to clear the tension he caused, and which he hated, at work. Most of all, he wanted to just not be in the dungeon that has been the office. He ran the first two miles with no music, just the sound of his feet hitting the pavement in almost a meditative run. As he passed the two-mile mark, Edward's mind drifted to Steve and how angry he was at him. He turned on heavy rock for the next two miles, realizing he may look crazy throwing imaginary punches into the air as he ran. The louder the music, the faster he ran. Finally, after he was almost sprinting, Edward slowed to a walk for the final mile, realizing he had some hard choices to make.

Steve made no attempts to follow up with Edward at the end of the week. Edward wasn't sure if Steve had talked to Michael, and it pissed him off. Edward knew he needed to stick to his word, or Steve would call his bluff going forward. Still, Edward had yet to go toe-to-toe with Michael, and frankly, he didn't know if it was worth it. What was he fighting for? After all, it was just a job. He told himself that at least a few dozen times when he first accepted it. Yet now he felt responsible for the team, his team. It was a bit rocky at first after Maggie left, but the team had always liked Edward. They fully accepted him as their leader now.

As Edward walked into his apartment, his cell phone rang.

"Hey, Mom. Good timing. I just got back from a run. How are you?"

"Edward, son, I haven't heard much from you lately. I don't know that we've touched base in the last two weeks."

"I know, Mom. I'm drowning at work. It's been crazy…"

Before he could continue, his mom cut him off. "I thought this was going to be just a job for you. Didn't you move back here to prioritize family? Edward that's not happening."

Edward paused before responding. Her timing was impeccable. How did she always know when to hammer down with the mom guilt? Maybe mothers always know. Yet, she wasn't wrong.

"Mom, I know you're right. I was just considering that myself this morning. I promise you I was. I'm not just saying that because you called to lay on the mom guilt."

"Son, I didn't call you to lay on the mom guilt. You don't want to talk with me? Don't call. That's on you," she said matter of fact.

"I called to tell you that your grandmother is declining fast. Fast, Edward. I had hoped that you would go see her of your own volition, so that when you looked back, it was because you prioritized her, and not because your mom called to remind you."

"Jesus, Mom, so this is *not* mom guilt?"

"Grow up, Edward. And forgive me for saying, but fuck you, you arrogant little shit. It isn't all about you. Your grandmother, her whole life, prioritized you. Do you remember a time when you needed something that she didn't help? A time when you were in some tournament or some event that she wasn't there to watch? I shouldn't have to guilt my 31-year-old son. He's a man. At least I thought he was. Now prove to me, to her, and to all of us that you're the man we knew."

With that, his mom hung up. It was the first time in a long time she didn't end their call with, "I love you." Edward looked at his watch. He was scheduled to spend the afternoon with Annie, but he hoped she would understand.

"Hi, Edward. What time will you be here today?"

"Hey, Annie, I hate to do this, but change in plans. I just talked to my mom, and things aren't going well for my grandma right now. I haven't seen her in a few weeks, and I really need to go spend some time with her. Can we look at time this week to reschedule?"

"Oh. Hasn't your grandma been the same for weeks? Can't you go visit her this week after work? You just told me the other day that you're going to work less because Steve has been taking advantage of you. I've been pretty understanding with how much you've been working. I feel like I barely see you myself. I was really looking forward to today, Edward."

Edward sighed. "I know, Annie. You're right. I don't seem to be doing well at anything right now."

"Except work. You've got that priority taken care of," Annie said coldly.

"Annie, I get it, but please believe that you're very important to me. I'm going to make this right. Listen, why don't you come with me? I'd love for you to meet Eltz. I'm not sure, unfortunately, that you'll have an extended period to get to spend time with her. I'd be thrilled if two of the most important women in my life could meet. Then the rest of the day I'm yours."

The phone was silent. Edward didn't want to push, but he thought that would be an easy compromise.

"I don't think so, Edward. Why don't you go spend time with your grandmother, and we'll touch base early in the week to plan time to connect."

Edward was confused when he hung up the phone. He walked into the laundry room to take off his sweaty clothes. He leaned on the washing machine perplexed. Annie was one of the warmest women he knew. Edward couldn't understand why she was so cold and dismissive at the idea of meeting Elsie. He was disappointed, but he didn't have time to dwell on it. He wanted to see Elsie before she went down for her afternoon nap.

Edward was on the road within 20 minutes. He considered calling his mom back to ask what he should expect, but after the "man up" smack down, he thought better of it. As normal, he walked into the facility carrying two coffees.

"Hello, sir. Welcome. Whom are you visiting today? Could I ask you to sign in please?"

Edward didn't recognize the nurse's aide. Surely it hadn't been that long since he had visited. He felt terrible. Edward shook his head, laughing to himself that his mother probably purposefully didn't tell him about the new staff to prolong the guilt effect.

"Elsie Wagner. I'm her grandson."

"Oh! Are you Peter?"

"No. I'm his younger brother."

"I'm sorry. The nurses and Elsie have been talking about Peter lately. He's been here pretty regularly the last few weeks. I haven't met him yet, though. I guess I didn't realize he had a brother. I'm just getting to know everyone's family."

Edward felt sick to his stomach. He was thankful Peter had been putting in effort to spend time with Eltz, but it reinforced how misaligned his priorities were.

"Is she in the dining room? I was hoping maybe I could have lunch with her."

"No, sir. She hasn't been getting out of bed the last few days. You are welcome to sit with her as long as you'd like. I don't know if she'll be awake though or not. It really just depends on the day."

Edward nodded his head understandingly. He grabbed the two coffees and walked toward Elsie's room. When he walked in, she was asleep. She was frailer than he had ever seen her. She lied on her side, all of maybe 90 pounds remaining. He could see her spine, every pointy aspect, jutting out of her gray sweatshirt. He leaned down to kiss her, noticing how pale she was. He whispered, "I love you, Elsie. More than anyone I've ever loved. If you're ready, then I will have to be as well."

He wiped the tears from his eyes as he sat in her chair in the corner of the room. He didn't know if he should wait for her to wake up or leave. Edward felt a dull ache in his chest like he was sitting there waiting for her to die. He quickly walked out to speak with the nurse's aide.

"Excuse me. How long does she sleep now? Do you expect her to wake up soon?"

"Oh, Edward, was it? I wish I could say. If I'm being honest, hospice comes in now to tend to her. I hate to be the one to tell you that, but she spends more time resting than awake now. We're all trying to just make her comfortable as long as the good Lord keeps her with us."

Edward's eyes welled up instantly, and he just shook his head. He quickly turned to go back to her room before the aide could see his face flush with tears.

As Edward walked back into Elsie's room, he saw her eyes were open, as if she knew he were there. He kissed her forehead as he leaned down to talk to her.

"Eltz, I brought you your coffee, but I think it's gone cold. I'll promise to keep bringing them as long as you'll promise to be here waiting to visit with me."

She shook her head slightly without saying a word, and Edward knew what that meant. He turned before she could see him cry again. It wasn't fair to her. It was time for him to be strong and support her. He tried to speak clearly, but the lump in his throat rendered that difficult.

"Ok, Eltz. I won't make you promise. I know you're tired. You know I'll never be ready, but I will do my best. I love you."

Again, she couldn't speak. She just nodded her head in agreement when he said I love you.

"Eltz, I'm going to go so you can rest. I promise to

come back Monday after work to see you. I promise."

He again leaned down to kiss her forehead before he left, and he could hear her faintly whisper, "Ok, my Eddie. I'll see you Monday."

When Edward got back in his car, he broke down and sobbed. After he thought he had composed himself, he started to dial Peter to thank him for continuing to visit Elsie, but he couldn't yet speak as he started sobbing harder again. He hung up quickly.

He wanted to call his mom as well to thank her for telling him to go visit, but his shame prevented that. He thought back over the last several weeks and how little time he made for his family. What spare time he did have, he was trying to spend with Annie, although admittedly, a lot of his energy ended up going to Maggie as well. He couldn't help but feel he was at the same crossroads he faced when he chose to leave Chicago. He again got his priorities wrong, and because of it, he lost out on time he could never get back. As he considered his time in Chicago, Kate crossed his mind for the first time in almost 6 months. He finally had made peace with the fact that someone who could walk away so easily never loved him in the same way he loved her. That was a very hard realization to accept, for it meant the happiest days of his life all felt fake. Edward felt very alone in that moment in his car.

The one bright spot in his life was Annie. He wanted to tell her how much she meant to him. He composed himself enough to dial.

"Hello, Edward. What's going on?"

"Hey, Annie. I just finished seeing Elsie. I'd really love to see you. I miss you, and you're right. My priorities have been wrong lately, and I want to make it up to you."

"Edward, I appreciate the sentiment, but I've been doing a lot of thinking. This just isn't working for me."

Edward was silent. He felt shell-shocked by her words.

"I enjoyed our time when we first met - how fun and lively you were, how full of life. But lately, as much as I've tried to be understanding, I've felt like an afterthought. When you weren't talking about work, it was about your crazy co-worker, and now your Grandma is dying. It's just all too much."

"Wait. The final straw is my grandma?" Edward asked incredulously.

"Not your grandma necessarily. The whole situation. I think it's great that you're close to your family. It's one of the things I liked most about you when we met. But if she really is close to passing, it's just another setback before we can try to build something. You'll be focused there. This is just unfortunate timing, Edward. I just can't do this right now."

Edward couldn't believe what Annie was saying. Admittedly, he had been a bad boyfriend over the last few weeks. Yet to say that impending mourning would prevent trying to build something together felt very cold. That wasn't like the Annie he knew at all.

"Annie, I don't know what to say. I guess I'll have to respect your decision. I want you to know I was falling for you, and just because I'm going to accept this doesn't mean I like it. But you're right. My grandma is probably going to pass soon, if not this week, and I am going to prioritize that. If that is a deal breaker for you, I think it speaks volumes anyway. Take care of yourself."

"I'm sorry, Edward."

He hung up after hearing her say that. It had the same intonation as when Kate said it. It felt like deja vu. Edward drove to a nearby liquor store to pick up a bottle of Jack Daniels before going home. After drinking more than half the bottle, he thought to himself as he prepared to sleep the afternoon away, *now I better understand why Maggie turned to booze. It really does ease the pain, even if just momentarily.*

Edward spent most of Sunday trying to stay busy to keep his mind occupied, as well as to stave off his hangover. He chose not to talk to anyone in his family because he wasn't emotionally prepared to have those conversations, and he was tired of crying. Ironically, Maggie was more on his mind than ever because he felt like he understood her even more now. He wished he could just sit down and talk to her again. He missed her intelligence, her laugh.

Edward was thankful by the time Monday morning arrived. Work would be a good distraction, despite the tense backdrop of late. Edward wasted no time in singling out Steve in the morning.

"Morning, Steve."

Steve looked like he was trying to avoid him, as he quickly ducked into his office. Edward followed him uninvited.

"I wanted to follow up on your conversation with Michael last week about filling Maggie's role."

"Edward, we didn't get a chance to talk about it. As I mentioned, we are currently on a hiring freeze."

"Thanks. That's all I needed. I'll take it from here."

Steve knew what Edward meant. He leaned out of his office as he saw Edward brazenly walk toward Michael's office. Steve figured it was all pomp and circumstance and that he'd stop short, but Edward called his bluff as he knocked straight away. Steve last saw Edward closing the door to Michael's office behind him.

After an hour, Steve wondered why he hadn't heard anything. There was no yelling. There was no storming out of Michael's office. He figured those were 2 of the most likely scenarios. He had seen Edward leave Michael's office a good 20 minutes ago. He wondered why neither had sought him out. He knew better, though, than to seek Michael out. It was better to let this play out on its own.

By 5 pm, Steve still hadn't received any sort of update from either Edward or Michael, so he walked toward Edward's desk to ask how the conversation went. It was barely 5:01 pm, and Edward was already preparing to leave.

"Calling it a night pretty early, aren't you, Edward?"

The minute he said it, Steve knew that was not the right conversation starter. Edward glared at him in response.

"I've decided to keep your hours," Edward sneered sarcastically. "Besides I have a prior engagement tonight. I need to leave."

"Well, before you go, I'd like to talk to you about your conversation with Michael."

"Sorry, I have to go now. I don't have time to discuss."

"Edward, it will only take a minute. It's not really up for discussion."

"You're right, Steve. It's not. I have to go now."

Edward boldly walked out, much to Steve's chagrin. Both he and Edward knew there was no real recourse in the short-term as Steve needed him at the helm of the Crandon team.

Edward's face was beat red with anger as he walked out of the building. His conversation with Michael hadn't gone as he had planned. Michael was receptive to speaking with him, even complimentary of the work, acknowledging how much effort he's put in since Maggie had left. That gave Edward the opportunity to make his case for filling her role as quickly as possible. Michael reiterated what Steve had said that he needed to figure out team dynamics and utilization before bringing in anyone from the outside. Edward knew better than to give Michael an ultimatum, as he may very well be fired on the spot. Instead, Edward was savvy enough to take his shot at Steve.

"Michael, I appreciate the career advancement and support I've gotten here, but lately, I've put work before family. I can't do that anymore. My grandmother is dying, and I need to spend more time with her. Steve knew that was the reason I moved back to Michigan, and since Maggie has left, he's done nothing to help with the overwhelming workload on Crandon."

"What do you mean, Edward? He's told me that he's stepped up to help the business keep running smoothly since Maggie left. Is that not the case?"

"If by running smoothly, he means he's asked me if I've got it all covered, then yes. If he means he's actually done any real work or helped with client conversations, then no. That would be categorically false."

"Edward, it took a lot of balls to come in here today to talk to me. I respect that it's because of your family. I'll take it from here."

Edward drove out of the parking lot not knowing exactly what Michael had planned, but he felt somewhat better by the fact that he made it known how useless Steve was. His anger subsided when he recognized that it didn't really matter anyway. None of it mattered. He was about to go see Eltz, and in that moment, nothing was more important.

Edward called his mom as he drove toward the nursing home. It would be the first time they had spoken since she called him out for being missing in action.

"Hi, Mom. How are you?"

"I'm okay, Edward. It's been a tough few days for me, as I'm sure you can relate. It's hard to see mom like that. You know you reach a point in life where you become the caregiver, and the roles reverse. Nothing really can ever prepare you to parent your parent. It's been a source of great joy, and admittedly, stress the last few years. And just like mom is tired, Edward, I'm tired."

"Wow, Mom. I'm sorry. I guess I had never really thought about it that way."

"Well, it's not something that I ever wanted to discuss.

I never wanted it to seem like I was burdened to have to help care for my own mother."

"Yeah, but mom, you're allowed to vent. Stress is stress. I don't think people would've thought you felt obligated."

"It's water under the bridge now, son. I think we're nearing its natural conclusion, and I'm filled with mixed emotions. I know. I mean I really know in my heart of hearts she's ready to go. I look at her, and I don't want her to be in this state. She is trapped inside her own body right now. It's selfish to want to keep her with us. I guess I'm just processing my own sadness, but you didn't call to hear me lament. How are you? What's new?"

Edward was surprised by his mom's words. He was half expecting her to still be upset with him, but her priorities, and her focus, were where they should be, on her mother. Edward wished he had better maintained his own priorities over the last few months. Work, deadlines, new projects - they'd all be there in 3 months. Most likely, he knew, Elsie would not. Add it to the list of life lessons she had taught him.

"Well, Mom. I took your advice and went to see Elsie this past weekend. I promised her I'd be back today. I left work promptly at 5:00 and am heading to see her now. I'm not looking forward to how I may find her. She wasn't good when I stopped in. In fact, she could barely speak. She didn't even sit up when I came in."

"I know, Edward. She told me you were coming Monday."

"She did?"

"Edward, you've been a great source of joy in her life. I stopped both days this weekend to see her. Like you said, she doesn't leave the bed much, if at all, but the one thing she said to me was, 'Eddie's coming Monday to see me.' You've given a dying woman who can barely move a little bit of joy in her last days. Thank you for stepping up."

Edward was silent, as he tried to hold back tears. The lump in his throat prevented him from speaking right away.

"Mom, I haven't done much right in the last few months. Hell, maybe even the last year. But I'm trying. I realize today may be the last time I see her. I don't know how to process that."

"I wish I could be of more help... because I wish someone could tell me the same thing. I think we just have to take it as it comes."

"I don't think we have any other option, Mom. Ok, well I'm pulling in to grab 2 coffees now before heading over, so I have to go. Love you."

"Edward, you know she can't drink it, right? I don't think she can keep down much but water these days."

"It doesn't much matter, does it? It's our thing, and I'm having coffee with my Eltz."

"I suppose you're right. Call me if you need me. I don't know that I'll be much help, but I guess we can cry together."

"Gee thanks, Mom. Gotta go. Bye!"

As Edward drove toward the nursing home, he considered calling Peter for additional moral support, but he didn't think it would be of much additional help. He knew he was stalling. It was one of those moments in life you know you must face, but for which nothing prepares you. As he parked, he took one last deep breath to compose himself. Elsie was waiting for him, and he knew he couldn't disappoint.

"Hi. I'm here to see Elsie Wagner."

"Ah, you must be Eddie."

"Edward, yes."

"Oh, my apologies," the nurse's aide said as she signed him in.

"She's been telling anyone that would listen that her Eddie was stopping to see her Monday. She's waiting for you."

All of a sudden, Edward felt a tremendous amount of pressure. She so clearly is anticipating his visit, he didn't want to let her down. Yet he wondered if she would even be awake. He didn't know what to expect when he saw her. He slowly walked toward her room, the last stall tactic he had left. As he entered, he was surprised to find her sitting up, awake in her chair - stunned to be more exact. She smiled a huge smile when he walked into the room.

"Eltz! Look at you. You're awake and chipper today."

She tilted her head gently and tried to raise her eyebrows in a sort of nod of agreement. She still barely had energy to speak.

"I brought you coffee. I'll set that right here. You can drink this later," Edward said as he winked at her, both knowing she wouldn't drink it.

"Eltz, I'm so happy you're awake today. I've been looking forward to our visit."

Edward smiled at her, as he held her bony, fragile hands. He looked into her eyes, both so alert, as if she saved all her energy for that moment. He continued to smile at her in silence, trying to capture that moment in his mind. Then she surprised him. With a clear and strong, yet quiet voice she asked, "Eddie, are you going to be ok?"

Immediately, tears streamed down his face. He leaned down and kissed her hands, which he still caressed in his own.

He looked up again to find Elsie somewhat scowling at him. "Don't you cry, young man."

Edward started to laugh as tears still rolled down his face. The irony of the moment too much for his fragile emotions. She was still the grandmother, and her concern was him, even now.

Again, he looked at her, and her face remained stern. His poignant moment was lost on her. Her focus was still on him. Again, with seemingly full concentration to speak the words, she asked, "Will you be ok, Eddie?"

"Eltz, I promise I'll be ok. You know if I had my choice, I'd never say goodbye. That's not God's will. You've taught me that. When it's our time, it's our time. I'll make peace with that. I'm doing ok otherwise. I'm finding balance with work. I will be ok."

"Eddie, there is more to life than work. I'm sad that I didn't get to see you find your true love."

"I already have, Elsie Wagner. I think it's you."

It was her turn to chuckle, if ever so faintly. The stern look returned to a smile. She squeezed his hand, acknowledging she felt the same.

"Eddie, I'm tired. Will you get the nurse to help me back to the bed?"

He nodded as he gently let go of her hands. He understood why she would be tired. He didn't know where she had found the strength for this visit.

By the time he returned with the nurse, Elsie was already asleep in her chair.

"Oh, I'm sorry, sir. She barely opens her eyes these days. I hope you're not disappointed with your visit. I'm sure she could hear you," the nurse said trying to offer solace.

"Oh, I'm not disappointed at all. I had coffee with my grandmother, like I always do."

The nurse looked at him questioningly. Yet he smiled in return. He then turned in Elsie's direction as she lie sleeping. He said aloud, "In fact, I'll be ok. I promise you, I'll be ok."

Eighteen

Renee picked up her phone to text Maggie, like she had so many times over the last few weeks. It was a force of habit, but she knew it was futile. Maggie wouldn't get the message. Renee tossed her phone on the kitchen counter in frustration. She missed her best friend, and despite their fights and difficulties of the last year, the last few weeks showed Renee how much Maggie meant in her life.

Renee poured her morning coffee and grabbed the newspaper to get her mind off Maggie. She didn't have much time before she needed to hop in the shower, so she decided to skim quickly. She'd read the local news and oddly, the obituaries. Having grown up in a small town, that too was a force of habit. This one she inherited from her mother. Her mother would say to her, "That's how you make sure you pay your respects when needed." Renee always thought it odd, yet she followed suit. Renee skimmed the names quickly. No one she knew. Renee also had started reading the names again to see if there were any vintage names that would be good for future baby use. Her biological clock was ticking, and she liked the idea of using a name from an earlier generation. One name today in particular jumped out at her. As she read the obituary, she made the connection - that was Maggie's co-worker's, Edward's, grandmother. After giving it a moment's thought, Renee picked up her phone to call work. She left a message on her boss's phone.

"Hi, Rick. Good morning. It's Renee. I'm not feeling well today, so I won't be in. Hopefully, I'll feel a bit better by tomorrow."

Renee then sent one more text before almost running to the shower. She figured she'd give them a head's up she was coming.

About an hour later, Renee pulled up to an attractive, white colonial home with a well-manicured lawn and a cute, gray-haired older man waving like crazy walking out of the garage to greet her.

"Renee, honey. What brings you back so soon? You were just here this past weekend. Don't you have to work today?"

"Good morning, Mr. Adams. I do; well, I did. I saw some news this morning, and I thought I should come tell Maggie myself. How is she doing today?"

"She's up this morning. She's laughing. We had breakfast together. It's a good start to her day. I honestly think she's getting better. I think her doctor was right to prescribe a break for her. I am slowly seeing signs of my daughter coming back."

"Well, I hope so! I miss her like crazy. Just this morning I went to text her, and I knew that would fall on deaf ears. I can't wait to have my partner in crime back."

"Yeah, after losing Brian and leaving her job, and then the drinking mixed with emotional outbursts, her mother and I were pretty lost as to what to do. After running a few tests, her doctor recommended a psychologist to process the last year. That doctor was pretty quick in her diagnosis - our poor Maggie had a nervous breakdown. She recommended turning off the phone, social media and other outlets and having her take some time away from the stress of the outside world."

Renee, of course, already knew all this. Mr. Adams had repeated this story to her almost every time she had visited in the last few weeks. Renee was the one exception to the outside world Maggie's parents would allow. Renee knew he just needed an ear to listen, as this had been hard on them as well. Plus, as he had aged, he often would repeat his stories. She thought it endearing.

"So, Renee, what is the news? Is everything okay? I want to make sure we don't rile her up."

"Oh, I hope not to, Mr. Adams. I saw in the paper this morning that one of Maggie's former co-workers had lost his grandmother. I figured she'd want to know. Plus, it was a good excuse to come see her again."

"Was she close to this co-worker?"

Renee didn't know how to answer that question. One of the benefits, yet pressures, of being a best friend, is you are privy to knowledge that not everyone has. After having quit her job, Maggie finally had admitted to Renee she most likely had feelings for Edward. Confusing as they were, she didn't know how to process them. To be first rejected by him when she tried to kiss him and then betrayed by him for his own promotion, it really was the final escalation in a tumultuous year leading to her breakdown. Yearning, embarrassment, grieving, frustration, anger... it was all too much for Maggie.

"I'm not sure I'd describe them as friends, Mr. Adams. They did, however, work closely together. I just figured she'd want to know."

"Head on in, love. She'll be happy to see you."

"Good morning, my darling!" Renee chimed as she hugged her best friend.

"Good morning to you too, Mrs. Adams. Thank you for allowing me to stop by on such short notice."

"Oh Renee, dear, you are always welcome. You know that."

"Great. Counting on it. When did you say you were cooking your famous veggie lasagna again? I'll make sure to stop by that night," Renee chuckled as if she were a high schooler visiting after school.

"Hey, Mags, could we head downstairs? I was hoping we could chat in private."

Maggie nodded, as she grabbed her friend by the hand as if they were going to the basement to play Barbies.

"Renee, I'm so happy you came today. My parents are driving me crazy. They have been so amazing the last few weeks. I feel bad even saying it, but girl, I am losing my mind."

"Again?" Renee sneered sarcastically as they both erupted in laughter.

"I hate you! You big diva!" Maggie quipped in return.

"Seriously. I'm going stir crazy. My dad is treating me like I'm 12 again with little ability to make my own decisions or pour my own coffee. I get it. I was a basket case. I admit it. I probably even needed this break, but I feel better than I have in a long time."

"Yeah when I got here, he made it sound like you were just starting the recovery process. I didn't want to get into it with him."

"Thank you. It's going to come to a head here in the next week or so. I feel like I'm ready to go home, but I'm sure they're going to push back. I think they have come to like having me here. It has given them a bit of a sense of purpose I think. They've been wonderful. I can't say it enough, but it is time. I'm hoping when I see my psychologist next week that she agrees."

"Maggie, this is me. You don't have to justify it to me."

"I know, but I just feel bad whining when I couldn't have done it without them. I owe them so much. I was in a really, really bad place."

"Oh, I know! Girl, you were a hot mess."

"Gee thanks, Renee."

"If I can't say that to you, who can I? I'm equally as happy you're getting back to your old self. That's why I'm ok coming today to tell you what I learned this morning."

"I'm not sure I like the sounds of that. Is everything ok?"

"For us? Most certainly. I did, however, read this morning that Edward's grandmother passed away over the weekend. Something in my gut told me you'd want to know."

"Oh," Maggie said quietly, as she furrowed her brow, looking down to make sense of the news.

"Maggie, are you ok? Should I not have mentioned it?"

"Oh, no. I'm really glad you did. Thank you! I need to go to the calling hours. I was just thinking how I was going to explain that to my parents."

"What? The calling hours! Girl, have you lost your mind again? Why would you go to the calling hours of a woman you never met? I figured perhaps you'd want to send a card or something."

"Renee, when Brian died, Edward came to his calling hours. He didn't have to. He barely knew me at the time, and he didn't know Brian at all. And let's be honest, I was a total bitch to him when we first met. The only reason Edward would come is because he's a good man. He came out of respect. He was a good man to try to help me when my drinking got the best of me. I should go and show the same respect, and if the moment presents itself, apologize."

"Was he a good man when he screwed you over at work?"

"Renee, thank you for being so protective. I love you for that. I've had this conversation with my psychologist, and as I've processed, I've had to acknowledge my own role, and my own culpability, in how everything transpired. Certainly, Brian dying played a large role in changing the course of my own reality, but I must own my actions. I can't blame Edward for my attitude with Steve, or even prior to that, not fighting for a promotion, and not leaving if I didn't feel rewarded. After a loveless marriage where I accepted complacency, I did the same with work. I just waited around hoping to be recognized. I made certain choices. I can't play the victim."

"Wow, ok. I think you are strong enough. This is my Maggie. I won't object if this is what you feel you need to do. Welcome back, bitch."

"But you'll come with me, right? I'm strong, but I'm not Wonder Woman!"

"The things you don't do for your best friend. I guess I'm going to the funeral home."

"Thank you so much! Pull out your phone and look up the calling hours, would you? My parents won't let me anywhere near the internet. I just got nightly news privileges back last week. Do you see what I mean? I'm sort of cut off here, and I don't know how much more that I can take now that I'm feeling better."

"Just don't rush recovery, ok, Mags? I don't want to see you back to where you were. Promise me."

"I've got a plan to stay focused, Renee. Now, let's look up the obituary."

Renee wasn't sure it was the best idea her friend ever had, but she certainly could appreciate the sentiment. Edward would be busy visiting with so many people that any interaction with Maggie would be limited to a couple of minutes max. Renee decided not to fight her on it, although she knew it most likely meant lying to Maggie's parents, which didn't thrill her.

The calling hours were that afternoon, and the funeral would be tomorrow morning. Renee considered that had she waited a few more days to tell Maggie none of this would be an issue.

"Mags, we'd have to go today. I can't take off tomorrow to go with you to the funeral. Are you ok with that? Are you sure you're up to going so quickly? It's pretty abrupt to put yourself in that situation."

"Renee, I need to go, before I lose my nerve. Plus, I need to close this chapter of my life. If I don't go tonight, what am I supposed to do call him up for lunch? I think that would be more awkward. I can go and quickly pay my respects, offer support and apologize. Then I will have closure and can move on."

"Fine. What are you going to tell your parents?"

"I'm not going to tell them anything. You're going to tell them that we're going to lunch. They can't say no to you."

"The shit I don't do for you. Go get ready, and I'll sweet talk your dad. You owe me!"

Maggie nervously looked through her closet. She needed to wear funeral-appropriate attire but also wanted to look attractive. She grew increasingly frustrated as she rummaged through endless pant suits and boring cardigan sets. Finally, she found a dress she had worn only once before. It was a black, sleeveless pencil dress, cut at the knee and very form fitting. Because it covered her shoulders, it was professionally sexy as Brian described it when he saw her in it. She had worn it about 7 years ago to an advertising awards dinner, one Brian wouldn't attend with her. More recently, she chose not to wear it, for she didn't feel particularly sexy. Today, though, it was her best option. The dress fit better than ever.

When Maggie walked out to join Renee, who was sitting in the kitchen chatting with Maggie's mom, Renee couldn't believe it. Maggie was stunning. Her hair was pulled up, and she was wearing a modest pearl necklace. She looked like Jackie Onassis.

"Excuse me. Where's my friend Maggie? I wasn't expecting Elizabeth Taylor to be joining me for lunch."

"I just figured it would be nice to look my best now that I feel my best. Thank you for noticing, Renee. Are you ready?"

"Maggie, dear, are you sure you're up for going out today?" her mom said softly.

"Mom, we all knew this was a temporary arrangement. I can't stay holed up forever. Besides, I'm not even leaving. I'm coming back here. I'm just going to a nice lunch. I need to slowly start resuming my life. Please do not worry. I'll be back later. Where is my phone?"

"Maggie, dear, are you sure you need your phone? You

know your doctor said to take a break from social media and such. I never knew all what she was talking about."

"Mom, it's been weeks. Please stop worrying. It'll be ok."

"Ok, but only because you're with our dear Renee. I know she'll get you home safely."

"You betcha, Mrs. Adams. Nothing to worry about."

Maggie's mom hugged her as if it were one of the last time she'd see her daughter. Maggie had to pry herself away. She again reassured her mother she'd be fine, before giving her dad a simpler hug in the garage.

As Renee pulled out of the driveway waving to Mr. Adams, Maggie sighed, "Can you believe those two?"

"They care about you. They just don't want to see you hit rock bottom again."

Maggie nodded knowingly, as she stared out the passenger window of the car. It had been weeks since she had gone anywhere, and the idea of going to the funeral home seemed better in theory than it did in that moment. Her heart raced faster as they neared the funeral home. When Renee parked and turned off the car, she reached for the car handle to get out. Maggie stopped her abruptly.

"Wait. I'm not sure I can do this."

"What do you mean? This was your idea!"

"I know, but now that we're here, I'm not sure he'd want to see me. I didn't know this woman. I'm just supposed to walk in there like we're old friends? Like I hadn't totally upended his life in the last year, in the worst possible ways?"

"Tell me about it! That's what I was trying to ask you in your basement. So, what do you want to do?"

"You tell me, Renee. What should I do?"

"Mags, you know I can't. This is your call. There obviously was a reason why you thought you needed to do this. How are you going to feel if you don't face Edward?"

Maggie sat quiet for a few minutes. Renee let the

question linger in the air and knew better than to add any more commentary. The sound of silence was uncomfortably awkward. Renee was staring out the driver window as to not stare at Maggie. Renee jumped when Maggie finally blurted out, "I have to go in!"

Nineteen

Edward had arrived first thing in the morning to the funeral home to help his mom. Calling hours would start at 11 am, and she insisted on arriving by 9 am to make sure everything was perfect. He knew his father and brother wouldn't be as patient or supportive of the minor details that seemed to matter to his mother today, so he volunteered. She was doing relatively well, but after having served as her mother's caregiver for much of the last few years, she just felt numb. As they walked into the funeral home together, she was racing through the things she wanted Edward to do before people starting arriving. She seemed to be on auto pilot. That is until she saw her mother's body.

"Oh, Edward. Look how beautiful she looks."

Edward nodded in agreement. Yet this frail woman, as nice as they made her look, was not the stout, strong woman he had known most of his life. He put his hand on his grandmother's, "Oh Eltz, what am I going to do without you?"

His mother wondered the same thing as tears streamed down her face. After thirty minutes of trying to finish setting out pictures and breaking down into hysterical tears, Edward told his mother to go sit in the family area and have some tea. He would handle the rest. She looked around to make sure her mother's final wishes were taken care of before finally agreeing.

"Edward, wait. One more thing. I had mom's favorite bible verse printed on a canvas to hang by the casket. Would you make sure to get an easel and set it up for me?"

Edward knew exactly which verse it would be. Ecclesiastes 3. Elsie would often quote this to support her family and reinforce God's plan.

Edward ran back to the car and got the canvas out of the trunk. When he entered the main room, the funeral director had already set up the easel. Edward placed the canvas and took a few steps back. For the first time in years, he read the complete verse as he blankly stared at his fallen hero.

To everything there is a season, and a time to every purpose under the heaven:
A time to be born, and a time to die; a time to plant, and a time to pluck up that which is planted;
A time to kill, and a time to heal; a time to break down, and a time to build up;
A time to weep, and a time to laugh; a time to mourn, and a time to dance;
A time to cast away stones, and a time to gather stones together; a time to embrace, and a time to refrain from embracing;
A time to get, and a time to lose; a time to keep, and a time to cast away;
A time to rend, and a time to sew; a time to keep silence, and a time to speak;
A time to love, and a time to hate; a time of war, and a time of peace.

Edward closed his eyes and silently cried. He hadn't wanted to cry in front of his mother. Edward opened his eyes and reread the words, *A time to be born, and a time to die.*

It was as if he could hear his grandmother saying again, "Don't you cry, young man." He had to laugh as he wiped his tears.

Edward looked at his watch. He had about 45 minutes left before calling hours would start. He hurriedly finished putting out the remaining pictures and then ran to the family area.

"Why are you in such a hurry?" his mother asked.

"Because I want to have one last cup of coffee with just me and my Eltz before everyone arrives."

He poured two cups and carried them into the visitation area and closed the doors to the room behind him. His mother knew better than to disrupt them. Edward sat for a while just staring at Elsie's body, sipping his coffee and thinking about a lifetime of memories. Finally, he looked at his watch and knew he couldn't delay any longer.

"Well, Eltz. This is probably our last cup of coffee for a while. I guess I'm happy for you. I know you're with grandpa now, in a better place. I'm still not sure how I'm going to manage without your advice, your love, your humor, your support...but I guess I'm going to have to figure that out. I can only hope you felt like you got as much out of our relationship as I did, because it doesn't feel like it. It feels like I took and took. I'm sorry I was absent all those years I was in Chicago. Maybe this is my last lesson - the value of time. I'm just not ready to say goodbye, but I guess I have to. People will be arriving any minute. So, let me say this Elsie Wagner - thank you and I love you."

Edward leaned down to kiss his grandma's forehead before heading to open the doors to the visitation room. People had already started to arrive, but his mother had politely welcomed them and asked them to wait. He hugged his mother tightly and whispered, "thank you."

By 3 pm, Edward grew tired of welcoming his extended family to the funeral home. Edward was weary of small talk and reminiscing. He also noticed most people that had come to pay their respects were part of a couple. While he knew he was surrounded by family and friends, it felt very lonely to be going through this alone. He looked at his grandma, and he was filled with sadness that the woman he loved most would never get to meet his future wife.

After thanking his Aunt Nancy for visiting, Edward

needed a break. He headed to get some water. While the water seemed to help, Edward just needed another moment before facing the crowd, so he walked out the back door of the funeral home to get some fresh air. He stood cross-armed staring blankly into the sky thankful for the moment's reprieve. He was startled when a hand touched his shoulder. He turned around to find Annie with outstretched arms waiting for a hug.

"Oh, Edward. I'm so sorry for your loss. I know how much your grandma meant to you," she said as she embraced him suddenly.

"Annie, I'm surprised to see you. Thank you for coming, but I'm a little taken aback."

"Edward, our timing was off. I didn't handle the demands of your job and family well. To be honest, though, there was more to it than that. Losing my dad last year really took a lot out of me. I wasn't emotionally ready to handle death again. That was too draining on me," Annie said as she looked at the ground, her voice trailing away.

She reached for Edward's hands and gripped them tightly. "While I know I didn't know your grandma, I wasn't sure I could provide the level of support you'd need from a girlfriend. I panicked. I pushed you away. Not purposefully. I reacted emotionally, and over the last few days, I've had time to process my emotions. When I heard your grandma had passed, I knew I needed to be here for you. Can you forgive me?"

"Annie, honestly, I haven't given much thought to you and me. I don't mean that harshly or to hurt you. But when you broke up with me, I was pretty sad, lonely. Yet, at the same time, I could focus my energy on Eltz."

"Of course. As it needed to be! I'm happy you had that time with her too. I guess I'm asking if perhaps when you're ready, if we could try again."

Edward tilted his head, looking at her puzzled. She was

stunningly beautiful, and he still had the instinct to want to kiss her. She was a fantastic kisser, but he didn't know if he had the capacity to date again in the short-term.

"Annie, I'm so touched that you came today. It means a lot considering how things ended with us. Thank you for being honest with me and providing a bit of context. I never was quite sure how things could go from so good to done in a matter of days. I'll own up to my part in not prioritizing us. I just don't think I can think about dating again right now. I'm sure in a few weeks when the dust settles, I'll be able to make more sense of what I want, but for now, I have to ask for patience."

Annie nodded understandingly. "I want to go pay my respects to the woman that helped shape you into the great guy you are today," she said as she kissed him on the cheek before heading into the funeral home.

Edward shook his head in disbelief. "What the fuck was that? I didn't see that coming today. Eltz, is this your way of pushing my love life forward? Got any other tricks up your sleeve today?"

Edward looked at his watch. He had already been outside for 25 minutes. He knew he needed to get back to the visitation, as there were another 2 hours to go. He sighed deeply.

"Edward, where have you been? I haven't had a chance to look for you. There just have been too many people," his mother said hurriedly as she saw him re-enter the funeral home.

"Mom, calm down. I was only gone a few minutes. Did I miss someone that stopped to see me?"

"Oh, on the contrary, my son," his mother chimed as a cheshire cat grin crossed her face.

"Mom, you're freaking me out. What's going on?"

"You didn't miss her. She's inside waiting for you."

"Who? Annie? I know we talked outside. She said she wanted to come pay her respects. I told her I wasn't ready

245

to deal with it today."

"Who's Annie? If you weren't ready to deal with her, you better brace up then, young man. Kate is in there."

"You've got to be fucking kidding me! What the hell is she doing here?" Edward started to sweat immediately as his face turned flush.

"She said her mother told her about mom's passing. She must've seen it on my Facebook wall. I forgot we're friends."

"I thought she was in London. Why is she in Detroit?"

"Edward, she came to see you."

"Dear Jesus God, the ghosts of girlfriends past part 2 at my grandmother's calling hours. This is Elsie's doing. She's playing Love Connection from the great beyond."

His mother laughed out loud at the irony. "Edward, you have to go talk to her. She came all this way to see you."

"Mom, I don't owe her anything. She certainly didn't give me an explanation when she just up and left. She said she couldn't marry me, and that was it."

"Edward, it's a visitation. There are no expectations that you'll be able to talk with any one person for more than a few minutes. Just say hi and thank her for coming. You have a ready excuse to speak with other guests."

"Going back outside would be the easier option, Mother."

"I doubt she's going to leave until she sees you. So, you can either go now, or put off the inevitable. I say go rip off the bandage. Now, who's this Annie? Point her out, I want to scope out bachelorette number 1."

Edward didn't indulge his mother's curiosity. Instead he marched back toward the casket, in an almost soldier like way. He didn't look around the room, nor was he trying to find Kate. It didn't matter, within minutes, a familiar voice said his name.

"Hi, Edward. How are you coping? I know how much your grandmother meant to you."

"Hi, Kate. Yes, she was the best. I could count on her always. That's a rarity in today's world."

Kate picked up on the subtle jab but let it go.

"And how are you, Edward?"

"Kate, why are you here? I thought you were in London. Surely, you didn't fly all the way back just for my grandmother's funeral."

"Edward, I came to pay my respects. You are important to me, and she was important to you. I wanted to be here for you."

"Why now? It's been how long? *'I'm important to you?'* What the fuck is that? We haven't talked since you left. What's really going on?"

"Edward, don't make a scene. This is your grandmother's visitation."

"Oh, I think she'd be proud of the way I'm handling this. I'm sure she's enjoying the front row seat. She wasn't too keen on how you treated me."

"Edward, what do you want me to say? That I needed to go take that opportunity for me. That I knew if I didn't, I'd never be able to live with the *'what if.'* I had the experience. I learned a lot, but I moved back to Chicago a few weeks ago. You're the first person I wanted to see."

"Kate, time didn't just stand still. I didn't sit around waiting for you. I moved on, as crushed as I was. I was ready to build my life with you."

Kate started to rub Edward's arm softly. "I didn't expect you to wait. I knew the chance I was taking and what I was giving up when I left. I just had to do it for me."

Edward moved her hand away quickly. "Right. You knew what you were giving up, and you still chose to leave. I guess I should thank you. I was able to move back home and spend quality time with Eltz before she passed. I am so thankful for that time."

Kate centered herself in front of Edward, as she put her

hands on both his elbows and looked into his eyes. He still hadn't seen anyone with eyes that blue.

"Edward, Eccliastes 3. It's right there. Look. *A time to weep, and a time to laugh; a time to mourn, and a time to dance.* Maybe, just as Elsie said to both of us when she was alive, that everything happens for a reason, when it's meant to. You needed to come back home to be with her, and I needed to go take this opportunity to find myself. And do you know what I realized? That you're the man I'm meant to be with."

"Kate, today of all days... Really? This is the shit you're dumping on me today. Did you expect in my weakened, emotional state that I'd be so thankful to welcome you back?"

"No, Edward. I came with no expectations actually. I wanted to pay my respects because I still love you, and I couldn't imagine not being here for you. I wasn't planning on telling you that today, though. Yet, here we are."

"Kate, I can't. Not today. I don't want to deal with this. Thank you for coming. I need to continue visiting now."

"Edward, truly, I had no expectations but to want to give my support to you and your family," she said as she quickly hugged him. "My number is still the same if you should want to talk."

As Kate turned to leave, Edward shook his head in disbelief. He turned to Elsie's body. "Oh, I'm sure you think this is a real laugh riot, don't you Elsie Wagner? I'm good with today's round of surpris..."

Before he could finish that sentence, he saw Maggie and Renee in the receiving line.

"Elsie, you've got to be shitting me. I guess you always did say everything happens in 3's. Well ghost of girls past 3 has entered the building. Ol' Malbec Maggie in the room. Gee thanks, Eltz."

Edward continued visiting knowing that he'd have to face Maggie within the next few minutes. He noticed she

248

had lost some weight since he had last seen her. She looked healthier too, more well-rested. He had, in fact, never seen her look so beautiful.

"Hello, Edward. You remember, Renee."

"Hi, ladies. Thank you for coming. I'd like to say I'm surprised to see you, but nothing surprises me anymore. It's been quite the day. Maggie, how are you?"

"No, Edward, how are you? I'm so sorry for your loss."

"Thank you. I think she's in a better place now. I'm thankful to have had time with her in these last few weeks. I'm at peace with how we said goodbye."

"That's good to hear. For the most part, I felt that way when Brian died, but it was different. He wasn't in his 90s. I only wish I had had more time."

"Maggie, I have to ask. Why did you come today? The last I saw you, you were so angry. I couldn't even get a word in edgewise to try to explain."

"Wow, Edward, going straight for it."

"Well, Mags, you wouldn't believe the day I have had even if I told you. At this point, I've lost my patience for pleasantries. So, what gives?"

Maggie playfully smacked him on the arm for calling her, 'Mags.'

"Honestly, Edward, I wanted to pay you the same respect you paid me when Brian died. My time away has provided a lot of clarity into my own actions and what I have to take ownership over. I want to apologize to you for how I behaved, for what I put you through. I also need to thank you for making sure that I was always safe, despite my reckless behavior. I wasn't expecting necessarily to say that at the casket, but I don't know that there ever was going to be a good time."

"Oh, don't worry, I'm sure Elsie is loving hearing you apologize to me. She's had quite the show today."

Renee and Maggie looked at each other quizzically. Maggie was just relieved to have said what she came to say.

"Well, Edward, I won't take up anymore of your time. Best of luck with everything in the future. Thank you again for everything, and my deepest condolences."

"Maggie, wait. Where've you been? Jan has tried to reach you for weeks."

Maggie looked shocked. She looked down at her shoes sheepishly.

"Edward, I guess honesty is part of my therapy so I'll tell it to you straight. My parents staged an intervention. I had a mental breakdown. Between work, my drinking, my anger toward Steve, my unprocessed feelings after Brian died, and my feelings for you, I snapped. Per doctor's orders, they took away my phone and access to social media until I healed."

Maggie still looked down at her feet as to not make eye contact with him. Edward immediately looked at Renee when he heard the words, 'my feelings for you.' His eyes showed heavy confusion. Renee's eyes grew big as if to say don't ask me.

"Maggie, what do you mean your feelings for me? What feelings?"

Maggie shook her head as she answered, "It doesn't matter now, Edward. It just doesn't matter. Again, I'm so sorry for your loss. With deepest respect to you and your family."

Edward stood a bit stunned. He wanted to ask her if she was planning to come back to work, or even go back to work in general. He wanted to ask her if she was ok, if there was anything he could do to help. As he watched her walk away, for the first time, he recognized he had felt something for her too. He couldn't deny that he wanted to protect her, and that he missed her. Maggie stopped to read the canvas near the casket.

'*To everything there is a season, and a time to every purpose under the heaven: A time to be born, and a time to die; a time to plant, and a time to pluck up that which is planted.'*

She re-read the canvas three times, as tears rolled down her face. For all that she had gone through, it gave her hope that perhaps there was a reason - a purpose for all her anguish, her embarrassment, her struggles. As she began to read it again, she was in full ugly cry mode as the emotions of the last 2 years bubbled over. Suddenly, she was enveloped in a hug. Edward held her closely as he patted her back.

"I'm sorry too, Maggie. I never wanted to fight with you either."

"I'm not crying because of you, Edward. I'm crying because of that canvas. It's as if it's speaking to me, consoling me for what I've gone through."

"It was my grandma's favorite bible verse. She would often recite it to us as well for consolation and guidance. It wouldn't surprise me if she weren't speaking to you, reading you this."

"But why me? She didn't know me."

"Because she knows I care about you."

Maggie returned her face to Edward's lapel and sobbed. After a minute, when neither Edward nor Maggie were moving, Renee parted them and took Maggie's hand.

"We need to go, Edward. We're holding up the visitation line. We're sorry again for your loss."

Maggie continued to cry as they walked toward the door. All she could do was turn and wave to Edward, no words would come out.

"Edward, who was that? I've never seen that woman before," his mother asked.

"That was my former co-worker, Maggie. She's had a really hard go of it lately, and I think this just brought back a lot of emotions for her. It was nice to see her again. That was cool of her to come pay her respects."

"Young man, I've known you your whole life. I

watched you go embrace that young woman and hold her. That was not a hug you give a co-worker. She means something to you, doesn't she?"

"Mom, I don't know how to answer that. Just when I thought I could focus on grieving and moving on with my life, Annie, Kate and Maggie all show up at my grandma's calling hours. And guess what. They all indicated they have feelings for me. I can't process that today."

"Well, they all realized what an incredible young man you are, and so dapper. Don't think I haven't noticed all the women here noticing you."

"Mom, they're all extended family and old women."

"Edward, that doesn't mean they can't appreciate what a handsome man you've turned into. Digressing a moment, so what are you going to do about your lady quandary?"

"Mom, I don't know. I honestly do not know. And frankly, today isn't the day I'm going to figure it out. Tomorrow, we bury my best friend. That's really where I need to focus."

Twenty

Edward was thankful Annie, Maggie nor Kate came to the funeral. It was enough of a shock to see them at calling hours. It allowed him to focus on his grieving. Despite knowing Elsie's condition had been worsening for weeks, the funeral was still numbing for Edward. He held his mother's hand most of the day, and even in his 30s, was comforted by her touch.

Edward knew he would not be going to work on Monday, and he was tentative the rest of the week depending on how he felt, although he didn't feel obligated to tell Steve that. Edward had made sure Jan was up-to-speed on all the latest projects. He felt confident she would help manage the few days he was out. Steve felt differently. On Tuesday morning, Steve had left Edward a message on his cell phone.

"Edward. It's Steve. You've had a few days here over the weekend plus Monday to take care of your family obligations. It's Tuesday, and I would've expected you to be in today. I'll see you in the office tomorrow."

Edward hadn't answered when he saw who was calling. In fact, he didn't listen until late Tuesday afternoon. He instantly regretted it.

"What a passive aggressive asshole! What kind of nerve does that guy have?" he said as he slammed his car door.

Edward had just gotten back to his apartment after having stayed with his family the last few days. He had planned on going back to the office in the morning, but now he would take an extra day out of spite.

"We're given 5 total days for bereavement. I have only taken 3, and he's calling me talking about my obligations? He must've forgotten those 10 pm dinners I had at my desk, foregoing my family obligations, the motherfucker."

Edward stewed the rest of the night, alternating between sputtering to himself and outright yelling in his apartment. In a moment of clarity under a hot shower, he thought to himself, *Edward, what are you doing? Why are you expending so much energy for this guy? He's a total tool, a piece of shit that won't matter to you in 5 years. Get a grip, bud.*

It calmed him down at least for the rest of the evening. When he awoke in the morning, he decided he'd take the high road and return to work. He recognized it was more to get out of the lonely solitude of his apartment than it was to appease Steve.

In lieu of office coffee, Edward stopped for 2 hot coffees and smiled even though he knew the second coffee was for Elsie. She was with him in spirit. For the first time since she passed, he felt a moment of happiness as he sipped his coffee walking into the office. It was short-lived.

"Edward, nice of you to join us. I wasn't sure if you were going to milk this for the rest of the week. The least you could've done is to give me some kind of notice as to your plans. I'm growing weary of the attitude. It's like you're picking up where Maggie left off," Steve said as he met Edward at his desk. Edward hadn't even taken his coat off yet.

Edward stood silent for a moment. He looked around his desk. He looked at the pile of open projects on his desk. He looked at prints of some of the outstanding work they had done in the past year hanging on his cubicle wall. He looked at the post-it notes of to-do notes he left for himself last week. It was as if time had slowed to a quarter speed.

"Are you not even going to acknowledge that I'm talking to you, Edward?"

Edward snapped out of his trance. His gut reaction was

again to punch Steve in the face. Instead, he took another sip of his coffee before picking up the stack of open project files and handing them to Steve.

"These are for you. They're your responsibility now. To your point, I'm picking up where Maggie left off, and I'm leaving as well."

"Bullshit! Maggie was an emotional wreck. You're a bit more grounded than that. Besides, she had insurance money. You're just going to give up a senior director salary with no replacement? I think you're smarter than that, but thanks for showing me your cards. I'm sure Michael will appreciate knowing where you stand."

Edward didn't appreciate the veiled threat. He pushed Steve aside as he left his cubicle and walked the length of the hallway. Without knocking, he opened the door, greeted with an angry look from Michael.

"What the fuck do you think you're doing? Who the fuck do you think you are, Edward? Is your head up your ass? Never barge in here without knocking again!"

"Michael, you won't have to worry about that. I'm resigning effective immediately. I no longer will tolerate your management style nor the cowardice and intimidation of your henchman out there. I gave you an opportunity to fix this, and apparently it wasn't a priority for you."

"Edward, let's calm down. You know we value you and need you leading the Crandon business."

"Oh really? With my head up my ass? Is that the value I bring? It's the first fucking day back after burying my grandmother, and I have to deal with that jackass threatening me? No, I'm done. I warned you about him. I told you to fix it, and you didn't. Best of luck to you and your organization. Thank you for the opportunity. With your confidence in Steve, I'm sure he's more than capable of running the account better than Maggie or I apparently did."

Michael didn't say another word. As most bullies do,

he knew when he was matched. Instead, he just shook Edward's hand and gave him a parting head nod.

As Edward started collecting his things at his desk, he heard Michael yell, "Steve, get the fuck in here!"

Edward didn't much care what came of their conversation. He was at peace with his decision, although Steve was right in saying he didn't have as good of backup plan as Maggie had. If Edward had learned anything over the last 3 months, it's that time is the only truly valuable resource. He wasn't going to waste any more of his energy on Steve.

While Michael and Steve were behind closed doors, Edward felt obligated to call Sheila personally with the news of his impending departure.

His call went to voicemail. "Hi Sheila, this is Edward. I wanted to connect with you today if possible. It's somewhat timely…"

He stopped mid-sentence as he saw Sheila was calling him back.

"Hi, Sheila. I was just leaving you a message."

"Hello, Edward. Yes, I was just walking into my office. I am running meeting to meeting today. I talked to Jan last week about an upcoming initiative I'm working on, and she told me about your grandmother. I'm so sorry. When I saw it was you that was calling I figured it must be somewhat urgent for you to call me on what I assume is your first morning back."

"Sheila, thank you for your condolences. Yes, it is timely, so I appreciate the quick call back. I wanted to tell you myself that I will be transitioning from the Crandon business effective immediately. I have thoroughly enjoyed your partnership and being challenged by you to be better. I think the whole team is proud of the work we did together."

"Wait, Edward are you serious? First Maggie, and now you as well? No! We don't want to endure another change in account leadership. What the hell is going on over there? And what do you mean you're transitioning? Did Steve put you on another business? If so, I'm calling him next."

"Sheila, no. It isn't that. I resigned this morning. I will be leaving the agency."

"Edward, are you sure? Was it something we had done as a client? I know we can be very demanding."

"Absolutely not! This work has been some of the most challenging and developmental of my career to date."

"Then, why, Edward? First Maggie leaves abruptly, and then you leave in the same way."

"Sheila, I respect you, so I'm not going to be frank. I have a difference in leadership philosophy, and therefore, it's time to pursue other opportunities."

"Well, Edward, considering the situation, my question was rather rhetorical, wasn't it? I had already concluded that. I hate to see you go. Thank you for all your hard work. I wish I had gotten the chance to say the same to Maggie. She never returned any of my phone calls, which seemed uncharacteristic for her."

"Well, Sheila, as luck would have it, I just recently saw Maggie. I'm sure if you give her another call now, you'd have more luck reaching her. I want to wish you continued success. Take care, Sheila."

Edward was sure Steve would be pissed when he learned he had called Sheila. That gave him immense pleasure. What he had to do next, however, did not.

Edward knocked gently on Jan's door. "Hey, may I come in?"

"Yep, but you have to make it fast, Buster, as I am running to a meeting in 5 minutes. I'm glad you're back. It's been so crazy while you were out."

"Oh Jan... Well, I can make it fast, but you're not going to be glad for long. I resigned this morning."

"What!" Jan shrieked in disbelief. "Close the door. The

meeting can wait. What in the world happened, Edward?"

"Jan, I just reached my boiling point this morning. It's not worth it. Life is short, boy oh boy, have I learned that in the last few weeks. I just don't want to be angry anymore. I don't want to be consumed by work, and certainly not for that guy. He's not worth it."

"Which one?" Jan snickered.

"Take your pick!" Edward laughed, as he gave Jan a sad look. "I'm going to miss you most of all, Scarecrow."

Jan gave Edward an uncharacteristic hug. "I'm going to miss you too, but I understand your point. I hope you know what you're doing. You make a good living here."

"Jan, I'll land on my feet. I need to figure out life, anyway. I haven't had time to do that since starting here."

Jan started to tear up. "Ok, I'm not doing this. I'm going to my meeting. You have my digits!"

Edward walked back to his desk filled with melancholy. He didn't want to do a grandiose goodbye tour. He would send a brief email later thanking everyone for their work. He wanted to sneak out as quickly as possible, to no avail.

"Edward…"

He looked up to see Michael standing at his cubicle.

"I talked with Steve, and I better understand your position. He explained to me how hard you've worked and the emotional toll following your grandmother's death. So, I will overlook this morning. We don't want to lose you. Let's talk about how we can realign teams to have you not report to Steve."

"Michael, is that what he told you? That I was emotionally taxed following my grandmother's death? Nothing about his passive aggressive management or total disregard toward my family obligations? How callous he was this morning to me about her death? '*My milking it*?' Michael, thank you for making the effort. I truly do appreciate the opportunity and the work I got to do over the last year here. I just think my time here has come to an end. I hope if the time comes you'll act as a reference for me based on the work I led on the Crandon business."

"Of course, Edward, and please know, you're always welcome back."

Edward shook his head appreciatively, knowing that was unlikely. He didn't know what the future would bring, but he didn't envision a second tour of duty here.

It didn't take Edward long to finish boxing up his belongings. As he got into his car, he considered texting Maggie to tell her about his own magnificent resignation - how he finally got to tell both Steve and Michael off. He thought she'd appreciate it, or she may have several months ago. He thought about it for a minute, but then wondered why she would care now. He didn't want to stir up old emotions, especially after she seemed to have moved past it.

Edward wasn't sure what to do about Maggie. He wasn't sure what to do about Annie or Kate either. As he drove away, he considered going out on a date with each now that he had plenty of time on his hands. He wondered if it was worth it. There was so much baggage with each. Perhaps it was better to move on completely. He turned on the radio. He didn't have to decide right now. At the first stop light, he texted Maggie.

Sheila will probably be calling you.

Maggie responded right away.

Ok. I do owe her a call back. She had called a lot when I was off the grid. Do you know what she wants to discuss?

Edward didn't respond. Edward decided going off the grid himself is what he needed to heal and rejuvenate. Edward spent much of the next 2 months traveling to see old friends and vacationing. While he certainly didn't have an insurance policy to live off, he did receive an inheritance from Elsie that he felt was well used to go live life. He didn't go completely offline, but he did avoid social media and his phone as much as possible. In the weeks following Elsie's funeral, both Annie and Kate reached out twice. Edward didn't respond to either. He felt somewhat like an asshole ignoring them, but he wasn't sure what to say. He really didn't know what he wanted, and he didn't feel the offense was any worse than either had perpetrated against him.

Edward also wasn't sure what he was going to do when he returned to Detroit. The rest of his family was relatively healthy, so there was no longer a pressing need to stay in the area. He had spent much of his time there working, so his social circle was limited. He just wasn't ready to make any life choices yet.

Edward spent the last few days of his rejuvenation tour on the beach in Mexico. He knew it was time to get back to the real world when the hours started to feel interminable. What once felt like meditation in watching the waves turned into a slow form of torture.

When he arrived back in the US, he turned his phone on to find a series of texts from Maggie.

Edward. We need to connect. I talked to Sheila!

Edward? Where are you? I heard you quit! Why didn't you tell me?

Edward! I thought we were on decent terms. Why are you ignoring me?

Edward, are you ok? I'm starting to worry.

Ok, Edward. Perhaps you need space too. I will have to respect that. Just wanted you to know the agency lost the Crandon business. I guess Sheila gave it to Michael about what a weasel Steve is and how she's not working with him anymore. Comeuppance! Take care of yourself.

Edward started to laugh out loud on the plane, as his fellow passengers gave him funny looks. He felt sad for the larger team as a whole and hoped no one would lose their job, but couldn't help but feel vindication for both Maggie and him.

"Hi, Mom. How are you?" Edward said as he answered the phone from the baggage claim.

"Hi, honey. Dad and I are just driving into the airport now to pick you up. See you in a few minutes."

Edward was happy to see his parents after having been gone for so long. The car ride home was mostly filled with mundane updates, but one topic piqued Edward's interest.

"Honey, your grandmother's tombstone came in last week. It looks so nice. We went again last week and put out a wreath. You'll have to go see it this week."

Edward hadn't been to the cemetery since the funeral. He had left town shortly thereafter. He wanted to see the headstone, but he didn't want to face the reality that she was really gone. He had largely ignored it emotionally while he was away.

It was a pattern in his life of late. Edward had intended to connect with Maggie the week after he got back on what Sheila had told her, but he never seemed to get around to it. With each passing day, he felt less interested in it, almost as if it were a previous lifetime. He felt the same way about Annie and Kate. He wanted to look forward to new beginnings, not linger in the past. He had scheduled a series of out of state interviews in the ensuing weeks. He wasn't even sure he'd be there in 2 months to make it worth trying to rekindle.

Knowing he would be flying out again soon for interviews, he made time to visit the cemetery.

"Well, Eltz, I'm finally here. Where've I been? Well, I guess I've been everywhere but here. Thank you for the money. I had a great time out living life. I feel like you'd be proud of me. I wasn't focused on work or obligations. I was focused on making memories. I'm not always good at that. I know you're always proud of me, but you know what I mean. Did I meet any girls? None that I'm ready to bring home to you. The last time we were together you sprung three on me. You just couldn't let the last chance go by to try to find me a wife, could you? Well joke is on you. I don't think any of them are 'the one.' I think it's best that I move forward and start fresh. How do I know? I don't know. I'm just doing the best I can, mainly because I don't have you here to guide me! Well, I know you're with me always, but it just isn't as easy to hear you. I wish I could ask you what I should be doing with my life."

Edward touched her engraved named, *Elsie C. Wagner*. He sat in silence in the cemetery for another 30 minutes hoping for some greater clarity just by being closer to her in spirit. He thought about the funeral and the comedy that was facing Annie, Kate and Maggie in direct succession. He thought about the tears he shed and his final goodbye. As Edward got up, feeling no more inspired, he finally saw the other side of Elsie's tombstone. There it read:

To everything there is a season, and a time to every purpose under the heaven.

He again felt the comfort of this, as if he heard it directly from Elsie. Edward knew the next step would unfold as it was meant to.

Edward had interviews in New York City, Chicago and Atlanta first. He had applied for agency jobs, corporate gigs, and even some non-traditional roles. He was open to the universe and letting it guide him to where he needed to be. Despite having a strong portfolio of work and experience, offers were not coming as quickly as Edward had expected. Not being located in those cities had proven to be a sticking point in a competitive job market.

After several weeks of intense interviews and travel, Edward settled into a Friday night with beer and sports. He was looking forward to a quiet evening, although he wished he had someone to share it with. He had avoided dating altogether recently.

"Well, bud, perhaps one good rejection deserves

another, hey?" Edward said to himself as he considered the recent jobs he didn't get. "Guess there's no time like now to get back to online dating. Shoot me now!" he grunted as he begrudgingly opened his laptop.

After flipping through several profiles that didn't catch his interest, Edward stopped cold when he read the profile titled, *To Everything There is a Season.*

Hi, my name is Maggie. I'm starting my second act excited about finding love again. It's taken me a while to get here, but I was recently reminded that life happens in its own time.

To everything there is a season, and a time to every purpose under the heaven:

A time to be born, and a time to die; a time to plant, and a time to pluck up that which is planted.

I read these words at a moment when I was still pretty lost, and felt guidance from a woman I had never met. It renewed my faith... my faith in God... and my faith in myself. I never got to meet her, but she helped me more than she'll ever know.

So now, if you're not totally scared away, I'm looking for something quite simple. Honesty, laughter, wit, and a smidge of ambition. If you can handle that, message me!

Edward thought back to his conversations with Elsie about Maggie. She had told him not to judge her, for he didn't know what she was going through. She had called him out on his feelings for her, even when he wouldn't acknowledge them himself. She had even brought her to the funeral home, of that he was now sure.

Edward looked up to the ceiling. "Well, well, well. Perhaps the last laugh isn't on you after all, you old sage. You just couldn't let this go, could you?"

Edward quickly typed a message before hitting send.

Hi, my name is Edward. My efforts haven't always turned out for the best, but I always had the best of intentions. I'm looking for new beginnings, and if you're open to a fresh start, I'd like to ask you out.

Edward smiled as he closed his laptop. He was confident of the response. He got up and picked up the picture of him and Elsie on his mantle.

"Thank you. I only wish you got to meet her, but then again, you already changed her life. I love you, Eltz."

Made in the USA
Lexington, KY
10 October 2017